PRAISE FOR THE QUEEN'S CURSE

The Queen's Curse by JF Rogers delivers an exciting and satisfying conclusion to *The Cursed Lands* trilogy, in which half-elf Princess Colleen and her merry band of companions venture into a wondrous and yet dangerous new kingdom. Rogers seamlessly mixes a fantastical adventure with a powerful message of faith and perseverance in difficult times. If you loved *The King's Curse* and *The Witch's Curse*, this one is a must-read.

Gina Detwiler, author of the *Forlorn* Series

THE
QUEEN'S
CURSE

THE CURSED LANDS BOOK 3

J. F. ROGERS

NOBLEBRIGHT
PUBLISHING

www.noblebrightpublishing.com

The Queen's Curse - The Cursed Lands Book 3

Edited by Brilliant Cut Editing
Cover design by 100 Covers

Paperback ISBN: 978-1-955169-22-6
Hardcover ISBN: 978-1-955169-23-3

Published by Noblebright Publishing
Sanford, Maine
www.noblebrightpublishing.com

Blessed *is* the man who endures temptation; for when he has been approved, he will receive the crown of life which the Lord has promised to those who love Him.

— JAMES 1:12

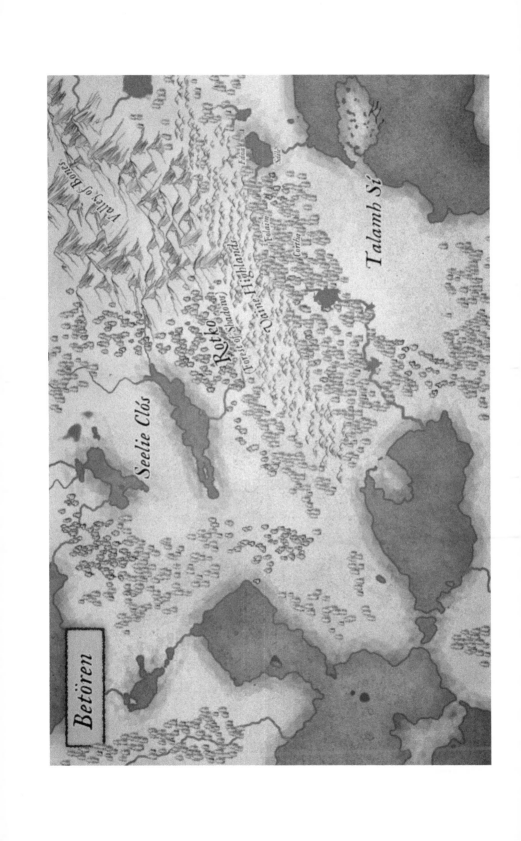

PRONUNCIATION GUIDE

PEOPLE

Alajos \ AH-lah-yosh \ a rebel fae

Alpertti \ AL-per-tee \ Queen Rhiannon's advisor

Auberon \ O-bər-ahn \ King of Talamh Sí

Eerika \ EH-ri-ka \ the princess

Eerikki \ EH-ri-ki \ King Auberon's father

Fallon \ FA-lən \ Colleen's adopted mother

Beagan \ BEE-gun \ Colleen's adopted brother

Corwin \ KAWR-win \ Colleen's adopted brother

Egon \ EE-gahn \ a rebel fae

Hadwin \ HAD-win \ a human

Hiisi \ HEE-zee \ a gargoyle-like creature

Iida \ EE-Dah \ Colleen's maid

Iisakki \ EE-sah-ki \ the dragon, nicknamed Sakki

Kohl \ kohl \ a rebel fae

Liam \ LEE-əm \ the Defender

Ludek \ LOO-deck \ leader of the Kapinallis

Maija \ MAH-yah \ Queen Rhiannon's younger sister

Mikko \ MEE-koh \ a fae guard

Nialla \ NEE-al-ah \ Colleen's adopted sister

Niilo \ NEE-loh \ Leader of the elfin army

Noita \ Noy-tah \ the witch

Pepin \ PEP-ən \ the pech who made Drochaid

Pirkko \ PIR-ko \ a member of the Saoirse Trodaí

Reko \ REH-ko \ a member of the Saoirse Trodaí

Rhiannon \ ree-ANN-ən \ Queen of Seelie Clós

Ruuta \ ROO-tah \ Colleen's lady-in-waiting

Ryan \ RIE-ən \ Colleen's adopted brother

Rhys \ REES \ a boy who joins Colleen in her quest

Silja \ SEEL-yah \ an ogre's daughter with piglike features

Taneli \ TA-ne-li \ a member of the Saoirse Trodaí

Ulla \ OO-lah \ a dragon

Valtteri \ VAHL-te-ri \ leader of the Saoirse Trodaí

Vilppu \ VIL-pu \ a driver

Yaeger \ YAHG-er \ a rebel fae

GROUPS

Fasgadair \ fahs-geh-deer \ Ariboslian vampires

Gachen \ gah-chen \ an Ariboslian race of shapeshifters

Kapina \ KAH-pee-nah \ rebels

Kapinallis \ KAH-pee-nah-lees \ rebel group

Pech \ peck \ an Ariboslian race of small, strong people

Saors \ SEE-ores \ those who have been freed

Saoirse Trodaí \ SEE-er-shay TRAH-day \ freedom fighters

Vapaus \ vah-pows \ a rebel group

PLACES

Ariboslia \ air-eh-BOWS-lia \ the realm where Colleen grew up

Betören \ beh-TUHR-ən \ the realm Colleen is in now

Folaím \ FALL-eem \ the veiled forest city

Koulu \ KOO-loo \ a fae school

Notirr* \ no-tear \ a village of mounds in hills occupied by the Cael

Sáile \ SOH-leh \ a fishing village

Seelie Clós \ SEE-lee clohs \ the seelie court across the Divide

Rotko* \ ROHT-goh \ the Divide, aka the forest of shadows

Talamh Sí \ tall-um she\ King Auberon's kingdom

THINGS

Äiti \ eye-a-tee \ mama

Aivopestä \ I-voh-pest-ah \ a potion that makes people believe Auberon
is God

Croí \ kree \ a spelled tree in Folaím

Isä \ ee-sah \ father

Jumala \ YU-mah-lah \ fae word for God

Käärme \ KAH-are-may \ large serpent/wormlike creature

Keino \ GAY-no \ a synthetic version of aether

Lapsi \ LAHP-see \ child

Muisti marja \ MOO-ee-stee mahr-yah \ a banned ingredient in the memory-erasing spell

Nuudelit \ NOO-deh-lit \ noodles

Pakana \ PAH-kah-nah \ an insult for an unbeliever

Socrú \ suh-CRU \ bond mark

Täydellinen \ TAOW-del-ee-nehn \ a crystal

Unohtaa \ oon-off-tah \ a potion that erases memory

Töykeä \ DOH-kyah \ rude

Turas \ TUHR-us \ a large megalith

Tyhmiä \ DEWH-mee-yaa \ fool

Värikäs \ VAH-ree-kahs \ the color of aether smoke

Vastalääke \ VAHS-tah-lah-geh \ antidote

Zorac \ Zohr-ack \ a demon

*trill the r

ONE

I looked back at the wall of ethereal lights waving a slow but steady farewell, searching for signs of Sakki. The air crackled and popped, questioning my loyalty. I could no longer see my beloved dragon. Birds twittered on this side of the Divide. Try as they might, their joyous symphony couldn't stop the sorrow welling up in the dragon-sized hole in my heart. The pit swelled with each step away from him. An invisible band between us stretched, threatening to snap us back together once I stepped too far. Maybe it would have had our bond not broken.

Sakki. My cry sounded pitiful, even to me. And I knew he wouldn't reply. He couldn't.

Liam scuffed the plush grass. A look passed between him and Ruuta. Her glamor-enhanced eyebrows lifted, and he shrugged. Though they despised one another, they cared for me and seemed at a loss for how to help me.

I tugged my sleeve to inspect my bond mark. My socrú. Evidence of my bond with Sakki. It was still there. That was something. I fingered the tattoo-like markings that had appeared the moment we first touched, and I smiled a sad smile. The others returned my pathetic smile. My heart squeezed red tears as I choked back a sob lodged in my throat.

1

Nay. I straightened my spine and quickened my step. The sooner I fixed whatever had broken between us, the sooner I could return to him.

Guilt nagged at me like an overindulged toddler. Restoring my bond wasn't supposed to be my goal. I was on a mission for God. He had a purpose for me, not that I understood what it was. All I knew was I was supposed to go to Queen Rhiannon. But for what? Guidance? Could she restore my bond with Sakki? How could I trust anything she said? She served a demon!

God, I don't get it. Not at all. But You know what You're doing. Help me take one step after another, trusting You all the way.

As the day grew brighter and we strode farther away, the waving lights marking the Divide were no longer visible. The effervescent air worked to clear my mind, but images of Sakki held me captive. My feet itched to get where I must and do whatever was required to return. If only I could skip the journey and fast-forward to the end with Sakki and me together and the bond restored.

But God had other plans.

He *always* had other plans.

Did His plans include returning to Talamh Sí to restore the order I'd destroyed? *Just what do You have planned? If only You'd let me in on Your secrets.*

Despite my hurry, I couldn't make my feet move faster. I might as well have worn concrete shoes rather than riding boots, though the soles were wearing thin and my feet were tired from all the cubits I'd forced them to cross.

Hiisi seemed to sense my sadness. He glanced back at me from atop Liam's shoulders with giant eyes full of empathy and jutted his chin upward as if to say, "chin up." Not that my strange little gargoyle friend would talk that way. Nay. He'd say something like, "Lift you head. You no sad."

Ruuta kept surging ahead. Then, realizing she was traveling with baggage, she slowed, waiting for us to draw near enough before she rushed ahead again.

Liam waited for me. He squeezed my upper arm with a sympathetic hand. My sadness must be affecting my energy. It didn't leap within me at his touch as it normally would.

Was that another effect of the witch's curse? Had it not simply broken my bond with Sakki, but something within me? Something that affected my obvious connection with Liam too? Or had sadness merely dulled my senses?

If only I'd listened when God told me to put on the ring. If I'd obeyed immediately, none of this would have happened. Liam and I could explore whatever was growing between us. And my bond wouldn't have broken.

But Sakki still would've stayed behind to protect the Divide. There was no changing that stubborn, scaly beast's mind. And besides, if Sakki stayed behind and I didn't desperately need to see Rhiannon to fix our bond, would I still agree to go with Ruuta to the demon-serving queen? Or would I want to stay back with Sakki?

I shook my head and scoffed at myself. *Stop thinking about all the what-ifs and deal with what is.*

If only Sakki could reply to my silent conversation with some sarcastic retort.

"All will be well." Liam eyed me askance. "You'll get Sakki back. At least now you know he's safe."

"That's true." I breathed in that encouraging detail and tried breathing out all the negative thoughts swirling endlessly in my distraught mind.

Light in. Dark out.

Light in. Dark out.

Breathe. Just breathe.

Sakki is safe.

Great is Thy faithfulness...

"Come see this." Ruuta's excited voice filtered through the leafy woods.

I followed Liam and Hiisi past the curtain of trees rustling in my wake to an opening. It reminded me of the ridge where Liam showed me my father's city, Talamh Sí. Both views stole my breath, but this was different. Before us lay a city of mighty misshapen trees. Buildings defied physics to nestle among them. The air buzzed as if charged with power, and an ethereal glow lit all of Seelie Clós. And there, taller than the city in the foreground, stood a castle the magnitude of which I couldn't comprehend. The entire city would have lain in the castle's incomprehensible shadow if it didn't shed its own light.

I gaped. There were no words.

Had the humans seen this city and tried to mimic it with iron and stone? Their attempts fell short. Far, far, far short. Despite my pull back to Sakki, something about the place tugged me forward. Comforting winds lazed past me.

Cooooool LEEEEEEEN.

I stepped toward the ledge.

Two

Bits of earth skittered from beneath my feet and bounced down the sheer cliffside. Liam snatched my arm.

"It knows my name. My real name." I tried to walk against his pull.

"What are you doing?" He swirled me to face him.

I eyed his hand on me, barely feeling his touch, then craned my neck to the view of Seelie Clós. "What?"

"Were you about to walk off the cliff?" He snagged my chin between his thumb and forefinger and forced me to look at him.

"Nay, I—" As I stared into his ocean eyes, I jerked back into myself. "What happened?" I glanced at the city, then gasped at how close I stood to the edge and jumped away. Once I was at a safe distance, my attention snapped to Liam. "It's like... it called to me." My eyes drifted again.

Liam grasped my shoulders, turned me away, and pulled me into the woods. He whipped his head at Ruuta, urging her to follow. "What's happening to her?"

Ruuta pressed her lips into a thin line, trying to suppress a smile. "It's her home. Part of her longs to be here. I feel it too."

He narrowed his eyes as if to say he had different, more nefarious suspicions as to the cause. "I'm not sure she should go."

I ripped myself from his grip. "What?"

He gawked at me. "You said it called your name. Your real name. What does that even mean?"

"It called me Colleen, like it knew I preferred it to Eerika. Like... it *knows* me."

"And you don't find that alarming?" He stepped back, his questioning expression passing back and forth between us. "What do you think of this, Hiisi?"

"Me no know." Confusion raised the throaty voice behind me. Then a velvety arm curled around my leg. "Me never been here."

More radiant than ever, Ruuta rolled her eyes at Liam. This place must be energizing her, bolstering her glamor. "Don't listen to him. You're on a mission to see Queen Rhiannon. Your God told you to see her. We just made it through the Divide. There's no going back, should we care to at this point."

"Well, we could..."

Despite Liam's opposition, relief relaxed me. Then my gut squeezed. How could I feel relief at continuing to see my aunt? I needed to find a cure for the bond and get back. I couldn't let whatever pulled at me steer me away from my mission.

Flickering lights buzzed past me. Then another. And another.

"Pixies!" Ruuta squealed out in childlike glee. "They sensed your sadness."

The pixies hovered around me, rustling like leaves fluttering in an updraft. They smelled like fresh grass, but also a bit bitter, like candy that had gone stale.

Something landed on my hand, and I nearly swatted it before realizing it was a pixie. It clung to my thumb and adjusted itself to remain upright as I brought it to my face. The others closed in. Tiny people smaller than my thumb with translucent wings and covered in gold-colored fur. They flashed mischievous smiles under luminous overlarge eyes. The one on my hand left my thumb and alighted on my palm with a bow.

Glowing dust clouded around me, and I breathed it in. I wafted it away as I coughed. "What"—cough, cough, wheeze—"was that?"

"They favored you with pixie dust." Ruuta beamed. "A rare privilege. How do you feel now?"

I checked myself. The sadness was still there, but far away. Just beyond reach. Tension left me, and I felt—"Peace."

Ruuta's smile widened, and Liam's eyebrows squeezed together, turbulent waves crashing in his ocean eyes.

Fear struck me like Noita's lightning. If I'd learned anything in this world, it was that I didn't know it well enough. Anything could sidetrack me. Much already had, or I'd be home right now. *God, I have to get back to Sakki. Please let nothing stop me from getting back to him.*

Hiisi clung to my leg, and his solemn gargoyle face tipped up at me, his overlong limbs tightening like constricting snakes. "Me no leave you. Me guide."

I still didn't know what that meant. Did he even know? He hadn't guided me out of the Divide following the King's Road, but he had miraculously appeared in the käärme's stomach and helped me escape.

Liam's jaw tensed, and his temples pulsed. "I will do everything in my power to ensure you return."

Ruuta's laugh sounded like a nervous horse whinny. "Don't be melodramatic. Once you experience the city, its effects will wear off. You'll still love it, but you can leave. I did."

I stiffened, pointing an accusatory finger. "How do I know this isn't all part of some grand plan to lure me into serving your demon? How can I trust you at all?"

When she flinched as if I'd struck her, I winced over being so harsh. I'd never seen her look so hurt. "I'm sorry. I—"

"Don't apologize to her." Liam raked a hand through his thick black hair, leaving it adorably tousled. Some fell across his forehead, almost reaching his eyes. "You've every right to be suspicious."

Ruuta held up a hand. "It's all right. There is nothing the princ—" Her eyes widened as she glanced around, then leaned in to whisper. "My apologies. It's not safe to speak of who you are outside of Queen Rhiannon's protection."

Creeping crabs. Was that true? I craned all around, my nerves recoiling. Hadn't she said something about it being unsafe for royalty? I whispered back. "Why is it unsafe?"

"I'll explain later. But know this: Queen Rhiannon will realize we're here, and when she does, she'll send a knight to escort us. Until then, if you come upon any fae, do not make eye contact. And if one greets you, respond with the proper greeting. When the sun is up say, 'May the sun shine upon you.' At night say, 'May the moon shine upon you.'"

"What happens if I don't speak to the demon worshipers at all?" Liam gripped his forehead and rubbed his temples.

Her face twisted, her eyes blazing. She whirled toward him, her dainty chin jutting up and her ungloved hands jamming on her slim waist. "If you value your life, *human*, you won't utter such things."

She said the word *human* with such ferocity, Liam and I both stepped away from her.

Her eyes widened. She sagged like she'd been possessed and felt the demon flee her body. "I—" She closed her eyes and huffed out a breath to compose herself. When she was ready, she tried again. "I'm trying to help you. It's beautiful, yes, but don't let that deceive you into lowering your guard. This is a dangerous place." She nodded to the rifle across Liam's back. "And you need to hide that. Human weapons aren't allowed here."

"How can you tell me this is a dangerous place and to hide my rifle all in one sentence?"

"At best, it will be taken from you. At worst, you will be killed for it."

He shrugged the weapon from his shoulder and tucked it under his coat. It wasn't hidden well, but it was better than strung on him out in the open. "I'll find a place to stash it while we're here."

He didn't mention his pistol, but since it was hidden, he'd probably keep it on him.

"What makes this shiny place so dangerous? Magic? Creatures? Deadly plants?" He softened his tone and held a hand up to ward off any more verbal attacks. "It would be helpful to know what to be on guard against."

"The fae can be deceptive. They have their reasons for what they do. Their motives and magic are unpredictable."

"And you got so mad when Fergus said not to trust the fae." Liam scoffed, forgetting himself again.

I smacked his arm to get him to stop.

She huffed. "You say you can't trust me, but you can. Queen Rhiannon and I both want Colleen to return to Talamh Sí to ascend the throne." Her hand moved toward the stone around her neck as if readying to compel me. Then, seeming to realize her error, she dropped it. "I promise you. I will stop at nothing to return you to Talamh Sí."

While I couldn't trust her word, she could offer nothing more, so it would have to be good enough.

God, You brought me here. Help me trust You to see me through and back to Sakki.

THREE

We walked to the city through a celestial garden across uncharted terrain, pregnant with unknown wonders. Homes made from twisty ethereal trees gave way to gold, silver, and diamond buildings reflecting sunlit prisms. Crystal streets and grassy paths linked unimaginable opulence, the band holding the city's crown-jewel buildings together.

The grass beneath my feet appeared wet, but it didn't dampen my shoes. Glistening flowers of indescribable variety lined the paths and embellished otherwise empty spaces. Pixies hummed as they flitted about. Trails of pixie dust dissipated behind them.

Where was all the traffic? For a city of this size, vehicles and people should clog the streets, ships sailing above. Some people—fae—wrapped in shimmering translucent cloaks and capes that shifted and moved with their bodies, stepped out of a shop, then disappeared in a cloud of orange.

A beautiful woman holding a child's hand neared. Like everything else, their dresses sparkled beneath their cloaks, seeming to give off their own light. Facial glamors, similar to Ruuta's, matched their clothes and accentuated their beauty. The little girl's was simpler, more understated. They smiled as they passed. But I caught something in their eyes. Distaste?

The little girl spotted Hiisi and screamed, pawing at her mother to be picked up. "Äiti!" Once the mother secured the child in her arms, the duo blinked out—disappeared—like the image on the teleview when the connection cut.

"Where did they go?" I walked around where they'd been, giving it a wide berth in case they were still there.

"The ones who disappeared in an orange cloud used a spell. The woman with her child had the gift of teleportation and didn't need one. But whether they're gifted or use a spell, most fae teleport. When we walk, it's for enjoyment, not necessity." She heaved a heavy sigh. "Sadly, I don't have the gift, nor have I a suitable spell. We'll have to walk."

I sensed her feeling disadvantaged. I felt it too, without my ability to see auras. But why couldn't I now? Was it this place? Or had Noita broken more than just my bond? I leaned close to Ruuta. "Can you see auras?"

"No. No one can."

"But you said—"

"I know what I said. All fae can see auras, but not here. Members of the public safety committee decided that reading a person's emotions was an infringement of their privacy. Therefore, we have enacted wards to subdue auras."

"Subdue?" That sounded bad. My feet refused to go further. "As in... are you taking their emotions away? Are you manipulating minds like my father had?"

She spun around, blinking. "Of course not. We merely hide their expression to prevent them from being seen and interpreted. Such suppression doesn't affect one's emotions in the slightest."

That may be, but given that I was a foreigner in yet another foreign world, reading emotions came in handy. And I was used to it. Not having it felt more like a disability than it probably felt never having the ability at all.

What would the fae think of us?

I ran a hand down at my torn and dirty riding clothes, fiddled with the wild tangle of my blonde curls, and resisted the urge to smell myself. We were a disgusting mess. A blemish on the pristine beauty—except for Ruuta. Then I looked at Hiisi. I'd come to adore his hideously cute face. He could've been an animated gargoyle with his gray skin and matching clothes seeming chiseled from stone, though his skin felt soft, velvety. His wide flattened head and the hooked fangs protruding from his lower lip were something from the nightmare we'd left behind, belying the sweet spirit that dwelled within.

If only she knew him. He was endearing. Caring. God's servant.

"Wait. How did that little girl see Hiisi?" Were there some who believed in God here?

"I can see him now too." Ruuta tucked a tuft of stray blonde hairs behind her ear.

"You see me?" Hiisi ran to catch up with Ruuta and stumbled, trying to look up at her. "You believe?"

"Yes, I see you. No, I don't believe in your God." She slowed, giving his short legs a break. "I expected to see you once we reached Seelie Clós. Nothing that exists in this realm can hide. Just as you were visible in the dragon temple, here, wards protect us from such deception."

That was harsh. I didn't think of her inability to see him as a deception, but a side effect of unbelief. It would have been easier if he'd remained invisible. "Is he going to have that effect on everyone?"

"Probably. But they can go elsewhere." Ruuta waved it off. "Once we get to the castle and change out of these clothes, I'll teach you to beautify yourself as the rest of the fae do." She jerked a thumb toward Liam. "And make him look like a fae."

"But you just said there was no such deception here." My head throbbed, all this confusing me already.

"You can't hide yourself entirely, but with the right spells, you can alter your features."

"You're not turning me into a fae."

The way he spat out the word fae chafed. "*I'm* part fae."

Liam caught my attention and smoothed the disgust from his face, his face morphing into an apologetic smile.

She wrinkled her nose at him. "You'll have to make do with a bath. And suitable attire."

"I couldn't give two figs about what these fake people think of me."

Ruuta spoke over Liam. "And we may be able to make Hiisi look a little more... appealing."

"No. No, no, no, no, no." Hiisi shook his head so hard I was surprised he didn't lose his balance and fall over. He punctuated his objections by stamping his foot. "Me stay me. God made me. No change."

I picked him up and carried him on my hip. He clung to me as Beagan had when he was a baby—like a koala—but with longer arms and a firmer grip. "It's okay, Hiisi. No one needs to change you." If Hiisi disgusted the fae, well... let *them* disappear.

We continued along a flower-lined crystalline path, and the sky darkened. A ship's woody underbelly passed overhead.

"Don't move!" I yell-whispered.

Had they seen us?

FOUR

Creeping crabs! I tugged the air, wrapping us in my veil. How hadn't I heard it sooner? Now that I was paying attention and the ship was upon us, it was impossible to ignore the whirring motors and loose wood creaking above. Faint shouts from the crew floated on the wind.

We waited until the towers of trees, leafy canopies, and shiny buildings hid us and the whirring dimmed to a faint hum before our frozen positions thawed. Even then, I didn't remove my veil. "Do you think they saw us?"

"Unlikely. Though your veil didn't work. There are wards, remember?" Ruuta squinted into the sea of orange flowing across the horizon where the ship had disappeared. "Even so, I doubt they're even looking for you. That was a cargo ship."

"So the merchant ships are running again." Liam's voice was rough and deep with fatigue. "That's good, right? Talamh Sí must be falling under some kind of order."

Ruuta's shoulders rose and fell in a single languid motion.

Why did that worry me? I didn't even want to be queen. Why not let them do whatever they wanted? Who cared?

But if the Vapaus had gotten control, what must life be like for the citizens? Judging from what I'd seen, they cared about their own freedom—nothing else, including lives. They killed Pirkko and Valtteri. They didn't care about people.

Faces from my travels came to mind—Kieron O'Donal, his family and their farm, Pauli from the school I visited, the other children, Floyd O'Malley in my father's prison cell, Fergus in the highlands, Carr and Fiske in Sáile. They all needed help.

Help the Vapaus was unlikely to offer.

Creeping crabs. I did care.

But now, I needed to end this part of the journey. Though unsure how I felt about spells, I'd have given almost anything for a spell to transport us. Or a horse. Did they have horses around here? Even a loud autocar would do. I needed rest.

I scuffed my foot on the even ground, nearly tripping myself and ruining a clump of grass. The grass fixed itself, showing no signs of disturbance, reminding me of beò feur. But this was regular grass, not little creatures that resembled blades of grass. What in Ariboslia?

I had to stop thinking like that. We weren't in Ariboslia. Or Talamh Sí. Or in the Divide. Each place I'd been to in this realm was like a different world unto itself. Why should Seelie Clós be any different? I'd never understood one before being thrust into the next. And I'd left each one different from what it had been when I'd arrived. And not necessarily for the better.

The Divide would be better off with the witch gone, but what about Talamh Sí? My father's curse was wrong, keeping people from knowing the true God. But there had been order when my father ruled. What kind of chaos would I return to? When would it ever be safe to return?

I didn't understand what God was doing. Why send me to Queen Rhiannon? What could she do to help me, and why would I want to accept her help? She served a demon. Would taking her help be like accepting help from the demon she served?

Liam glanced over his shoulder and must've noticed me staggering. "Let me take him."

Hiisi opened his sleepy eyes and reached out to help Liam peel him from my arms. Liam smelled crisp and woodsy like the forest after a thunderstorm. Hiisi settled in, wrapping his arms around Liam's neck, and closed his eyes again. Soft snores escaped his gargoyle mouth.

Liam leaned in to whisper. "You know, he's kind of cute despite looking like something from a nightmare."

"He is." I smiled and tripped on my own feet again and watched the grass fix itself. "Did you notice the grass?"

"Yeah." He quirked his lips and wrinkled his nose. "Everything around here is probably under some fae spell. The place reeks of it."

I sniffed. "I smell nothing." Other than him.

"No. Not actually smells—it's just everywhere, and I don't like it."

"Oh." I wasn't sure how I felt about it. It was beautiful. Mesmerizing. And it was a relief after Noita's horrors. As the light of day dimmed, the illumination from the lights grew ever more intense. But it was all a facade. As fake as Ruuta's face glamor. Even if I didn't like it, I preferred to see things how they were.

God, You helped me see past the witch's living nightmare. Can You help me see past the fae magic too?

Nothing changed. Was it different here? Maybe the fae magic wasn't an illusion. Maybe it changed the structure of things. I had so much to learn about how fae magic worked. Then again, wasn't magic evil? I should focus on getting to Queen Rhiannon and getting out.

A figure materialized in Ruuta's path. Liam plowed into her. I stepped on the heel of his boot and disturbed Hiisi's sleep.

I shuffled to see the intruder. A male fae from the looks of him. His slightly feminine face couldn't overpower his physique. Armor hugged his thin, yet muscular, frame and shimmered like a million gems refracting the light in impossible ways.

"May the moon shine upon you, Ruuta." His words slipped together with a musical quality—melodic. With no signs of stubble, he, too, wore face glamor. Pointed ears gave away the elfin ancestry all fae possessed. His blond hair, cut in an unfamiliar style, was very short on the sides, almost shaved, showing off his ears. The top of his hair, pulled back into a bun, didn't move when he gave a sweeping bow. His armor tinkled with dainty clinks as if it were made of glass. "May the moon shine upon you and yours, Your Highness."

"Mikko!" Ruuta grasped his armored forearm, their history clear in the way they looked at each other. "May the moon shine upon you as well." Her laugh rang out, pleasant and light, as she hugged him.

Once they peeled apart, Mikko bowed again. His ice-blue eyes resisted shifting their gaze from her to me. They lost their softness and never quite met mine. "Allow me to escort you to the castle." He gripped a stone around his neck and twirled his finger.

Our surroundings disappeared. When they solidified again, I teetered to keep from toppling in a grand room aglow in silver and gold lights and open to a panoramic view of the garden city. A dim twinkling melody wafted from some place far away.

"Princess Eerika." A stiff man crooked an arm and bowed at the waist. Beneath hair perfectly white, styled, and trimmed, green eyes as sharp as the finest blade peered from skin soft and youthful. "May the sun shine upon you. Alpertti at your service." Something about him was familiar. But why would anyone here be familiar? Then I remembered.

"I saw you on my father's teleview."

The man grew taller, but not out of pride. His unearthly green eyes narrowed. "Your father allowed you to partake in our confidential meetings?"

Creeping crabs! I'd been eavesdropping. Why, oh why had I mentioned it? "Uh, not exactly." I wrung my hands together. "I heard a strange noise and—"

Ruuta stepped between us. "The princess need not explain herself, Alpertti."

"Of course not." Alpertti's gaze switched past me. He clasped his hands behind him and snapped his feet together.

"Princess Eerika. At long last." The regal voice floating down upon my shoulders had to be the queen.

FIVE

I spun. Encased in a sparkling gold gown with a matching crown gleaming atop blonde hair arranged in swoops and curls, she smelled of roses and opulence. Her skin shimmered in the light like fireflies twinkling in the dusk. She bore a striking resemblance to the pictures I'd seen of my mother as well as Sakki's image of her. But such images could never capture her iridescent eyes that seemed both green and blue at once. Stunning jewels draped across her breastbone shone brighter from her charm. And yet she exhibited so much more than mere beauty. Her commanding presence demanded respect and undefiled attention.

How could I ever compare to such a queen?

I faltered as I curtsied. Heat blossomed up my neck. "May the moon shine upon you."

Queen Rhiannon laughed in time to the background melody, and the winking lights seemed to dance along. She gripped my grubby hands in her gloved ones and squeezed. "I have long awaited this day. If only your mother could be here to see you too." Her eyes glistened, turning bluer.

I searched their aquamarine depths. Was she sad? I had assumed she'd be a heartless ruler. But what had given me that impression? When I learned she served Zorac, I thought the worst of her and expected her to be like Noita. Maybe she just didn't know God. Maybe Zorac was all she knew. Could I help her come to know God?

Nay, I'd tried that with my father. It hadn't worked. Every time I tried, he erased my memory.

But it had worked in the end. He was with God now.

God, give me wisdom to know what to do. Do I get close to her and help bring her to You? Or do I steer clear since she wants to bring me to Zorac?

Queen Rhiannon eyed me up and down, then did the same with the others without revealing her thoughts. She lifted her chin and peered down her pixie nose at Liam. "Is this your defender, Liam?"

He removed Hiisi from his shoulders, widened his stance, and clasped his hands behind his back.

How did she know all that? Then I remembered Alpertti's conversation over the teleview and relaxed. She was the reason Liam remained my defender. Father would have gotten rid of him. "Aye, he's with me."

"Very good. He shall remain your defender here as well. Thank you for seeing my niece to me." She narrowed her eyes and lifted a finger to Hiisi. "And what is this?"

Hiisi shrank away from her, pressing into Liam's leg.

"This is Hiisi." I squeezed his shoulder. "He helped get me through the Divide."

"Well, then. Any friend of my niece is a friend of the seelie court. You are welcome here, Hiisi. Particularly if you are skilled with traversing the Divide. Perhaps you can share your secrets."

Hiisi wrinkled his nose.

"I thought it impossible to cross without wards and feared for your safety, niece."

Though I'd been prepared to hate her, how could I not soften toward her? She was so... likable.

"Tell me"—she paced a slow circle around us—"did you happen upon the witch in your unfortunate travels?"

"We did." I lost her as she circled behind me. "She's dead."

"Dead, you say?" Rhiannon stopped over my left shoulder. Her gloved hand fluttered to her mouth to cover her shock. Then she recovered herself. "How did that come about?"

"Liam shot her." I jabbed a thumb toward him.

"After we restored her soul." He faced forward, not tracking Rhiannon's movement. "It was a team effort."

"And what became of the Divide after her demise?" Her face remained placid as she paced, but her voice quivered.

"The light returned. My dragon is there, protecting it." My voice hitched, hating to say the words aloud.

"Well, good for you." Her smile failed to reach her eyes. "And how did the witch look? Was she the fearsome-looking creature of whom I've heard tell?"

Who would she have heard it from? Anyone who entered the Divide remained trapped. Nay, humans passed through. "She had horns like tree branches." I almost added that she'd looked like a normal fae when I was in her home. What held me back?

"Just as I've been told." Queen Rhiannon's thoughtful gaze sharpened. "Ruuta."

Ruuta snapped to attention and curtsied. "Yes, my queen."

"Bring the princess to her rooms. Get her cleaned for dinner." Queen Rhiannon waved a regal hand toward Liam. "Place her defender and the creature in the nurse's quarters."

"Very well, my queen." Ruuta moved to show us out, but I held back.

"Uh, Your Majesty?"

"Let there be no regal titles among us, child. You are my niece. We are family." She smiled a warm smile that set me at ease. "Call me Aunt Rhiannon."

"A—aunt Rhiannon?" I stuttered. "May I make one request?"

"Name it, child. Ask me for anything in my kingdom, and it shall be yours."

"I—that is, Noita the Witch did something to me. It affected my bond with my dragon. Is there something you can do?"

"Well..." Her eyes flickered from blue to green as she blinked. "The fae know little of dragons and their bonds, not having had such experiences ourselves."

My heart crushed, making me slump.

"But my gifting with spells is unparalleled." She chucked my chin. "Take heart. If anyone can puzzle out the witch's spell and find an antidote, it's me. And I will do everything within my power to restore you."

It wasn't what I wanted to hear, but it was something. All hope was not lost. I breathed out a relieved breath. "Thank you."

She smiled, brightening the room like a warm spring day after a brutal frost. "There's nothing I wouldn't do for you, my child. Now go. Rest before dinner. I'll have the cooks prepare a grand meal for your homecoming."

Homecoming. That wasn't at all what I thought of this venture. It was more of an inconvenience, a means to restore my bond and return to Sakki. But I smiled in return, hoping she couldn't read my true feelings even without my aura. The last thing I needed was to offend my host, particularly if she had any kind of power over me.

Six

Ruuta delivered us through the gardens along a luminous pillar-lined corridor. Everywhere we went, that faint tinkling melody followed us. The white floor shimmered with silver and gold, twinkling in time to the music. Flowering vines climbed the pillars. Lush leaves cast a soft shade over pale pink blossoms that gleamed like pearls. I caught my breath.

But something was off. It was all too... perfect. There were no shadows. No breeze. The heavy scent of cinnamon bread didn't belong here amongst gardens and away from kitchens. No weeds or insects blighted the impeccable flowers. I touched a petal as we passed, and my finger slipped right through.

Fake. Everything was fake. Something about that disturbed me to no end.

Several rights and lefts turned me around until I lost all sense of direction. Each walkway looked the same. The exact same. With all their magic, couldn't they use different scenery... different flowers? Whoever designed this place had gotten lazy. No matter which way we turned, the garden view remained, along with the cinnamon-bread scent. What *was* here, an empty corridor? My vision swam as I struggled to make sense of what my eyes beheld. "How will I ever find my way around this place? It all looks the same."

"You can't tell?" Ruuta threw a confused look over her shoulder, but she didn't stop walking. "When you tap into your fae abilities, you shouldn't have a problem."

"Doesn't help *us* much, does it?" Liam's thick lashes obscured his eyes as he cupped a hand around Hiisi's head, the little fella trotting to keep up.

"Good. Perhaps it will prevent you from wandering about on your own."

Hiisi smiled up at Liam, unconcerned.

But these so-called fae abilities, whatever those were, didn't help me either. They were about as untapped as possible. I was part elf, after all. Maybe my elf side suppressed my fae side. I hoped it wasn't part of a trap.

Nay, I wouldn't explore that rabbit trail. God told me to come here.

God, please tell me what to do now that I'm here.

We followed Ruuta into a gazebo offering a view of the gardens on all but one side, which was a solid wall. The floor shifted. I splayed my hands to keep my balance. "What is this?"

"It's a lift." Ruuta waved, and the gazebo lifted us into the air.

Hiisi yelped and leaped into my arms as I stepped away from the edge to the only wall. Liam pressed in close.

Ruuta laughed. "You can't fall." She moved close to the edge and held out a hand. It seemed to connect with something solid midair. "There's a wall. This lift is as enclosed as your human lifts. But it's prettier than those nasty iron cages."

It may be prettier, but it was also far more anxiety inducing. I'd never get used to this place.

Would I be here long enough to get used to it?

What a terrifying thought. I hoped not.

The lift came to a smooth stop, though the slight lurch made my stomach consider giving up what little it contained.

"Whoa." Hiisi buried his face in my neck.

Ruuta swung her hand again, and the wall vanished. We followed her along another hallway that appeared to overlook the gardens below on one

23

wall, but it was probably fake. At least I could see that I stood many floors up, not on the main level. I didn't need fae abilities for that.

She led us to double doors burnished in gold etched with an intricate leaf pattern. "These are your private quarters. We have it spelled so none may enter without permission. Once you learn to cast permission spells, you can allow and prevent visitors at your discretion. Until then, we will do it for you. We have wards protecting the castle and extra precautions surrounding your quarters for your added safety and privacy."

She pushed the doors open to a sitting room where several fae worked. Their matching purple frocks, glittering with silver, swished as they flitted about. Items materialized with a wave of their hands—a stack of wood ignited in the fireplace, flowers bloomed in vases, and a cart with tea and cookies materialized beside a table on a balcony overlooking the gardens.

The air smelled of freshly baked cookies and carried a hint of smoke and honeysuckle.

"This is the sitting area." Ruuta led us through the fae who stopped to curtsy and greet me, never meeting me in the eye, then continued about their business. "You'll recognize your servants by their attire."

We passed a room feigning to be an outdoor garden with a natural pond and waterfall. Smooth stones and greenery surrounded the water. A servant waved her hand over a pool, coaxing steamy tendrils to arise. With another wave, flower petals floated on the surface. The sweet lavender scent and promises of complete relaxation drew me in.

"This is your bath." Ruuta waved to an open door across the hall. "This is your closet."

That was a *bath*? I couldn't wait for the tour to end so I could escape into it. I dragged myself away and gasped at the countless gowns and shoes lining the walls. Jewelry in cases stood beside a couch in the center. Fallon would be searching for her precious jeans amongst all the sparkles. Picturing my mom made me chuckle. But the laugh faded.

We moved on, and Ruuta displayed an enormous bedroom that put my room in my father's castle to shame. And that had been massive compared to the humble rooms I'd shared with other orphans in Notirr or my tiny room in Cian. But this place? I'd need a map to make my way around the massive bed.

A sob lodged in my throat. Would I ever get home? I didn't need all this extravagance. I only wanted to fix my bond with Sakki, do whatever God tasked me to accomplish here, restore Talamh Sí, and get home to my family. Such an impossible task list weighed me down.

Would I ever see my family again... at least to let them know I was safe? Well, as safe as a fae-elf with royal blood could be in these cursed lands? They must be off their heads with worry. How long had I been gone? The time I'd spent in the Divide and all the times my father had erased my memory had scrambled my brain. No wonder Rhys hadn't been able to explain much about his time there.

Rhys. I choked on another sob. How could he give up his life like that? But then, because of him, Sakki was still alive. We all were. Other than Samu. But he'd helped restore the Divide and reunite with his dragon. And Rhys got what he wanted too. He was with God now.

Thank You, God, for letting me see his spirit rise and know he's with You.

I hadn't realized what a gift that was until now. And Samu. While I hated that they sacrificed themselves for us, it comforted me to know they were beyond all pain and experiencing nothing but the pure joy of being with God. A joy I looked forward to experiencing someday.

"Well?" Ruuta jabbed my upper arm. "What do you think?"

I must've blanked out. Though I stood in the entryway, I paid little attention to the room beyond its enormity. The massive tree consuming the center dwarfed my father's, and no cage contained it or the birds fluttering about the furniture. Were they spelled not to poop on my things?

"I suggested they add the tree, like in your room at Talamh Sí. Queen Rhiannon thought it a brilliant idea."

"It reminds me of the croí tree in Folaím." Its leaves and tiny purple flowers seemed illuminated from within.

Ruuta beamed. "It is a croí tree." She gathered a branch, brought it to her nose, and inhaled. "Don't you love the scent?"

"You mean it's real? Not an illusion?" I stuck my nose into the blossoms she offered and sniffed. The minty fragrance calmed me. Was that a natural calming effect of the flowers or a fae additive? I didn't remember this scent from the tree in Folaím. But then, the bulk of the flowers had fallen. I'd been mostly to blame for that. A tinge of guilt zapped me.

Nay. I dare not carry guilt for something I hadn't created. I hadn't known who to trust. Turns out, I was right not trusting the Saors. They tricked me into helping them without letting me know they intended to draw the citizens from their homes and cause a distraction by setting a ship on fire. If Sakki and I hadn't come to the rescue, how many would have died?

But in their minds, the ends justified the means.

Did they? The people were free now.

My heart squeezed like fruit in a juice press. Again, I fell victim to distracting thoughts. Must focus.

Fix bond. Return to Sakki.

Fix bond. Return to Sakki.

"When will Rhiannon work on restoring my bond?"

"First things first." Ruuta wrinkled her nose. "You stink and need a bath. You can discuss the matter with Queen Rhiannon at dinner." She turned to Liam and Hiisi. "Come, I'll show you where you'll sleep."

I grabbed Liam's arm, keeping him from leaving me. "Will they be far?"

Ruuta pointed beyond the croí tree. "They'll sleep in an adjoining room through there. And I'll stay here with you as I did in Talamh Sí. You won't be alone."

I released Liam and watched them disappear around the tree.

God, please let us complete what needs to get done and return to Sakki. I winced at a disturbing thought. *Let us get out of here alive. All of us.*

SEVEN

My tired body relaxed into the soft bedding, feeling clean and savoring the light lavender scent on my skin and infused in my pillow. But what was that annoying tinkling sound? Was I the only one who heard it? It sounded like pixie dust popping in waves.

At least it distracted me from my thoughts. I stared at the tree branch shadows waving on the arched ceiling.

Tink-ah tink tink. Tink-ah tink tink.

Would it never stop? It wasn't a steady sound, like the ticking clocks in my father's castle. After a time, that may have *helped* me sleep. But the notes dancing around my ears like a pesky bug, scaling up and down, becoming louder and softer, would never lull me to sleep.

But it might drive me mad.

Tink-ah-dee tink-ah-dee tink.

"Ah!" I flopped over, pressing the pillow to my ears. But my hot breath warmed my face. I needed fresh air, so I flipped to my side, crushing the pillow to my exposed ear.

The sound filtered through.

Tink-ah tink. Tink-ah-dee tink.

Earplugs. I needed earplugs.

Wait. Liam had stuffed the horses' ears with cloth when the ship's alarm scared them. I flung the covers away and stepped onto the soft rug in search of bits of cloth to stop up my ears. I tiptoed past Ruuta's bed, past the closet and washing room to the sitting room. A cool breeze ambled my way, chilling my arms.

The doors were open. I sneaked toward them and peeked outside. Liam sat in a chair with his feet up, crossed at the ankles, resting on the railing.

"You're still up?"

He yanked his feet to the floor and spun. "Colleen? Why aren't you asleep?"

"Can't. That incessant music, or whatever it is. Isn't it driving you mad?"

"What music?"

I moved to sit in the empty chair beside him and listened.

Tink-ah tink tink. Tink-ah tink tink.

"You don't hear that? I can't escape it. It follows me wherever I go."

He took the blanket from his lap and placed it around my shoulders. "Maybe it's in your head."

That was a terrible thought. I wrapped myself in the blanket. "Thank you. F–for the blanket... not the idea that I'm losing my head from a sound only I can hear."

"There's nothing wrong with tipping off your rocker a little, just don't knock it over." He smirked. The moon shone on him, casting a shadow over his forehead from his spilling hair, but illuminating his ocean eyes. They sparkled with humor, and a tremor ran through me. He reached out, laying his forearm on the armrest, his hand awaiting.

Did he expect me to take it? My heart thundered. My fingers stretched and recoiled with indecision until they connected. Energy surged from the spot, sending charges racing through me without purpose. He curled his fingers around mine. The pulsing electricity subsided into a comforting warmth.

He smiled at me, squeezed my hand, and gazed up at the moon. "Beau-tiful, isn't it?"

"I thought you hated it here."

"I'd rather be home, no question. But there's no harm in taking a breath and enjoying God's beauty... even here. I don't know what's real and what isn't. But that"—he dropped his elbow on the other armrest and pointed up—"no fae manipulated that. That's God's handiwork all the way."

"The moon the witch kept over her hut was pretty impressive."

Liam cocked his head so he was looking up at me. With the new angle, a shadow fell over his eyes, but I knew the unimpressed look he was giving me all too well. Then he turned toward me. "I'm glad you're here and we finally get a moment... alone."

My heart skittered, searching for a place to hide. I held my breath. "Aye?"

"Aye." He chuckled. "I love the way you talk. Your accent. The way your tongue rolls when you say certain words."

"I don't have an accent. You all have accents."

He released my hand and pulled his chair closer. My heart pounded out new rhythms. He gripped my chin, drawing my face toward his. Closer and closer until his ocean eyes filled my view and my head swam away in them. Then his lips touched mine, and everything within me ignited. The sensation dissipated, and I opened my eyes. His searched mine. The warmth in them melted my soul. A small smile curved his lips, making his eyes shine and my heart flutter before he kissed me again. The world fell away, and there was only me and him—

"Why aren't you in bed?"

We broke apart, and the world came rushing back into existence. The annoying music blared around Ruuta's rigid form. I jumped to stand as if I'd been caught doing something wrong. Though I hadn't. "I—we—Nay, we couldn't sleep."

She frowned. "Between your exhaustion and the sleeping potion, I expected you to be out until morning."

"Potion?" I racked my brain, but I didn't remember her giving me anything.

"In your drink. At dinner." Ruuta disappeared inside.

I rose to chase after her, then remembered Liam. Unsure of what to do or say, I shrugged. "Sorry. I should go."

He quirked his lips and nodded. Though I longed to remain, I chased after Ruuta, catching up to her outside the closet. "You put something in my drink without my permission?" All the negative emotions toward my father for slipping me a drink to erase my memories came rushing back, pushing out all I'd felt with Liam, and I was ready to rage. "How could you do something like that to me?"

"Queen Rhiannon commanded me, and I cannot refuse my queen." Ruuta moved to a chest of drawers by her bed, removed a vial, and swirled it at me. "You want to sleep, don't you?"

"That's not the point." I huffed. "You should've at least told me. Aren't you my lady-in-waiting? Aren't you supposed to serve *me*?" Creeping crabs. Now, I sounded so spoiled, flashing the princess card, but what choice did I have?

"Of course. But the queen is my higher authority. I must do her bidding." She waited for me to enter the bedchamber and closed the door behind me.

How infuriating. "Fine. I'll discuss it with her."

That seemed to satisfy her. She held the potion out to me. "Put three drops on your tongue. That should be enough."

I glared at the potion. While part of me wanted to refuse it based on principles, the rest of me desperately wanted sleep, so I obeyed. And after what happened with Liam, would I ever sleep again? I touched my lips, and my heart squealed with glee at the memory.

"Am I going to have to keep you two separated?"

"Huh?" I yanked myself back to reality. "Nay. Why would you need to do that?"

"Even I recognize his beauty... for a human. He is a delicious—"

"Okay." My blood soared to my face as I fought the urge to clamp a hand over her mouth. I did *not* want to have whatever conversation she was starting.

Ruuta rolled her eyes with an exasperated sigh. "I only mean to say that now is not the time for distractions. Even pleasant ones. There will be plenty of time for that later." She waved me off. "Now get back into bed before you pass out where you stand."

"I highly doubt—" Waves of dizziness flowed through me. Unsteady, as if I crossed the deck of a rocky ship, I splayed my arms and softened my knees. Back in bed, I'd barely covered myself when the sleeping potion took over, shutting out the torturous melody.

EIGHT

A crash and the skittering of shattered glass startled me. Heart pounding, I bolted upright. My head felt sluggish like I was still in a dream. "What was that?" I whispered in the dark. But no response came. I fumbled my way through the covers to the edge of the bed and slipped to my feet. "Is anyone there?"

Still no answer.

I padded across the soft rug. Ruuta wasn't in her bed.

"I'll kill you!"

My head jolted toward Liam's murderous voice. No amount of anger could mask his fear. My heart pounding harder, I charged to his room, then slowed.

"Liam?"

Moonlight revealed his shape and the gun in his hand ready. But he jerked his aim as if he couldn't quite find his attacker.

"Liam?" I clung to the doorframe, peering around it, praying he didn't confuse me with whatever he intended to shoot. With my fuzzy head still clinging to sleep, this felt like a dream. But the soft fabric under my toes and the cool stone or crystal I clung to told me this was real.

"Someone—*something*—was in here hovering above me."

"Hovering over you?" But that wasn't possible. "Were you having a nightmare?"

"No—"

Light accosted the room. My eyes reeled from the sudden onslaught, and I squeezed them shut.

"Is something wrong?" Ruuta asked. "I heard a crash."

I blinked away the pain, adjusting to the brightness one blink at a time. Something shiny glittered on the carpet. Glass, crystal, or whatever the bedside lantern was made of now lay shattered on the floor. I passed through the entryway toward Liam, careful to avoid the shards.

Hiisi came running, crashing into my legs. I picked him up.

"You saw it, didn't you?" Liam asked Hiisi.

He trembled and buried his face in my neck.

I rubbed his back. "What happened?"

"I was asleep and felt a weight pressing on my chest. Something—a ghost or something—hovered over me." He rubbed his throat and coughed. "It tried to strangle me."

"Are you sure it wasn't just a dream?" Even as I asked, I somehow knew it wasn't. The fear in my heart took on new life, and my hand fluttered to my throat as if mine were next.

"It was real." The venom-infused words slithered past clenched teeth.

I wheeled on Ruuta. "Do you know what he's talking about? Is there someone here, under a veil?"

"Impossible. The wards protecting the castle are too powerful. No veil could withstand them."

"A spirit then? Could something here come and go like a ghost?" I felt the chain and followed it to my father's ring. My heart found solace in its presence. If only I could go into the spiritual realm and chase down this spirit, if that's what it was. But I couldn't do that, not without God's say-so.

She huffed through her nose in an unbecoming way that seemed cold, even for her. "There's nothing of the sort. He's perfectly safe."

"Then how do you explain what happened to me?" He flung his arm toward his bed, his tendons protruded from his neck. "I didn't imagine it."

What was that on his neck? I stepped closer to investigate. Redness ringed his neck, thicker on the sides, marking where the hands had squeezed.

"Look at his neck." I yanked on his collar. "There's a bruise forming. *Something* tried to strangle him."

"He probably did it to himself." She scoffed again and turned back the way she came.

I reached for the budding wound. "It's impossible to leave marks like that on yourself."

Liam veered away before I could touch it.

"How are you awake? That sleeping tonic should have knocked you out two times over. Go back to bed." She motioned to the sharp pieces of the lantern scattered across the floor. "Careful where you step. The servants will clean it in the morn."

Sometimes, her cruel nature boggled my mind, but this was beyond anything I'd seen from her yet. The moment I felt she was out of earshot, I vented to Liam in a hushed voice. "How can she be so indifferent? And to deny it happened at all... despite the evidence?" I scoffed. "Something's up with her."

"Colleen." He grabbed my wrist and pulled me to sit beside him. "Watch your feet."

I avoided the broken shards and sat. Hiisi crawled up his bed to sit on Liam's other side and pat his leg.

"Are you all right?" His touch ignited the energy within me and almost made me forget the scattered landmines at our feet. I really should pick it up myself before anyone got hurt.

He leaned in to whisper. "Something is wrong with this place. We need to leave."

"But we just got here." I spoke too loudly. My gaze flicked to the door to ensure no one lingered. I lowered my voice. "We fought for our lives to get through the Divide. We can't turn back now. We still need Queen Rhiannon's help."

"But if something is trying to kill me—"

"Nothing is trying to kill you." I was sounding as cold and uncaring as

Ruuta. With a deep sigh, I squeezed his hand and tried again with more compassion. "You won't die."

"You don't know that. Rhys is dead. Samu, Valtteri, Pirkko, Taneli—"

My heart grieved for each fallen name.

"—all dead. You can't guarantee I'll survive." He adjusted himself to peer deep into my eyes. "If I'm not here to protect you—"

"You will be." I clutched his hand as if I could hold him together through my touch.

Light in. Dark out.

Light in. Dark out.

Breathe. Just breathe.

Great is Thy faithfulness...

I slowed my racing heart, my breath. As I repeated the words, I pushed my renewed calm into him as I had with Clover. Whether it worked or not, I couldn't be sure. But sleepiness was taking me over yet again, so I rose while I could still stand. "I should get back to bed."

He wouldn't release my hand, and in my clumsy sleepiness, I almost stepped on the crystal. "Sorry." He realized his error and let go. "Please think about it. The Divide is safe. We can return to Sakki—"

"But my bond is still broken."

"You'd be with him, even if it wasn't the same."

"But I still need Queen Rhiannon's help to restore my father's kingdom."

"Maybe you should leave it to the humans to sort out for themselves."

What a tempting proposition. I'd love to return to the Divide... to Sakki. And I'd never wanted to be queen. Maybe we could all return to Ariboslia. "I'll think about it."

That seemed to satisfy him. He nodded.

"Take care of him," I said to Hiisi.

He stood and pointed to the bed beneath his feet. "Me stay here."

I chuckled. "Looks like you're sleeping with Hiisi tonight."

"Stay over there." He shooed Hiisi toward the opposite edge. "And no hogging the covers."

A face-splitting grin overtook Hiisi's face, and he buried himself under the blankets. Liam rolled his eyes, but he failed to restrain his smile as he slipped into bed. Now that they both were in better spirits, I felt more comfortable leaving them.

I craned around the room for a light switch. "How do I turn off the lights?"

"I don't know. Ruuta turned them on." He groaned and flung the blanket over his head. "It's fine. I'll sleep with the light on."

That would drive me insane. But if he could handle it, I'd let him. As I closed the door, I spoke through the opening. "Sleep well."

His voice filtered through the closing door. "Think about what I said."

Oh, I'd think about it. And despite the sleeping potion and my fuzzy head, it would probably keep me awake the rest of the night.

NINE

Birds twittered, their song covering the melody that seemed to go on and on for eternity. Sunlight warmed me. The calming scent from the croí tree wafted my way. It seemed more invigorating today. Still, I groaned, not wanting to wake. It had been so long since I slept so well, and I was comfy. Too comfy. I didn't want the feeling to go away, and anything I'd face the moment my feet hit the ground would sap me of all good feelings.

The last thing I remembered was Liam's request. He wanted to leave. And with good reason. But first, I had to find out what Rhiannon had to say. I couldn't have come all this way and never get a moment of her time.

Then I remembered the kiss. Giggles bubbled up as I replayed the memory again and again, stirring and restirring the whirlwind of emotions a simple kiss brought on.

Flashes of other memories came back. The amazing bath. The incredible dinner. And what was the sleeping gown Ruuta had given me made from? It was the most comfortable thing I'd ever put on my body. It shamed even selkie materials. Maybe I'd sneak it into my pack when it was time to leave.

If I ever left.

I'd been here almost a day already and had gotten little information from Queen Rhiannon. She hadn't stayed at dinner long, excusing herself yet again.

Today. She promised we'd talk today. One day closer to returning to Sakki.

Ugh. That meant getting out of bed.

But I'd see Liam again.

I peeled the cloudlike covering away and slid my feet onto the soft floor. The temperature in the room was perfect. Not too warm and not too cool. I eyed the croí and cringed. They planted the tree here to soothe me. Instead, it taunted me, conjuring the image of the one in my room in Talamh Sí and the one in Folaím. Both were triggers, reminders of all I'd lost.

I squared my shoulders and turned away, aiming for the closet. Ruuta appeared with a gown, her own high-waisted lavender dress alight with gossamer amethyst embroidery.

"Oh, good. You're awake." She laid a mountain of glistening fabric at the end of my bed. "I thought that extra sleeping potion might knock you out longer than intended."

"Sleeping potion?" I racked my brain. Right, what she'd given me hadn't even been the first dose.

"Get dressed. Queen Rhiannon's schedule is full, and we must get to breakfast before our meeting." Ruuta disappeared into my closet while I carried the armload of clothes behind the dressing panels.

It took me a long while to shift through the material to find how to put it on. After I donned the white layers shimmering with purple and silver, I couldn't relax my arms at my side without brushing fabric—how annoying! Then Ruuta insisted on doing me up with magical makeup. Her hand swirled over my face in precise strokes. She then gathered up my curls, twisting and jabbing them with silver prongs. When she was done, she showed me the mirror. Shock stole my breath. I cringed.

"You don't like it?" She gaped.

It was beautiful in a showy, not-at-all-me kind of way. And excessive.

Meant for a costume party, not whatever my everyday life now looked like. At least my hair still covered my pointy ears. Though I didn't need to hide them anymore, I still preferred them tucked away. "It's nice, but"—I prodded my face to see if the illusion would smudge or erase... anything— "is it necessary?"

She continued to gawk. "Nice? Nice is a comfortable bed or a warm slice of bread. You're *stunning*." Realizing I wouldn't agree, she shrugged it off. "This is our way. You are royalty. You must look the part."

"I doubt Liam will like it," I mumbled.

She scoffed. "Who cares what goes on in his mind? He's a waste of brain matter, if you ask me." She carried on, uttering insults under her breath.

When she released me, we went to meet Liam and Hiisi in the sitting room. My stomach jiggled, vacillating between an excitement that made my spirit want to leap from my skin and run to Liam faster to a dread that made me want to curl up like an opossum under the bed and play dead, hoping he'd never find me and see me this way.

Liam's eyes widened at my approach. He jumped to his feet in a dark uniform similar to his uniform in Talamh Sí. His mouth parted. Then he flattened his lips, and his choked-out cough barely hid a laugh.

Hiisi cocked his head and squinted as if I might look more like me from another angle.

"Don't say a word." Hot anger killed my excitement and dread. I wagged a finger at them.

"I wasn't. I—"

"Not a word." I snapped my raised finger to Liam, cutting him off.

He slammed his mouth shut, but his lips still twitched. If only I could wave my hands and erase that expression. Or kiss it away. I blushed at that. Hopefully, this magical makeup kept it concealed. Yet he seemed to sense something. His gaze lingered too long. Something new and mysterious in his ocean eyes ramped up the heat on my cheeks before he dragged his gaze away and smirked at Hiisi, who shrugged in return.

Hiisi grabbed my hand and waddled alongside me through the halls. I relaxed, grateful for the distraction and that Liam walked ahead of us where he couldn't see my face. What was happening to me? What was it about Liam, about a little kiss that sent my body reacting in such strange ways? It's as if my heart forgot how to keep time and my senses failed to function properly—ignoring some things and heightening others. And why, oh why, did my blood keep rushing to my face?

Perhaps suppressed auras and excessive fae glamors were blessings.

In our travels through the corridors, I glimpsed Liam's neck. Fresh bruises peeked out from his collar, and my innards twisted. *God, please keep him safe. Please let my time with Rhiannon be worth all this or make it clear to me if we should return home.*

After several turns, a trip back down the gazebo lift, and more turns to addle my mind further, we reached the dining room. Beautiful pastries and fruits decorated the table, and a wonderful aroma of fresh-baked bread and cinnamon beckoned. The moment we sat, Queen Rhiannon entered, regal with her understated facial glamor, elegant silvery gown that probably had fewer layers than mine, and matching crown. Was that the same one she wore yesterday? Or did she have different crowns to match her attire, like shoes?

"May the sun shine upon you, niece." She smiled warmly. "I trust you slept well."

Surprisingly, I had, despite the interruptions. Why did I feel so well rested? The sleeping potion? I'd better broach the subject of slipping me potions uninvited. "I, uh—"

Ruuta elbowed me. Why? To stop me from making my request or—Oh, right. "May the sun shine upon you as well, A–aunt Rhiannon." Calling her that was going to take some getting used to. It didn't roll off my tongue.

She beamed. "My apologies for leaving you at dinner prematurely. I've a few things to attend to this morning as well. The return of the long-lost princess created quite a stir. Ruuta will deliver you to me after you break your fast. We'll begin our instruction then."

Instruction? She's supposed to fix my bond. Protect me from those who want to kill me in Talamh Sí. Those didn't require any instruction. "Okay. Thank you."

She gave me a small bow and a big smile. "Go in the light of the sun."

"You, ah, go—" Ruuta hadn't instructed me on this part, but Queen Rhiannon had disappeared out the door anyway. "Was I supposed to say that go-in-the-light thing?"

Ruuta swallowed her bite, dabbed at her mouth with her napkin, and returned it to her lap. "Only the greeting is necessary. Fae will consider you rude and get a negative impression of you if you don't greet them properly. And a fae's mind is impossible to change once it's set. It is customary for the person retreating to excuse themselves by saying 'Go in the light of the sun' or the moon, depending on the time of day. But none expect a reply."

"I didn't greet her," Liam said past his mouthful. His gaze flitted to me and sparked.

"You're a human." Ruuta's bored expression said it all. "No one expects anything of you, and our impressions are already poor. Nothing you can say or do will change that."

Silent laughter rocked his shoulders. He'd barely finished chewing before shoving another half a pastry in his mouth. Hiisi stood on his chair to reach for a star-shaped fruit. Neither of my friends would ever be accepted by the fae, but they didn't care. I wished I didn't.

Why *did* I care what the fae thought of me? I shouldn't. Liam would say they're demon worshipers, so who cares what they thought? Hiisi would say he didn't want to be anything but what God created him to be, only not in so many words. They were both so confident in themselves. Shouldn't I be as confident? Especially if I was to become a queen?

I was about to eat my last bite of a butterberry tart, but my stomach felt like it might reject all I'd already ingested, so I dropped it on the plate. "Shouldn't we get going?" I wiped my hands on my napkin and covered my scraps with it.

Hiisi leaped from his chair, and Ruuta stood and smoothed her dress.

"But—" Liam motioned to all the food. More than we could eat. He grabbed a few more items and joined us, eating as he walked.

I didn't know what *instructions* with Queen Rhiannon would entail. Would she try to get me to do things I disapprove of? I couldn't even ask her not to slip me potions without permission. And she served Zorac, a demon. I had to tread with care. Put up boundaries, at least.

We walked in silence—other than the melody haunting me.

God, please give me wisdom and protect me. Protect all of us.

TEN

Ruuta led us along crystalline hallways, each carved and shaped into a different archway. The crystal reflected on the floor, creating deep shadows interspersed with pools of blue and purple light. Our shoes rapped along with sharp echoes.

Everywhere, we passed fae who stopped to curtsy or bow, not meeting my eye. As the crowd thickened, I stiffened my spine, growing more and more uncomfortable. While no one would look at me, they had no qualms glowering at Liam. Or worse, jumping away from Hiisi with frightened squeaks.

My fingers itched to wrap us in my veil. It wouldn't work, anyway.

At an enormous room lined with pillars covered in flowering vines, glimmering lights shone above. Rather than illuminating the high sapphire-slab ceiling, they made it seem as if there was no ceiling. Instead, it resembled a starry night sky.

Amid the eye-averting, bowing, curtsying crowd huddled a group that stuck out like red shells on a sandy beach. They wore goggles and aviator caps with straps waggling about their ears.

Humans!

And not just any humans. Aviators. Did they come over on the ship we saw yesterday? Or were things settling down in Talamh Sí and trade reestablished? I started across the floor to speak with them, then stopped. What would they think if they knew I'd fled my father's city to Queen Rhiannon's aid?

But they saw me. I locked eyes with the tallest male among them and sucked in a breath. Whoever he was, the lift of his eyebrow and the way he tracked me made it clear—he recognized me.

Ruuta was getting further ahead. Liam pressed on the small of my back to get me moving. So I hurried after her onto a platform. The audience hushed as we passed a golden throne giving off its own light. When we reached a low-threshold door blending almost seamlessly into the diamond-encrusted wall, the droning chatter resumed, and a knight opened it for us.

Queen Rhiannon stood from a central table carved of pure ivory. I think I smiled back before gawking at the octagonal space. Windows with gilded gold frames spanned two stories high on four crystal walls seemingly lit from within. Two twisty trees with pink blossoms flanked a waterfall flowing from the ceiling to the floor behind her. I couldn't avert my gaze. Its rushing waters, accented by twittering birds flitting about, washed out the annoying melody.

This was her *office*? I'd never get any work done in a place like this.

The door closed, cutting off the conversations beyond.

"M–may the sun shine upon—"

She held up a hand to interrupt me.

Creeping crabs. Was I supposed to wait for her to greet me first? Was there a royalty hierarchy order to these things?

"First lesson—one is only required to greet others with such formality upon the first meeting of the day."

"Oh." I cast my gaze down at the hemline covering my sparkling shoes. This would never work. I couldn't even greet others properly.

"Don't lose heart, niece. You'll receive no condemnation from me."

My heart warmed. How did she have the power to fill or deflate me with a word? Was it a problem within me? A spell? Whatever it was, it wasn't good. Not good at all. *God, don't let her have any power over me.*

"You've a growing company of courtiers, Your Majesty." The knight's stern voice rumbled like a distant thunderstorm.

"Their needs stem more from curiosity than necessity, no doubt." She beckoned Alpertti standing beside her desk. "Take accounts from those gathered and compile them in order of importance. Forward pressing matters to me and make appointments for the rest. Turn away newcomers unless they have urgent need. My long-lost niece has arrived. Surely, my subjects will understand."

Alpertti clicked his heels together, bowed, and left the room.

"I noticed some humans out there. Aviators. Does that mean trade between Talamh Sí and Seelie Clós has resumed?"

She lifted her chin, her eyebrows twitched. "Whomever they are, they're likely seeking keino, which I've not supplied Talamh Sí with since the insurrection. Nor will I until you assume your rightful place on the throne. So, if it's keino they're after, Alpertti will inform them of my terms and send them on their way."

"But how can you do that to the people? Without keino, everything will shut down—the factories, schools, farms, everything. The people will go without power, food, water—"

"It will all be restored the moment you return."

"Then let's go." I cut her off in my eagerness.

Queen Rhiannon stifled a laugh as she pumped her hand in the air to slow me down. "I'm delighted to see your eagerness to accept your role as queen."

I wouldn't go *that* far. While I hoped to help the people, I still waffled about being queen. I wrung my hands together.

"Would you be willing to return now?" She skewered me with a pointed stare.

"I, uh—"

"Are you willing to wait to fix your dragon bond?"

I hated the idea of waiting or going to Talamh Sí without him. But with only one dragon to protect the divide—

She inched as she inspected my face. "Even if it meant taking the throne by force?"

I shrank back, swallowing... hard.

She relaxed, giving me more space. "Not to worry, niece. I'll not make you do anything you're unprepared for. The humans Alpertti's in contact with are aware of my terms. Not a drop of keino will leave Seelie Clós until you are seated upon the throne with a crown upon your head. As of yesterday, they've been unwilling to concede. As for whoever stands in my court today, I'll not give them an audience unless they're here to discuss the terms of making you their queen or overthrow those who wish to prevent you from taking your rightful place."

"Should I be there when you meet with them?"

"Let's wait for Alpertti to determine if a meeting is warranted. Until then, use this time to learn about your fae side." She motioned to the puffy chairs facing her white desk as she smoothed out her dress and seated herself. "Please sit, won't you?"

Liam and Hiisi stood behind the chairs while Ruuta took her position at the furthest one from me, waiting for me to sit first. Where was all this politeness when she wasn't in the queen's presence?

The pillowy chair hugged me—at least as much as my billowy dress allowed. While I could sit here all day, I itched with urgency. Now, not only did I have a dragon to return to, but people who needed me. Well, not *me*, per se. They needed keino. But it seemed Rhiannon would ensure that required them to need me too.

Hiisi slinked around the chair and crawled into my lap with the stealth of a cat, keeping his gaze on the queen the whole way. Once he was settled, he grinned up at me. I glanced over my shoulder at Liam, caught his eye, and silently questioned him. He replied with a shrug while Ruuta focused on Rhiannon.

"What are your thoughts about Seelie Clós and the fae?" Her throne-like chair framed her as if it had been constructed around her. But with her glittery dress and crown, she should've been standing or sitting on an actual throne greeting courtiers, not tucked in behind a desk.

"Um... It's interesting. But why won't anyone meet my eye? Are they afraid of me?"

"You're royalty, my dear. 'Tis only fitting they should treat you as such."

It didn't feel fitting. It felt odd. "But they don't know me."

"They're all familiar with your parents, and you are their exact likeness. If that were not enough, Ruuta is your escort. All the courtiers know she is your lady-in-waiting. And you're wearing royal colors. Only royalty may don that hue of purple."

"But isn't that what the servants wear?"

"Royal servants. But their entire wardrobe is dark, and their clothes are plain, setting them apart. Your dress is light, one of a kind, made of the finest materials our kingdom has to offer, and dappled with the royal color." She pressed her lips together and addressed Ruuta. "Have you taught her our ways? Spellcasting?"

Ruuta pulled one side of her mouth into a half frown. "Not sufficiently, Your Majesty."

Try not at all.

The tinkling melody brushed by my ears. "And what is that incessant music?"

"Music?" Rhiannon straightened and exchanged a curious look with Ruuta, who widened her clueless eyes.

"It's a constant melody that sounds like... like..." How to explain? They'd *really* stare at me like I should be locked away if I said it sounded like fairy dust popping. "Um, like tiny mallets striking glasses with differing levels of water."

Their confused expressions didn't relax, but they didn't seem ready to commit me to an asylum either.

"No one has spoken to me of music. Do you hear it at certain times? Particular places?"

"Ever since I crossed the Divide. I thought it was how this place sounded." Their blank stares incited me to blather on. "I mean, it was worse last night. But that's probably because I was alone and trying to sleep in the quiet... other than the music."

"The sleeping potion didn't work?" Rhiannon's eyes twitched.

"Nay. Ruuta had to give me more." Well, that hadn't worked out as I'd hoped. Rather than ask her not to drug me unawares, I'd encouraged her.

"More than three drops?" Rhiannon scoffed. "That should've been enough to put a horse to sleep."

"Ruuta gave me three more."

Rhiannon grew to new heights and threw Ruuta an incredulous look.

"She's part elf." Ruuta cowered, casting her gaze lower. "If three did nothing, I thought—"

"I'm surprised you woke this morning." Rhiannon steepled her fingers. "You're right to consider her elfin side. I wonder if that has something to do with the music you hear. We'll have to make note of deviances from fae norms."

Ruuta nodded eagerly. "Yes, Your Majesty."

Deviances? I wiggled against the silky chair, uncomfortable with them talking about me as if I wasn't here, discussing my "deviances." Not being a full-blooded fae didn't make me a deviant. How about my care for the humans they thought little of or my lack of belief in their demon god? Did they consider those deviations? I opened my mouth to voice my opinions, then clamped it shut.

Creeping crabs. Where was this anger coming from?

We were wasting time, and I didn't want to get sidetracked with learning the ways of the fae. I wanted one thing from her and one thing only. "Can you fix my dragon bond?"

Eleven

Rhiannon's eyes crinkled with humor yet revealed no wrinkles as she rounded the table and stood beside me. "If I'm to help, first, I must seek to understand the bond. May I see your socrú?"

"My bond mark?" To her nod, I shoved up the delicate petals of the sleeve covering my upper arm.

"Fascinating." Her cool index finger traced the lines. Then, tapping her lips, she returned to her seat. "I've only seen one such mark before on your father. From what I understand, the bond occurs the moment the elf touches the dragon's egg. Is that correct?"

"Nay. After the dragon hatches. Assuming the dragon hatches for you."

"And your dragon hatched for a half elf?" Her eyes, wide and inquisitive, reminded me of a child thirsty for knowledge.

I shrugged. "So it seems."

Palms planted on the ivory surface, she leaned over her desk, straining to catch every word. "Tell me what happened from when you encountered the egg."

"It called to me."

"In words?" She blinked several times and cocked her head.

"Nay, it was more like... it lured me. Like, it wouldn't let me do anything but come to it." I searched her face for understanding, then slumped at her unchanged expression. "I can't explain."

She held a hand out to stop me from giving up. "Like a magnetic force?"

"Yes." I breathed relief. She was starting to understand, though that wasn't quite right either. Still, I hadn't a better example to offer.

"The egg drew you in, and you touched it?"

"Aye."

"Then what happened?"

"It's like it shocked me or something. The egg cracked, and there was an explosion of lights. When the lights dimmed, a kitten sat among the broken shells." I laughed over my confusion at a cat hatching from an egg. But the ache from Sakki's absence—our broken connection—squelched the fleeting humor.

"When did the socrú appear?"

"Once I came in contact with Sakki. I petted his head, and lights swept from my hand, up my arm, and encircled me, leaving this."

"You didn't receive his energy *through* your arm, but *outside* it?" Her voice was like a warm summer breeze rustling through the trees.

"Aye." I'd never thought of that. Energy typically traveled inside, not out. "What do you think it means?"

Either she had mastered the art of impassivity or a glamor masked her expression. Either way, I couldn't read her to glean what she might be thinking.

The door opened, and the commotion outside invaded. Alpertti crossed the distance with hurried clicks, clutching a book, and bowed to Rhiannon.

"Returned so soon? Surely you haven't heard from all the courtiers present." She stood, and her dress fell into place.

Ruuta launched herself from her seat and motioned for me to rise too. Hiisi slid from my lap and used my leg to prop himself.

"Forgive the intrusion, Your Majesty. I've come upon an urgent matter and handed my inquiry over to the council." With two hands, he offered his book to Queen Rhiannon.

She opened it to the ribbon marker, then clamped it shut. "My apologies, niece. I've other matters in which to attend. Rest assured, the information you've provided me is useful. I will confer with my team of experts." She handed the book back to Alpertti. "Ruuta, show my niece around and teach her our ways. Help her understand fae gifts and spells."

"Is it the humans?" I sucked in a breath.

Alpertti narrowed his eyes, sharpening his gaze. "What do you know of the humans?" His voice, although a whisper, seemed to roar from all directions at once.

"Nothing. I—" Did he dislike me? I didn't get any warm and fuzzy feelings from him. Quite the opposite. But what had I done... other than eavesdrop on one conversation?

"Alpertti, is that any way to speak to the future queen of Talamh Sí?" Rhiannon admonished. "My niece. Sole heir to my kingdom?"

My stomach clenched. Was I to become queen of Seelie Clós too? I could barely handle the thought of ruling one kingdom, never mind two.

He bowed low, first to her, then to me. "Forgive my rudeness, Your Majesties."

"Bring the princess to the koulu." Queen Rhiannon almost floated toward the exit, so graceful I couldn't imagine her feet moving beneath that gown. Why wouldn't she at least tell me if the problem dragging her away involved the humans?

"Yes, Your Majesty." Ruuta bowed and backed away.

Once Queen Rhiannon and Alpertti disappeared, I spun on Ruuta. "I need to find out why the humans are here."

"Give it a moment, would you? Courtiers stay all day waiting for an audience. Even if they do speak to her, they're unlikely to turn around and sail home tonight. Visitors from Talamh Sí spend a day after meeting with the queen, at minimum. We can ask after them later. But for now, my queen has commanded me to take you to the koulu."

"What's a koulu?"

"Probably their place of demon worship." Liam scoffed.

"I suggest you watch your tongue, human. I can remove it like that." She snapped her fingers in his face.

Hiisi's gasp rang out from below. He clutched both sides of his oblong head.

I picked him up and cooed to him. "Ruuta will do no such thing, will you?" I said the last part in a warning tone.

With a slight tip of her head and a raised eyebrow, she seemed to say it was a possibility. When I glowered at her, she squared her shoulders. "I know how you both feel. You've made that clearer than the Täydellinen crystal. But please, it would be so much easier if you would keep your judgments to yourselves."

Liam flattened his lips into a whitish line. It probably took all his restraint to hold back comment, but his stormy eyes and reddening face said it all.

"Sorry, Ruuta. We will go with you. I'll try to learn what I can. But promise me we'll look into the humans when we return."

"So long as my queen does not forbid it."

"Fine. You have your limits. I do too, so know this while you're teaching me the ways of the fae, I'll not do anything I believe God would disapprove of. You're not a believer. I can't impose my values on you. But I am, and there are certain things I will and will not do. Do you understand?"

"Fair enough." She bowed. "Now if you'll follow me."

Instead of the hall where we'd entered, we exited another guarded door down some garden-lined paths. The sky was real. We were outside. I breathed in the fresh air and caught my first view of the castle from the outside. The building looked like enormous crystal shards jutting from the ground—not resembling its interior. Must be another seelie spell.

How would I understand anything about this place when I couldn't trust what I was seeing? Did I need to treat it as I had the Divide under the witch's curse? Should I ask God to help me see things as they were? Or did things not work that way here? Was it all an illusion or something else?

I had so much to learn.

Ruuta led us through a path to a shallow pool. Rather than go around, she strode forward, right into the water.

What was she doing? "Ruu—"

My cry cut short when she stepped on the water's glassy surface and kept walking. "What in Ariboslia?"

Having fallen behind the others, I hurried to catch up. I tested the water with a toe, then a foot, then my full weight. Silver and gold fish swam beneath me, and I grew woozy.

I hadn't realized Liam had come back for me until he gripped my arm to steady me. "It's okay. I've got it. Just needed a moment to adjust."

He released me but stayed by my side. I toddled out, certain it must be slippery, but it wasn't. My pace quickened to a normal stride. When we reached Ruuta and Hiisi, she spun, taking the lead, though there was plenty of room for all of us to walk side-by-side. She kept checking over her shoulder to ensure we were still behind her. Her shoes click, click, clicked, a metronome to the melody in my head.

If it weren't for her Zorac obsession, her unhealthy attachment to Queen Rhiannon, and her disdain for humans, she'd make a better queen than I would.

We approached a building more like something I'd see in Talamh Sí but made of an entirely different material. Tinted blue glass, perhaps? But I couldn't see inside. It blended with the sky.

"This is the koulu." She called over her shoulder.

I scrambled closer. "You never said what that was."

"A school." She stopped at the door and waited. A pink beam of light shot out from a circular protrusion and scanned her face, then the light blinked out, and the door swung open. "After you."

Liam stooped to peer at the thing that had spat out lights at Ruuta's face, but he came at it from the side to avoid being blasted. "What was that?"

"Security. It will see through any wards or spells and identify the person. We can't allow just any rabble inside." She raised an eyebrow at him. "Except for you, of course."

He fixed his unimpressed gaze on her as he passed.

We stood in an enormous stark entryway. A wall of the same pink light blinked on before us.

"Walk through it. It detects contraband." Ruuta stepped forward to demonstrate, then spun around, waiting for us.

Hiisi cocked his head and squinted at the light, then at me. I nodded.

As we were about to step forward, Liam splayed his arms to stop us.

Ruuta huffed and cast her annoyed gaze upward. "It's a scan. Nothing more. It won't harm you."

"Aren't I her defender? I should go through first." He tested the beam and broke through.

WEE ooo WEE ooo WEE ooo.

The blaring alarm felt like fireworks blasting at me from all directions. I covered my ears and squatted, certain the place would implode.

TWELVE

H iisi leaped, swaddling me in his arms and burying his face in my
neck. His legs latched onto my waist, his bare feet nearly poking
through the slippery fabric of my dress. A flashing red wall of
light corralled us in the entryway. Two male fae, dressed in red uniforms,
materialized within the boundary. More swarmed outside like insects
descending upon a rare scrap of food.

The obnoxious alarm stopped, but the light barrier remained.

"Relinquish your weapons," the fae closest to Liam demanded.

Liam hesitated, then tugged his pistol from his holster. Still, they
waited. So he lifted his right pant leg, unclipped a knife, and deposited it
beside the gun.

The guard collected the weapons as if gathering dirty socks. As soon as
they were all in his possession, the lights containing us disappeared. "Step
back, please."

"What are you going to do with those?" Liam's brow furrowed, but he
complied. Once he'd backed up enough, the pink light reappeared.

"We will destroy them. There is no need for weaponry in Seelie Clós."

"You can't! I'll need them when we go to Talamh Sí."

The officer held the weapons away from him. "Your Royal Highness, what have you to say?"

"Please return the weapons at our departure from the koulu. It is as he said. We will have need of them." Why did I feel the need to sound regal?

"Very well." The other officer bowed. "We will bind them with a safety spell until then."

My gazed pinged between the two officers. Beyond their uniforms, they were identical with their clipped hair other than what gathered on their heads like a pompom on the winter hats Aunt Stacy brought from America. But they had the same voice too. Were they clones? Or a visage of the same person? So unnerving.

While the guard with the weapons blinked away, his doppelgänger waved us forward. "Please step through the scanner."

Still holding Hiisi, I walked through the lights with Liam. I cringed, waiting for another blast, but none came. On the other side, I breathed easier.

"Forgive the intrusion, Princess." The officer bowed, then blinked out like a disconnected teleview.

Devoid of guards, the place was cold and empty. The dead air smelled of nothingness. Shiny white floors reflected the frigid light above. Our footsteps bounced off the empty walls and amplified, sounding as though dozens of people walked with us, but we were alone.

Ruuta led us through a door, and a cacophony of chatter poured life into the void. Greenery and blossoms of every color surrounded a cluster of tables where young fae gathered, eating as they engaged in lively conversation. The males and females were difficult to differentiate. They all wore the same pale blue robe. None wore facial glamors. Or, if they did, they appeared natural, pale fae skin-toned, without bright colors swooping around their eyes like butterfly wings. They all wore their long hair in a bun. The only clue of gender differences were broader shoulders, stronger jawlines, and prominent Adam's apples. I assumed those were the males, but I could've been wrong.

"The third students take their lunch first since they leave early for their assigned apprenticeships." Ruuta addressed us over her shoulder, the throng deadened her clicking heels.

The students' conversations trailed off when they noticed us. They gawked, some forgetting not to look me in the eye. As I caught their gazes, I smiled, but they remembered their etiquette and lowered their stares with a bow. Some students hushed others, waving to get their schoolmates to stop talking until they, too, realized royalty was in their midst and silence reigned.

Unsure what else to do, I waved. "What are third students?"

"Firsts are the youngest, typically between the ages of seven to twelve, depending on their ability's development. Seconds tend to be ages ten to fifteen. Thirds are twelve to seventeen. Again, the abilities matter more than the numerical age. Some progress at a faster rate and move on to apprenticeships to study under their masters sooner. I've heard of some attaining their apprenticeships as early as age eleven, but it's rare."

I tried focusing on what Ruuta was saying as we maneuvered through the students. But their silent stares unnerved me. Some students saw Hiisi and gasped. Two yelped and blinked out of existence. We made it through the eating area, and the chatter reached a new high as we ascended the stairs. Another door opened to another stark hallway.

"This is where the firsts study." Ruuta continued along the corridor to an entryway blocked by blue light.

When we peered inside, a woman noticed us. With a wave of her hand, the light fizzled out. "Ruuta. May the sun shine upon you." She saw me and gaped. Recovering, she dipped into a hasty bow. "You've brought the princess with you?"

The children's excited voices rang like chimes on a blustery day.

Ruuta elbowed me, prompting me.

"May the sun shine upon you." Would I ever grow accustomed to saying that?

"Come in. Come in. Your timing couldn't be more perfect. I was teaching the firsts about our histories."

We filed inside to find several fae children wearing pale-green gowns and sitting huddled on the grass. Eyes already too big for their slender faces widened, and their gazes tilted higher as I neared.

"Princess Eerika." One student spoke in a dreamy voice.

"Aye." I grinned at them.

The children giggled, and one said, "You."

Another said, "You talk funny."

The teacher's face elongated, and horror flared the edges of her eyes as she clapped so loudly she startled everyone.

Then I realized they thought I was saying I or they didn't understand what aye meant. Either way, I needed to clarify. "I meant yes, I'm Princess Eerika."

"Children, is this how you greet royalty?"

They all scrambled to stand and bow. Then, in a bad attempt to speak together, they chorused, "May the sun shine upon you."

"This is the royal princess. What else should you add?" the teacher prodded.

"Your Highness." Some spoke with dramatic flair, while some mumbled and others seemed to lip-synch.

"Do you have a moment to join us?" the teacher asked. "I'm sure the children would love to ask you questions, appropriate questions." She gave them a stern expression as she stressed appropriate.

They widened their eyes in innocence or nodded to demonstrate their willingness to comply. Some children sat.

"Do we sit before royalty?" When she cast a harsh look at the sitters, they hopped back to their feet. Then she motioned me toward her chair. "Please, sit."

"Of course." I gathered my skirt to sit and wagged a hand at the kids. "Please, join me."

With elated gasps, the children dropped to the grassy floor.

"You needn't sit on the ground, Your Highness." The teacher's long face paled.

"Nonsense. Why shouldn't I?" I made myself comfortable in my nest of shiny material, and the children's shocked faces melted into adoration as they scooted closer.

A child I somehow thought was a boy lifted his robe to walk on his knees, then planted himself at my side as Hiisi was climbing onto my lap. He aimed a tiny digit at him. "Can I touch your pet?"

"Me no pet!" Hiisi balked.

The kid fell backward, then righted himself. "It talks?"

"You hear me." Hiisi's jaw slackened. "You no hear me?"

"They're just children, Hiisi. They haven't met anyone like you before."

The children agreed with loud noes and emphatic headshakes.

"Well, children." The teacher clapped her hands again but with less intensity this time. "The princess's time is valuable. Perhaps we can learn more about her... ah..."

She seemed to need help. "Hiisi."

"Hiisi. Perhaps we can question the princess about Hiisi some other time. But today we're talking about the history of the royal family. Drawing on what we've been learning, does anyone have any questions?"

One child leaped to their feet, nearly toppling over a close student.

"Yes?" The teacher motioned for them to speak.

"Is it true you're going to take down the Divide?" Their cerulean eyes nearly popped out of their small head.

"Well, I–I don't know." My hands flailed, and I gestured to Ruuta for help.

"That is the prophecy, is it not?" Ruuta smiled at the child.

With a satisfied nod, they sat back down, and another student popped up.

"Let's try to keep our questions to the histories, shall we?" The teacher's eyes flashed a warning. "We'll talk about the prophecies some other day."

"Did King Auberon try to kill you?"

The teacher grasped the child's head and pressed them down to sit. "My most sincere apologies, Your Highness. The first years have much to learn. We don't ask royalty such questions."

Another child took their time to stand, keeping their gaze downcast.

"Yes?"

Their gaze flicked from me to the teacher. "Are all royalty Zorac's de–desend—"

"Descendants." The teacher nodded her approval. "That is a good question."

The student beamed, then returned to sit, their spine straight with all attention on me, awaiting my answer.

How could I respond to such a question? "I, uh, don't know much about my ancestry. You probably know more than I do."

The children all laughed as if that was the funniest thing they'd ever heard. Some rocked back while others pitched forward.

Ruuta cleared her throat. "Yes, Princess Eerika is the last in Zorac's line —the prophesied descendant."

Their gazes all flicked to me with renewed interest as they oohed and aahed. I tried not to squirm under their uncomfortable admiration—being a demon's descendant was *not* something to be admired. But at least children everywhere were all the same. The human children in Talamh Sí, the gachen and selkie children in Ariboslia, and now these fae children. Kids were kids, no matter how far I traveled.

Maybe that was because God created them.

And like the children my father had forced to take a curse to make them his mindless worshipers once they came of age, these kids didn't have a chance either. They were being lied to, told a fallen angel was something worthy of serving. They didn't know the real God, either. Nor would they if no one ever told them.

God, what should I do about that?

"Princess? Princess?" The teacher approached, and her eyebrows pinched together.

Oops. I'd gotten lost in my thoughts. "I'm sorry. What?"

"The children would like to know when you plan to return to Talamh Sí to become queen."

"Well, that depends. Some people are angry with me because of my father, so I need Queen Rhiannon's help. I also need her to help restore the bond with my dragon."

A child I assumed to be a boy launched himself off the floor. "You have a dragon?" He thrust his arms out behind him like a cape. Then, catching the teacher's harsh stare, he sank back to the floor, but his eager gaze returned and fixed on me.

"I do." I laughed, but the laughter turned sad. "Or, I did."

Another child popped up to chime in. "What's it like to have a dragon?"

"It's wonderful. It's—"

The teacher clapped, startling me. "All right, children. Our lesson for today is about the royal histories. Since the princess is part of our present and future, perhaps it's time to let her get back to her duties, and we can return to our lesson."

"Aw!" Disappointment rang out throughout the room. One child flopped sideways onto the floor and played dead.

The teacher pressed her palms together. "I'm sorry to cut our time short, but I'm sure you've more important duties in which to attend."

"She does." Ruuta bowed as she retreated. "Go in the light of the sun."

As I retreated from the room, glancing once more at the children over my shoulder, a terrible burden struck me. I'd made so many promises to my father's people. I had to make his wrongs right and help them. Now I wanted to help these children too. But I was only one person. I couldn't do it all.

God, if there's something I'm to do for these people, please make it clear.

The teacher brought up a three-dimensional image of Queen Rhiannon. "Students, who is this?"

"Queen Rhiannon," some said sooner than others.

"And this?" An image of my parents replaced Queen Rhiannon's.

"Queen Delyth and King Auberon," some said.

I'd never seen my parents together. Nor would I. And I had no memories of my mother, only Sakki's version of her. The hole in my heart missing my dragon, my fallen friends, and my family stretched.

"And who is this?" The teacher displayed a new image.

I sucked in a breath. Why did she have *her* picture?

"Princess Maija," the children chanted.

"Nay."

Heads turned my way. They mustn't have realized I hadn't left yet.

"Forgive our delay." Ruuta tugged my arm out the door. "Go in the light of the sun."

The blue light returned, blocking the entryway and shutting out the sounds within the room.

"What was that about?" Ruuta asked.

"Who is Princess Maija?"

"The second born in your royal line. Rhiannon and Delyth's middle sister. Your aunt."

"Nay. It can't be." I peered into Ruuta's and Liam's questioning eyes. "That was Noita. The witch."

Thirteen

Ruuta charged into an empty white room. No. Not empty. A white table and chairs blended into their stark environment, creating the least inspiring room in existence.

As soon as the door closed, she spun around on me. "Be careful what you say. Thank Zorac I had the sense to seal the entryway before those blasphemous words passed your lips." She yanked a chair from the table with a loud screech, making me cringe. Rather than sit, she gripped the chairback like she might tear it in two. "I hope no one overheard you speak such sacrilege about the royal family—*your* family."

Liam stood by the door, brooding. His ocean eyes turbulent, he fumbled with his empty holster. I was glad for his lack of weaponry.

"I know what I saw, Ruuta." I thrust an arm out toward the room we'd left. "That image? That was Noita."

"Why do you keep saying that?" She held her hands up and shook them, probably imagining shaking me. "We both saw her. Don't you remember the tree-branch antlers protruding from her head?"

"Do you believe those were her natural features? When she had me in her home—a home she claimed possessed no magic, mind you—that was her real appearance."

She paced, shaking her head as if to convince the floor what I'd said wasn't true.

"It was Noita. I'd stake my life on it."

She stopped pacing and leveled her gaze at me, jaw set. "Would you stake Sakki's life on it?"

I stepped back toward Liam, almost wishing he was armed. But rather than give in to my irritation that she'd even suggest such a thing, I gave it serious thought. It took less than a second. I was that certain. "Aye. If the woman in Noita's hut wasn't Maija, it was her twin. Or someone spelled to look like her."

Ruuta stared through me, obviously no longer seeing me. "That must be it. The witch spelled herself to resemble Maija to confuse you."

"Why in Ariboslia would she do that?"

"We're not in Ariboslia." Liam chimed in unhelpfully.

I rolled my eyes. "You know what I mean. There was no reason for Noita to resemble someone I'd never met."

"Unless she wanted to confuse you, should you prevail in reaching Seelie Clós, which you have. Even after her death, you're wasting energy on her. She makes herself appear however she wants."

I disagreed. But Ruuta got what she wanted. She'd planted doubt in my mind. "Well, where is Maija now?"

"She died when I was yet a child." Seeming to sense my waning conviction, she touched my shoulder. "We can investigate it later, but I'm charged with teaching you seelie magic."

"You're going to train me right now? When we have a mystery to solve?"

"I also have a job to do." She patted my arm, then moved back behind the chair she'd assaulted. "And no matter what happens, you're going to need to learn if you're to help with any kind of investigating."

"So, you *will* look into this?" Pinpricks of hope lit within me, splattering my soul like a starry sky.

She quirked her lips. "*After* our lesson."

Was she giving in to get me to do what she wanted? I supposed it didn't matter as long as she followed through. "Fine."

Hiisi and I took up seats next to each other. He jumped from his chair, pushed it to touch mine, then hopped back on. Kicking his feet and looking up at me with a wide smile, he folded his spindly fingers in his lap.

"I'm not sure I'm comfortable learning magic. It's—"

"Please, before you protest, hear me out." Ruuta held up a hand. "Fae *magic* isn't what you imagine. It's not whatever Noita was doing. She was using unseelie dark arts, toying with human spells, tapping into the spiritual realm, delving into things seelie fae don't toil with. Dark things. Seelie magic isn't 'magic' at all, but energy manipulation using our natural abilities."

"Like my ability to heal?"

"Precisely." She paced the length of the table. "When you heal, you're manipulating the energy that exists within the living thing. We're all capable of some inherent abilities, such as seeing auras. An aura is nothing more than energy. Its color corresponds with certain emotions. Some fae have other natural talents such as healing, glamors, protective wards—such talents require no spell or potion." She talked as though she'd never thought about this before and was making it up as she went along. "Some fae are more naturally gifted than others, but all spells take time to learn and master."

"And it's all just energy manipulation."

"Precisely."

"I understand healing and veils, but why use glamors? I prefer to see things as they are."

"It's not as if we do it to induce fear or to manipulate as Noita had. Most of us use glamors to decorate ourselves or our living spaces. It's used to enhance beauty. Is that so wrong?"

I couldn't find a good argument. Perhaps it wasn't wrong. I just didn't like it, so I shrugged.

"When needed, we use glamors for protection as you use your veil."

"Or deceive." Liam's voice wafted from the doorway.

She threw him her bored expression. "All abilities can be used for good or evil. Hands can be used to do good as well as cause harm, can they not? Humans make weapons and use them to decimate the elves."

He folded his arms and turned back to watch the hallway through the luminous door.

She dragged her gaze from him.

"How is my veil like a glamor? I'm literally pulling the air around us."

"Do you *really* believe you're somehow shielding those within your veil from sight by using air which—in its very nature—is transparent?" She gaped at me as if suddenly aware of my stupidity and hoping I'd say something to assure her I wasn't as dim-witted as she feared.

Unfortunately, I could give her no such assurances. I felt as brainless as she perceived me. My veil had never made sense. I only knew that it worked. When I blanketed us in air, we became invisible to outsiders.

"You *do* realize you use fae magic to alter the perception of those outside the veil." She continued to stare, practically begging me to assure her of my mental capacity.

"I guess that makes sense." I shirked away from her condemning gaze.

She puckered her eyebrows in a scowl. "How do you not consider that similar to a glamor? In both cases, you're altering vision. I'd argue that a veil is more difficult, as it requires blocking those within the veil from sight while maintaining the background. And you do this without understanding what you're doing?" Her gaze softened. "That is a true talent."

"I'm never going to understand this." I slumped. "Is it necessary?"

She reached across the table and squeezed my hand. "All our abilities stem from manipulating energy. Our minds use energy and control what we see. Consider how you perceive colors, for example." She plucked her skirt, caressing the purple embroidery. "What color is this?"

"Purple."

"Wrong. It's every color except for red and blue, which makes purple."

My brain hurt.

"All the other colors are absorbed while reflecting red and blue, making you see purple. We manipulate light, which is energy, to alter how objects are perceived. Understand?"

I clutched my aching head. I would never get this. "Nay."

"How are you able to heal someone?"

"I just... push my energy outside of me into them, encouraging the body's natural healing ability, speeding up the process, and they heal."

"You don't know what you're doing?"

I shook my head.

"Hmm." She pinched her lower lip. "Another natural talent... like your veil. You don't even understand how it works, yet you do it without giving it much thought. Forgive me for failing to teach you. Given your abilities, I'd assumed you'd had some training. It's rare, even with natural talents, for you to manipulate energy as you do with no additional training. No understanding..."

I perked up, beginning to feel less dim-witted, but now she stared into the abyss of stark white walls, tugging at her lip, at a loss as to what to do with me.

Still staring off somewhere distant, she faced me. "When I compel someone, I didn't know what I was doing either. I pushed my thoughts into others' minds, and my thoughts became theirs...to a limited extent. That's why I need the stone. And it's taken years of training and practice to develop my talent as I have." Her gaze focused on me. "Let's deal with the mechanics later. For now, just understand that all we're doing is manipulating energy, forcing it where we want it to achieve our desired outcome."

Hiisi climbed into my lap. Apparently, the chair was too far away.

"Spells are merely written forms of such abilities. When we're able to understand the mechanics of what we've achieved, we record it for others to recreate, depending upon their abilities. Spellcasting is when a fae reproduces a written spell or when fae come together to achieve something they're incapable of on their own. When you observe the gardens that aren't there, you're seeing energy artistic spellcasters have left of their shared vision. When you see the glamor on my face, you're seeing the energy I'm projecting. Since you don't yet know how to use glamors to enhance your beauty on your own, I've placed a spell around you that affects others. It takes time to understand how to imagine how you want to appear and project those alterations. But over time, you don't even realize you're doing it. It's a minor manipulation. Grander manipulations, such as changing an entire landscape, require multiple gifted spellcasters to project their shared vision."

Now my head was pounding in protest. "I don't understand all of this. What about potions like my father's curse?"

"Potions involve intermingling manipulated energy with items found in nature, typically plant materials. The compounds in those plants enhance spells, making them more potent and transportable. In such forms, anyone can use them, even humans." She cast Liam a sidelong glance, but he paid no attention to her.

"But you act as though this is all normal... good even. How is my father's curse, iv–ivo—"

"Aivopestä."

"Right. How can you justify making such a potion?"

"We don't. It's illegal."

"But—" I rubbed my temples to jump-start my manipulated memories. "*You* told me he was ordering lots of aivopestä and that other one he used to erase my memories. And Liam's. And countless others."

"Unohtaa?"

"Aye."

"Yes, Queen Rhiannon advised me that your father had been ordering them and was causing you and the people harm. She intercepted a shipment and banished those involved to Rotko."

"*She* intercepted a shipment?" Now my head throbbed. "But I overheard him on the teleview asking Alpertti for more." And that could only mean one thing.

Alpertti was involved in transporting illegal spells.

FOURTEEN

Ruuta's head shot back so far she nearly gave her slender face a double chin. Maybe she did. With glamors, who knew? "You're mistaken."

Liam gave up keeping watch, a similar dumbfounded expression slackening his jaw, yet a glint in his eye suggested this revelation confirmed his suspicions. Hiisi craned his neck to stare up at me.

"I'm not." I replayed the scene in my head. The strange noises, me tiptoeing to my father's quarters to investigate, and the tiny version of Alpertti in the teleview as the picture scrambled in and out. "They talked about stolen supplies. Alpertti assured my father that he'd send more. He asked if there were any other seelie potions he wanted too."

"And mentioned aivopestä by name?"

"Aye. And the other one too."

"Unohtaa?"

I nodded.

"How can you be sure? Your father—"

I cut her off. "My father may have scrambled my mind and my memories, but it's the order that's confused, not the memories themselves. And I

69

remember his conversation with Alpertti. After that, he fetched Rhys to give me more so-called wine." I kicked myself for drinking it each and every time. If I'd only remembered that I lost my memory each time I drank... But without my memory, that wasn't possible.

Ruuta gripped her mouth. "There must be another explanation. Those are not seelie potions."

"Well, Alpertti supplied them. And he called them seelie."

"I believe you." Liam scrubbed his smooth face, making a slight scratching sound. His scruff must be growing in already. "The question is, how high up does this deceit in the castle go?"

"There is no deceit!" Ruuta twisted her mouth. Her glamor winked in and out.

Another memory came to mind—Alpertti warning my father not to worry about Queen Rhiannon's reasons. Was that because Alpertti was acting of his own accord? Or was he protecting her? Should I mention it?

"Clearly, there is. I mean, Colleen's other aunt is the witch."

"She was not—" Ruuta clamped her mouth shut and raised her clawed hands toward Liam, ready to scratch or choke him. Which one remained to be seen, but she stopped herself, poising her gnarled hands midair before working her jaw and massaging her hands, then lowering them to her sides. She started out of the room and jerked to a stop.

Given Ruuta's reaction to Liam, it was probably best not to say anything else about the queen. I picked up Hiisi and stood. "Is something wrong?"

"Let's visit the library. That's as good a place as any to start our investigation. Then you'll see Queen Rhiannon has no part in any of this."

"We didn't say she did."

I held a hand up to Liam while Ruuta ground her teeth, biting back the many words she must've wanted to hurl his way. "Don't keep provoking her."

"I'm not trying to provoke her. Just clarifying that we have reason to suspect Alpertti of treason by trading unseelie spells to your father and your aunt may have been the witch. I don't know how that comes into play.

But as of now, we don't know if those things are connected and have no reason to assume Queen Rhiannon is involved."

That seemed to appease Ruuta. She unclenched her jaw.

"We'll start by researching your father's curse." She dug into her dress at her hip, slipping her hand past shimmery lavender that appeared spun more from light than fabric, and retrieved a pouch. Placing it on the table, she unrolled it to reveal vials held to the pouch by perfectly sized pockets. After selecting one sloshing with glittering orange, she rolled the others up and put them away. "This is a teleportation potion. Everyone, take a sip, then hold on to me."

I eyed the orange potion. Veins of gold sparkles refused to mix within it. "Will it hurt?"

"Not at all. It will be as if the room around you changes, but you stay the same. You won't feel a thing except for a slight tingling sensation." She wagged the vial in my face. "But we must hurry. Please."

Liam captured my arm as I was about to snatch it from her. "You first. Then me. Then Hiisi. *Then* Colleen."

"Fine." Ruuta took a sip and handed it to him.

After we'd all sipped the foul-tasting orange potion, Ruuta held out her arms. Hiisi's slender fingers clung to my neck so hard he must've left twiggy imprints as Liam and I gripped Ruuta.

The tingling sensation she spoke of set in, starting from my throat and stomach and fanning out until every part of me itched like mad. I struggled to grasp Ruuta's arm rather than scratch. As she warned, the room disappeared, and a library emerged around us. We broke apart, and I stumbled backward. After I firmed my stance, I scratched in vain at the itches. I couldn't reach them. They were internal. Then, as quickly as the itching came, it faded.

"How was that merely manipulating energy?" Liam planted his feet as he swayed.

I agreed. We were organic material too, not just energy. Did her potion break us down and reanimate us in another place? It made little sense. But we were in Ruuta's world, and we had a new distraction I couldn't afford.

While I should want to resolve the questions I'd invoked, I wanted to fix my dragon bond and leave this bizarre world where nothing made sense more.

God, You brought us here for a reason. Help me accomplish whatever it is and go home—with Sakki.

FIFTEEN

Libraries everywhere were the same, filled with rows and rows of books. This library was no different, but it was circular and shiny like everything else. Even the books seemed to glow. Was that more fae trickery? Could they mask the contents of a book if they didn't like something... or to pull a prank? A spiral staircase ran through the center. I searched up and down, unable to see the top or bottom. The library must be countless floors within a wide tower—if sight could be trusted. Ruuta's fingers ran over the bookbindings, pulled out books, and dropped them in Liam's arms.

"I can carry some." I put Hiisi on Liam's shoulders, and he climbed into place. We should make him a little shoulder saddle. I laughed at the idea, and Ruuta scrutinized me as she handed me a book.

After moving to another row, she thrust a couple more at me and took two more for herself. "This should do. Grab on."

"Don't we need more of that potion?" I asked.

"We only need to drink the potion once. It lasts about a day. We'll need to take more tomorrow."

I wanted to ask what happens if we transported when there was some but not sufficient amounts of potion left in our system, but we had enough distraction. We needed to finish this and focus on Sakki. Once we locked together, she teleported us to a cozy windowless room offering only a table and chairs within its glowing crystal walls. I waffled, almost dropping my books as she dumped hers on the table.

She thudded open a thick volume. "We're free to speak in here as we search for anything about those potions. A privacy spell covers these rooms."

I opened a book with care. The cover was so old I feared it might disintegrate at my touch. I eased through fragile pages, and my hopes of finishing this task vanished. The symbols were unrecognizable. "What language is this?"

Her head jerked up, her stare harsh. "You can't read elfin script?" She slumped into a seat, her scowl switching to Liam and Hiisi. "I'm sure you can't either. I'll have to find a potion for that later. Until then, look for this word." She spun her book and tapped a string of symbols I'd never remember without drawing it.

"Got it." Liam riffled through a book.

How did he do that? Then I remembered the map in the Divide. He only needed to look at it once, and he had the whole thing memorized. If only I had that ability.

Hiisi climbed onto the table and craned his neck to see. With a wide-mouth smile, he nodded and thunked a book from the pile. He kneeled before it. As he studied the pages, his tongue slipped from his mouth and licked his cheek.

Did he have Liam's ability too?

"Here's something." Ruuta dragged her book closer to her face. "It mentions unohtaa." Her finger traced the words while she barely breathed, then dumped the book, and huffed. "It doesn't tell me anything I didn't know. It's a banned spell. The book only brings it up to discuss the ethics of such spells that affect others' minds. Nothing here assists our investigation. No ingredients, nothing."

As I continued riffling through pages, I probably overlooked the word many times. "Why isn't your compulsion illegal? It affects minds."

"Yeah." Liam raised an eyebrow. "Compulsion may not be dark magic, but making people do as you say is pretty dark, if you ask me."

Hiisi's mouth dropped, the little gargoyle a perfect caricature of abject horror. Did he not know of Ruuta's gift?

"Oh, wipe the judgment from your eyes. I didn't hear any complaints when I was sneaking us in and out of the Atonement Center." She thumbed through pages, paused, peering closely, then tossed the book into the reject pile, and picked up a new one. "I admit, I took some liberties while in Talamh Sí. But in Seelie Clós, laws restrict what I can and cannot do."

Liam scoffed. "Such as?"

"My compulsion is acceptable as long as my suggestion doesn't have any lasting effects on the deeper-core processes of the mind."

"So, compelling someone to forget their family wouldn't be okay?" Liam stopped leafing through his book and braced himself on the table with his fists.

I cringed. My father had done such a heinous thing as to make Liam forget his family.

"Correct."

"But making someone forget they saw you as you sneaked past? That would be okay." He poised his question as a statement.

She jostled her head, tossing the idea in her mind. "It depends. In that instance, it's not the compulsion that's a problem but the reason for using it. Who are you trying to sneak past and why?"

"What about—"

Ruuta held out a hand to stop me. "I'm charged with teaching you, but I cannot do anything else until I resolve this issue." She shoved her book away and grabbed another.

"Seems to me you shouldn't be allowed to compel people at all," Liam grumbled under his breath. Then, ignoring Ruuta's scathing look, he turned his book and slid it her way. "Is this it?"

She searched the page. Her finger scanned the words, and she sucked in a breath. "Well, we know one ingredient—muisti marja. A berry. It's banned due to its use in affecting memory. Such an ingredient could cause a simple compulsion spell to snake its way into the psyche permanently."

"Like with my father's memory-erasing elixir."

"Precisely." Her fingers returned to their trek across the page. "The rest of the ingredients are too common. We need to find something uncommon enough but not unlawful to inquire after. We can't ask about banned substances with the sole purpose of manipulating memories without raising suspicion, particularly as royal court members."

Liam raised his hand. "What if I go?"

"Go where?" But even as I asked, I knew.

"Outside the castle to investigate. I could ask around—"

"No self-respecting fae would deign to answer to a human." Her wrinkled nose smoothed as she tapped her chin. "But if I were to put a fae glamor on you..." She shook her head. "No. No one knows you. And you would never pass for a fae. You'd get caught."

That sent my heart racing to panic speed. "What would happen to him?"

"A human caught asking after banned spells? There's no telling what anyone might do. You might've noticed we don't have a large human population. Human lives are of little value here. They have no rights." Ruuta returned to skimming through her books, chatting as she did, unaware of the knots she was tying in my stomach. "There are two types of humans— those who fled Talamh Sí and are, therefore, of questionable character and those who are enslaved by the fae, donkeys who transport goods across the Divide—usually contraband."

She sighed and continued to flip pages.

"Now that I think about it"—she scanned a page, running a finger across it, and moved on to the next—"the two are one and the same. Humans come to Seelie Clós because they're fleeing Talamh Sí and end up as slaves." Flip. Scan. Flip, flip, scan. "Either way, it's of little consequence to me. If you want to trot off into the hands of your new master to become their donkey, ferrying contraband through the Divide, or get yourself killed, have at it."

"Will that happen to Liam?"

My panicked tone stole her attention from her book. Her expression softened, and she patted my arm. "As long as he remains under the seelie court's protection, no harm will come to him." She returned to her search.

Liam pointed at me. "But she's the princess. Can't she free me?"

Shoving aside her book, Ruuta rose and paced her side of the table. When she started tugging on her lip, she noticed and clasped her hands. "I'm not saying I believe Alpertti was working with your father or that Queen Rhiannon may have been involved, but if—*if!*—Queen Rhiannon had anything to do with supplying King Auberon with unohtaa, Princess Eerika could do nothing to save you."

Panic squeezed my lungs, stealing my breath. I couldn't lose him too.

"As I said, as long as he's under Queen Rhiannon's protection, he's safe. But if Queen Rhiannon is behind any of this and catches you snooping, she'll dispose of you herself."

She was about as soothing as an aggressive porcupine. "Forget it. He's not going. I'll go."

"You can't." Her eyes glinted. "You have royal blood. Do you know how valuable that is on the unseelie market?"

My jaw hung open as I shook my head, numb.

"Neither do I." She plunked back down into her seat and stared into my eyes to impress the seriousness upon me. "Royal blood is the heart of many an unseelie spell—which you would know if you could read these books." She thrust a book my way, then dropped it. "Queen Rhiannon does her best to root out and banish the unseelie fae, but she can't catch them all. Those would kidnap you for your blood."

Hiisi yelped, ran across the table to me, and clung to my neck. "You blood stay in you."

I patted his back. "If it's so dangerous out there, why are you suggesting taking us?"

"It's safe as long as you're with me under protective wards."

"Then let's all go." Liam closed the book before him.

"We will. I just don't see how to do so *and* get the answers we need. Members of the royal court can't wander about inquiring after questionable materials. Unless we did it under the guise of an official investigation, but word might get back to the queen." She squeezed her eyes shut. "This can't be right. If Alpertti was supplying Auberon with illegal potions, he must've been doing so without the queen's awareness. She has no reason to help your father control his people. If anything, she wanted to dispose of him to seat you on the throne."

"Is it possible that, with the princess"—Liam caught my stern stare—"I mean, *Colleen*, and her mother missing, she might've wanted him to hold the throne and control the people until Colleen's return?"

Ruuta squinted like this conversation hurt her head as much as it did mine.

"Let's carry on with the investigation, then." He slammed all the books shut with no regard for their age or health and piled them up. "Let's go see this village and start asking around."

"We can't. Haven't you heard a word Ruuta said?"

"His puny human brain can't comprehend fae speech."

"I wish that were true." He yawned, then stretched. "What choice do we have? Do your glamor thing. Make me look like a fae, and we'll go together with your protective wards. What could go wrong?"

WEE ooo WEE ooo WEE ooo.

I slammed my hands over my ears to protect them from the alarm's assault. With a puff of pink smoke, a fae appeared.

SIXTEEN

Her stern expression contrasted with her playful hair—pink on one side and blue on the other, drawn into a braided bun where the colors wove together at the base of her neck. The alarm came to a merciful stop, though its echo pounded in my ears as she marched to the pile of books.

"Pardon the intrusion, but I'll need to verify your book selection." She walked her fingers along their spines.

Ruuta approached, reaching out, pulling back, reaching out again, then tucking an invisible tuft of hair behind her ears. "May I ask what set off the alarm?"

The intruder continued reading the titles without looking up.

I eyed Ruuta, hoping my expression voiced my questions.

She answered by turning down one side of her mouth. Her fingers fluttered as if searching for something to do. "Is there anything wrong with them? Perhaps they shouldn't be in the librar—"

"Not alone, they're not." She met Ruuta's gaze. "But together they raise suspicion of unseelie spell—" Recognition reached her eyes, which grew to the size of saucers. Her gaze darted to me. Her back straightened as if her puppeteer yanked her strings. "Your Highness! May the sun shine upon you." She bowed. "Forgive me. I didn't realize."

"It's okay." I breathed easier. "We were doing some research."

The blue-and-pink glamor marking her face was more understated than most I'd seen so far. Certainly more than mine. I'd have to ask Ruuta to do mine more like hers next time.

"We're not crafting unseelie spells," Ruuta added.

"Of course you're not." The fae barked out a laugh and covered her mouth, her eyes flashing. She waved her free hand, keeping her gaze low as she backed away into the corner from where she appeared. "You needn't explain anything to me. I'm sure you're working on the queen's behalf, so when she receives the alert, please advise her we've erased it from our logs. I'll expunge it straightaway."

"Alert?" The back of Ruuta's neck elongated. "What alert?"

"Certain book selections trigger the alarm and notify the royal office." The fae continued her retreat toward the glowing rear wall, eyes blinking.

"You mean, Alpertti?"

"Precisely." She smiled, loosing a nervous laugh. "Please assure him it was a false alarm. Go in the light of the sun." She bowed and blinked away in a puff of pink smoke.

Why was her teleportation cloud pink when ours was orange? Now wasn't the time to ask. Ruuta had collapsed against the table and fanned her face, her breath coming in heaves. I hurried to her side.

"This is bad." She heaved a strained breath. "So very bad."

"So, Alpertti will know we're researching unseelie spells." He shrugged. "Might make things easier."

Ruuta wheeled on him and gripped his collar. "How? How in Zorac's name does this make anything better? Do you know what he'll do if—no, when—he learns we triggered the alarm?"

"Uh, no." He tugged at his shirt in her clutches.

She unhanded him and stared unblinking and slumped. "Neither do I."

He smoothed his shirt. "I'm curious to see his reaction." His gaze flicked between Ruuta and me. "I'm not saying I know how he'll react, but if he's involved in supplying the humans with unseelie spells and finds out we're investigating, don't you think he'll do something incriminating?"

"Maybe." She pressed her lips together, closed her eyes, and worked to regulate her breathing. "No good will come from this."

"You can't know that." Right? I gulped.

"Well, *I'm* eager to gauge Alpertti's response."

"I think you're the only one."

Judging from Hiisi's grim expression, I'd say she was right. I didn't know these people and how they reacted to normal situations. No way would I be able to read their responses. And these people had been conducting royal business. Those types knew how to conceal their true feelings.

Another reason I'd make a terrible queen.

And if anyone should be concerned, Liam should. After what Ruuta said about humans, why wasn't he more disturbed? If something happened to him or Hiisi, I'd... I'd...

Ruuta gathered the books with agitated, jerky movements. "We need to return these."

Liam threw Hiisi on his shoulders, and we helped carry books, then followed while she returned them to their homes.

"Once we put these away, we should investigate the village." Liam grabbed my book stack since his was dwindling.

"After what just happened?" She crammed a book in its proper place and spun to face him, her slippery lavender skirt sloshing like water around her ankles. "You think it's wise to continue?"

He scoffed. "Don't tell me you're going to let this minor inconvenience stop you. Are you really that weak?"

"Do you expect to get her to do anything by insulting her?" I clamped my free hand on my hip.

He rubbed his temple. His expression softened. "If we're going to face trouble when we return, wouldn't it be better to go now, while we still can?"

"We can't go without permission. It would give Alpertti an excuse to take away all our freedoms. Then we'd never know his motivation behind doing so."

"Does he have that kind of power?" Liam closed in. "Or are you afraid that the queen herself might be involved?"

"It's not that simple." She pushed him aside and moved to another shelf. "We must return to the castle for Queen Rhiannon's consent. I know the rules. And even I don't roam about the villages without guards. I don't know what wards might be there. If Queen Rhiannon realizes we went without permission, I could lose my station. And if we're not locked in the castle for conducting an unsanctioned investigation, Queen Rhiannon will only allow us to tour the village if we have the royal carriage and guards. Otherwise, she'll say it's too dangerous and there's no purpose other than to make an appearance, a show for the people to assure them we're one of them."

Liam scoffed. "What's the point? We won't be able to get answers with everyone gawking."

Ruuta gripped the book atop his pile and leaned into it, staring into his eyes. "What would you have us do... go into the village in disguises and ask around after illegal spells?"

"Yes. That's what I'm saying."

"Without guards? Or proper wards?"

His countenance faltered. "You don't have wards?"

"I didn't set out this morning planning to launch an investigation off royal grounds."

He wrinkled his nose.

"What do you think Queen Rhiannon will do when she finds out? Because she *will* find out. No." Ruuta shook her head and replaced another book. "I know very little about the village, and you know even less. I don't know which establishments to check, who to talk to... what wards might expose us." She shelved two more books. "No. We need to make an official visit to determine if it's worth risking an unofficial visit and come up with a plan once we understand what we're up against."

SEVENTEEN

After Ruuta replaced the books, we teleported to the castle where our midday meal awaited us. Queen Rhiannon checked in between appointments and approved our plans to venture into the village as long as we took the royal carriage and guards. If she saw the library alert, she didn't mention it. She also made us promise to use a glamor to make Hiisi and Liam appear to be fae. Hiisi had a fit before relenting. Now he looked like the most sullen fae boy in existence.

As we bounced along in the horse-drawn carriage, I tried to avoid Liam, but my gaze kept drifting to the male version of facial glamor and the bun showing off pointed ears. Every time I smiled at him, his scowl deepened. "You weren't this upset about being transformed into a hideous wolf-man with horns."

Ruuta huffed. "That was an improvement."

"To this?" He prodded his chin. "Anything's an improvement."

She diverted her gaze to the window.

He didn't look bad, but I was glad he wasn't a fae. I much preferred his natural features and human masculinity. His ocean eyes remained the same, maybe larger.

For his sake and my curiosity, I tried to focus on the scenery buzzing past. Villagers saw us, and cries announcing our presence rang out everywhere. Attractive gardens and decor adorned every home and establishment. But as we passed, some brightened. More plants sprouted and decorations conjured than had been there moments before.

If they were trying to impress me, there was no point. I didn't know who owned those buildings, and they were fine before the excess detracted from their simplistic beauty.

Ruuta retrieved her pouch of spells. After selecting one, she tapped a few drops onto her palm and blew it away. A blue cloud expanded, filling our carriage.

Liam wafted it away. "What fae magic is this?"

The spell obscured our vision, then poof. It disappeared.

"A sound-blocking spell." She rolled her spells and pocketed them. "Now it's safe to talk. No one will overhear our conversation."

"You could've warned us." He coughed.

"One doesn't announce such a spell prior to enacting it for obvious reasons, and we've much to discuss. We won't be able to disguise ourselves in the queen's escort's presence. And it will be difficult to escape the crowd once they're alerted to royalty in their midst. We must keep this as the tour Queen Rhiannon expects. This will give you the lay of the land and allow me to locate any wards that might give us away. Tonight, we'll sneak outside the castle to conduct a proper investigation."

Liam gave a sharp nod. "Good. I want to sort this out as soon as possible. If Colleen isn't safe—"

"If any member of the royal party is involved"— Ruuta interrupted—"it must be Alpertti, though I can't understand why."

"Why are you so quick to assume it's him and not Rhiannon?" His fae ocean eyes flashed.

"What reason have I to suspect my queen? She could never do something like that, nor has she reason to. How would keeping the humans under a curse help her in any way?"

"How would it help Alpertti?" Liam asked.

Other than the scathing glare from the corner of her eye, Ruuta ignored his remark. "She's doing what she can to help, supplying them with keino—"

"Or aether."

"Keino." Ruuta glared at Liam like she wanted to murder him in twenty different ways. She dragged her gaze away and unclenched her teeth. "What good would come from helping your father's people worship him like a god and manipulating their memories?"

"Did it occur to your biased fae brain that she had to have known what Auberon was doing all this time? Think about it. The people are crying out for his blood because they think he made them kill the elves—then everyone falls in line? Following his every word? That would never happen."

Ruuta's eyes twitched like an automaton with conflicting commands.

What he said made sense. At the very least, Rhiannon was aware of my father's underhanded dealings and vile treatment of his subjects. She never intervened. But then, he was controlling humans. If fae didn't value humans, that must be true of Rhiannon too. Maybe she didn't care what he did with them. I eyed Liam and didn't mention that.

"Does this mean whoever helped my father was also working with Noita?" This was so confusing. Why hadn't it occurred to me when I'd overheard the conversation on the teleview? Then again, I hadn't known what they were talking about or that he'd been erasing memories, including my own. "Didn't he get the curse from her?"

"That *is* the rumor." Ruuta dropped her hands with a forceful sigh. "I understand things aren't adding up. But the conversation you think you overheard was between your father and Alpertti alone. While I admit to liking Alpertti and believing him to be honorable, it makes more sense that he acted without Queen Rhiannon's awareness. You don't know her like I do. Alpertti may have used his position to make some underhanded dealings for financial gain. I will find proof and have him banished to the Divide."

"Just when I was starting to like you again."

"Not helpful, Liam." I narrowed my eyes in warning which amused him, judging from his quiet huffs of laughter.

"How would you like a few more glamors to further enhance your masculine fae beauty?"

He glowered at Ruuta, sharpening the menacing gleam in her eye.

"That's enough." I felt like a parent of squabbling children. "We have enough obstacles to contend with without you two attacking each other." As much as I wanted to return to Sakki with our bond intact, perhaps God led me here to root out deeper problems. If I was to be queen, I'd have to protect my realm. Perhaps it started here.

God, reveal whatever is happening and what to do about it.

The carriage rolled to a stop beside an extravagant water fountain with a white statue of winged fairies spitting water.

A knight appeared with a bow and opened the door. "May the sun shine upon you, Your Highness."

More carriages before and behind us spilled out knights who set up a perimeter.

Liam exited first and assisted Hiisi, Ruuta, and me while the knight stood at attention. Fae flocked to a respectable distance oohing and aahing. Nay. A spell must've held them back. They formed a neat row with the knights standing guard.

Was it my imagination or did the fountain grow?

"This way, Your Highness." Ruuta bowed and led us through the parted sea of fae. They sang an out-of-synch chorus of the official greeting at different starting points so the one line never ended.

I waved and reached out to children holding out their hands while Hiisi watched everyone with unforgiving skepticism. Liam marched with a puffed-out chest behind us. They were sure to realize he wasn't fae by that walk.

God, help us.

EIGHTEEN

Ruuta led us into a cute building bursting with flowers that bloomed at our approach. The knights contained a growing cluster of fae wearing aprons with the same elfin script as the sign outside.

One female waved the others behind her and bowed. "May the sun shine upon you, Your Highness." She looked up and cried out at Liam and Hiisi.

Their fae disguises were gone. Did this place have a ward against them, as Ruuta had warned? She was right to conduct a test visit first.

The fae regained her composure. "Will you be dining with us today, Your Highness?" She kept her head high and her gaze low. She must've understood why we'd explore in public with disguises. And if she judged us for our company, she didn't let on.

"The princess has eaten her midday meal. Tea and a light refreshment should suffice." Ruuta glanced around the airy space to a balcony above. "May we sit up there? In private?"

"Whatever the princess wishes." The fae waved to a staff member hanging over her shoulder who flitted away. "And what of your pets, Your Highness? Do you wish them to join you?"

"Pets?" The fae thought of Hiisi as a pet, but she'd said pets... plural. What other pet?

Her glamor winked in and out as she stammered. "Your donkey and your"—she motioned toward Hiisi—"pet."

Irritation flared under my skin, but I bit back the retort. Instead, I took a deep breath. She was a victim of her environment. Anger wouldn't change her ignorance. "Aye, the *human* and Hiisi will join me."

"Very well, Your Highness." Head bowed, she retreated.

The girl our host had shooed away returned with some flustered fae filing out the door. "The princess's table is ready."

We followed the woman up the stairs to a table far too big for the four of us with an overabundance of food. So much for *light* refreshments. "Your table, Your Highness. Is there anything else I can get you?"

"That will be all." Ruuta dipped in a slight bow.

The woman returned the bow with a deeper flourish and blinked out in a puff of orange smoke.

"Did she call me a *donkey?*" Liam's twisted expression seemed more confused than offended.

Ruuta unrolled her spells and blew the same one she had earlier, engulfing us in a blue cloud.

Liam coughed. "Another listening spell?"

"The last spell is still in the carriage until it dissipates." She plunked into her seat in a very unroyal way. "This is worse than I feared. I rarely venture outside royal grounds and never with anyone in disguise. We'll be recognized everywhere we go and bring lots of attention upon ourselves." She slumped, swiping at her temple as if there were stray strands of hair.

"There are wards against glamors"—I pointed to Liam and Hiisi—"as you said."

"What's this donkey business?" Liam wouldn't let it go.

"I already told you. Most humans in Seelie Clós smuggle contraband across the Divide." She lifted a hand as if the answer rested in her gloved palm. "Like a donkey carries supplies."

Liam scoffed. "Pets."

Hiisi jabbed a thumb at himself. "Me no pet. Me guide."

"I warned you." The myriad petals of her sleeves fluttered as Ruuta gestured to the shiny space, bursting with fauna, then to the passing fae craning to catch a glimpse of us from below. "Fae value what they deem beautiful. Hiisi, you don't fall into that category, sorry to say. And they've never seen anything like you. They don't know how to categorize you."

Hiisi stood on his seat with a satisfied smile. "Me Hiisi again. Me happy."

"This is ridiculous." Liam plucked a bite-sized pastry from a platter and popped it into his mouth. "And what's with the caravan of knights? There was none of that at the school."

"The koulu is on royal grounds and under stringent wards. Even so, you saw the security measures in place entering the building." Ruuta's eyes glazed over. "If we're to make it past the standard wards, we need a stronger spell."

"An illegal spell?" Liam waited for her retort. Seeing none was coming, he picked up his dainty cup, fumbling with it in his oversized human hands before taking a sip. He winced and glared at the offending drink.

His response piqued my curiosity, and I blew the steam from my cup and sipped. The tea was a little earthy with a sweet aftertaste. I drank more.

Liam wondered at me. "You *like* that?"

"It's good."

He shook his head and swallowed another pastry.

"It's a fae thing." Ruuta took a dainty sip. "Humans wouldn't understand." She replaced her cup on the saucer. "We might as well return to the castle. I will search Queen Rhiannon's sanctum for anything that might help us."

"Can't we use your teleportation spell?" Liam's eyes tracked Hiisi rapping a round fruit on the table, then picking at the peel with his spindly fingers.

"Teleportation spells don't work traveling in and out of royal grounds. Otherwise, anyone could get in."

"But that knight teleported us inside."

"Mikko? Teleportation is his gifting. That's one of his purposes in

Rhiannon's employ. But it doesn't matter. Even he can't get in or out without her express permission. She covers him with a ward for such a purpose." Ruuta downed the last of her drink with grace. "This is pointless. Let's go. We won't accomplish anything out here. And there's no point in returning."

I didn't want to deal with that crowd. "What will happen when we leave? Will Liam and Hiisi look like fae again?"

"Yes. The glamors are still intact. The wards here subdue them. Can you see the faint webbing in the air?"

"Webbing?" I craned my neck, looking everywhere.

"Look that way, into the light. Adjust your eyes. There are thin strands of fae magic."

"Adjust my eyes?" What in Ariboslia was she talking about? I fixed my gaze where she pointed, squinting and widening my eyes, tilting my head this way, then that. "I see nothing."

"It takes practice. Or maybe your elf side limits you." She stood and held her arms out. "For now, let's leave the easy way."

Liam snagged two more pastries while I picked up Hiisi. We both latched on with our free hands. When the orange dissipated, we stood outside the carriage.

"There they are!" someone shouted.

A lively crowd gathered. We filed into our coach as the knights scrambled to secure us. I waved out the window. Once the trail of carriages loaded with knights was ready, the driver got us moving. Children chased, waving and shouting. "Go in the light of the sun!"

I returned the greeting until they fell behind and no more fae awaited us. Then I leaned against the backrest with a sigh. The rocking lulled me, and after a night with several disruptions and enough sleeping potion to knock out a horse, my eyelids drooped.

Our transport lurched to a stop, jerking me from my rest. Shouts and heavy footfalls surrounded us. Our seating jostled, and three rapid knocks sounded from the driver through the carriage wall, then one, then two more.

"What's that mean?" Liam asked.

"It means something has gone wrong, and I'm to teleport you away."

We all latched on, but nothing happened. No itching. No orange cloud.

"What's happening?" I asked.

"Why aren't we teleporting?" Liam demanded.

Pure horror flared the edges of Ruuta's eyes. "Someone is blocking my spell."

Nineteen

"Princess, exit the carriage." Something in the voice and the way they overenunciated each syllable prompted me to rise without thinking.

"Don't." Liam snagged my arm.

After a sharp yank, my arm freed itself without my input. Something severed the connection between my brain and my body. While my disconnected mind screamed to stop, my mouth made no sound, and my feet pressed on. My body served a new master. But who?

As I reached for the door, Ruuta jumped in front of me. She clutched her stone. Before she opened her mouth, I pushed her away. Waves of panic crashed over me as my body persisted without me. I tried to apologize, but my lips refused to utter the words. But I hoped my eyes reflected my horror for her to see.

"It's a spell." Ruuta panted. "Do something!"

Liam wrapped his arms around me.

Without thinking, I lifted my arms and broke his hold using a strength I didn't know I had. Then I shoved him back into the seat and exited the carriage.

Two male fae awaited me. Their dirty faces peeked through long, stringy hair. One had dark hair while the other had almost no coloring at all and pink eyes. An albino?

"Unseelie." Ruuta gasped behind me. "Pakana."

"Watch your words, royal dog." The dark-haired fae blew something from his palm, and a black cloud wafted toward us.

Something within me lurched, and my head felt heavy, like what was left of my mind wanted nothing more than to sleep.

"Princess, come with us."

When the albino fae spoke, I responded without question and moved to join him, my mind's new master.

Click.

"She's not going anywhere with you." Liam must have raised his weapon. I couldn't turn my head, but neither could I mistake the click of a gun ready to fire.

"A human?" Dark Hair smacked the albino's arm. "You didn't say they had a donkey with them."

"I didn't think royals used donkeys. But what concern is it to us if they travel with their trash?" The albino laughed, but his eyes weren't laughing. "Princess, take the gun from the human."

I stopped advancing and turned back to Liam, reaching for the weapon. But it was a weak attempt. Though the command came from elsewhere and I couldn't disobey, it didn't force me to act with speed or strength. Liam dodged me, took aim, and shot the albino. The gun's blast echoed in my ears and morphed into a high-pitched ring boring into my skull like a keino-powered drill. I wanted to cover my ears—stop the onslaught. Instead, I continued my wasted effort to seize the weapon. The air smelled like burning leaves and gunpowder.

The albino froze, hands clutching his chest. He lifted his hands, glanced at his bloody palms, and fell backward without blinking. My gaze flickered to him as I continued my vain pursuit of the gun—which no longer mattered. The pistol had done its job.

With the albino's vitality weakening, the pull to do as he commanded lessened, but I continued my feeble pursuit while Liam sidestepped my advances. As the albino coughed and gurgled, his friend dropped to his knees at his side and cradled his head. A red stain spread, dirtying his already filthy shirt. His head lolled back while he gasped for breath. Ruuta remained transfixed, watching the scene play out.

A tinge of copper wafted toward me, mixing with the sulfuric gunpowder scent. The albino's eyes glazed over, snuffing out the light. He was dead.

With a sudden rush, whatever had been controlling my movements vanished. I stopped reaching for Liam's gun and wobbled. Arms wind-milling, I regained control of my body and moved toward the others surrounding the fallen criminal. Though I wasn't in the spiritual realm, all I could imagine was the inky soul leaking from him into the ground.

"You're coming with us." Liam planted his feet and aimed the pistol at the remaining fae. With one hand, he reached under his coat at his waist and retrieved something shiny, then tossed it at Ruuta's feet. "Bind him."

Ruuta didn't flinch.

"What did you do to her?" I grabbed the bracelets attached by a chain. The key dangled from one side.

"She's under a spell." The criminal glared at me. "They all are."

Along the caravan behind us, statues of the knights dismounting, approaching, and arming themselves with potions littered the scene.

"Are they alive?"

"Yes, but they're not awake."

Ruuta's eyes were open and blinking. "She doesn't look like she's asleep."

"They're not awake."

"What does that even mean?" Fury heated my face as I unclasped the metal binds and leaned to put them on our captive.

He jerked his hands away. "Please, iron will burn me."

I didn't much care. "Then tell me what you've done with them."

"I told you. They're under a spell. They're not sleeping, but they're not aware of what's happening around them or conscious of passing time."

"Free them." Liam closed in on the unseelie fae with his pistol ready.

"I can't." The fae backed away from the dangling iron, and sweat beaded on his forehead.

94

"What happens if I kill you?" Liam placed a crooked arm under his hand to steady the weapon. "Will the spell lift like the one holding Coll— the princess?"

"No." He averted his gaze from the gun barrel. "That spell is in the air and took effect the moment they breathed it in. It won't lift for another hour at least."

"What about me?"

"It doesn't work on humans." He raised a shaky finger toward our carriage. "Or whatever that is."

A trembling Hiisi peered out from behind the carriage's front wheel.

"And the princess?"

"My friend cast a compulsion spell on her. It protected her from the stun spell."

"Why didn't she fall under it when he died?"

"Because it's already dissipating. And she's part elf. Her elfin side makes fae spells unpredictable."

I tugged off my gloves and threw them at him. "Put these on."

The prisoner struggled to squeeze his hands into my gloves, but his slender fingers were too long, so the excess material looked like webbing between his fingers. They were long enough to tuck his sleeves inside to protect him from the iron. Once he was ready, I clasped the iron binds around his wrists and locked them.

"It's safe." I coaxed Hiisi out from hiding, and he ran to me, slammed into my leg, and curled around me like a boa constrictor.

"What do we do now?" I peeled Hiisi off and picked him up. "Wait for the spell to wear off? We don't know how to get back to the castle."

"These guys wanted you for something." Liam yanked the criminal to his feet, his face reddening. "What was it? What did you plan to do with the princess?"

The fae replied with a sneer.

Liam dropped the fae and aimed his pistol at him. "Talk."

The fae struggled to sit in a proud position with his hands clasped behind his back. "I'll not utter one word to the royal dog's trash."

A shot rang out.

Twenty

My heart tried to flee my body, carrying my blood along with it as I gripped my ears to stop the renewed ringing. The fae had fallen sideways. Bits of grass and pebbles pocked his face. His stringy brown hair writhed like a dirty swinging mophead as he struggled to search himself for a gunshot wound with his hands bound behind his back.

"That was a warning, pakana. Next time, I won't miss. And I wonder" —Liam's fingers curled around the gun's grip—"what an iron bullet would do to your innards should you survive."

The fae's facade melted. His legs crabbed away, but without hands to assist, he fell on his back. "Please, no."

"What are you doing?" I lunged for the weapon. "You can't shoot him."

"Of course I can, and I will if he doesn't start talking."

"W–we were to e–ensure the p–princess wasn't h–hurt." His racing stuttered speech was hard to follow.

"What do they want with the princess?" Liam closed in.

"I don't know."

Liam hovered over the squirming fae.

"We were t–to deliver her to some address." His shaky voice couldn't keep up as he sputtered.

"What address?"

"Laaksoon." He spat out the address in a rush. "Vihreä 20 in Laaksoon."

"Under whose orders?"

"I don't know his name." The writhing fae flinched, backed away as far as the ground allowed, and twisted sideways as Liam snatched his collar and aimed the barrel at his head. "The orders come from higher up... from within the castle walls."

"How high up?" His question met frightened silence, and his ocean eyes flashed with turbulent waves. "Why would Queen Rhiannon or any of her court order the princess's kidnaping?"

Fury burned in the fae's eyes, making him bold. "Why do the self-obsessed royals do anything? Their ways are utter nonsense."

Liam tugged the fae's collar and spoke through gritted teeth. "If what you're saying is true, if the orders came from the royals, why assist them in whatever they're plotting?"

"C–coin." The hatred in the fae's eyes gave way to fear as he stared at the barrel in his face. "Lots of coin."

"To what end?" Liam's nose twitched like a snarling dog's. "What did they plan to do with her?"

"I–I don't know!" The fae's voice climbed to a new high. "I'm a runner. A nobody." He writhed away from Liam. "I was following orders."

"Like a donkey?"

"Liam!"

His gaze flicked to me, and the turbulence subsided. "Give me a name —something to go on—or I will end your life." Liam pressed the pistol under the fae's chin.

The fae's Adam's apple bobbed roughly. "He's a Kapina. Part of the Kapinallis."

"What is the Kapinallis?"

"A rebel group."

I sucked in a breath at an image of Taneli aiming his gun at me, ready to kill. He'd been part of a rebel group too. No, he'd been in a rebel group within another rebel group.

Would every government oppress some to the point of developing a seedy underbelly of rebels? And what would happen should those people gain control? They would inevitably oppress those who had oppressed them and others. Then a new rebellion would rise, and the madness would continue time and time again. Was there no way to win this insane game? Everyone fighting for themselves, not caring what happened to others as long as they achieved their desired outcome? Madness.

Liam broke my thoughts. "Are there rebel spies in the castle?"

"I don't know." The fae swallowed against the gun to his throat. "I swear it!"

Was that a wound forming where the gun had touched him? Was it made from iron? "You're hurting him!"

Keeping the gun leveled at his captive, Liam grasped the fae's arm and yanked him to his feet. "Either there are rebel spies, Colleen, or the queen is working against you. Either way, the castle isn't safe for you."

I eyed the burn around the fae's neck. None of us was safe in the castle. "But where can we go? According to Ruuta, it's not safe for me outside the royal grounds, either."

"What if Ruuta's being lied to?"

"What if she's not? We need Rhiannon's help, remember? That's why we're here."

"If Rhiannon is here to help us, she will. But this might be our only chance to find out. If we wait around for the knights to waken, they'll take the prisoner and return us to the castle. We'll have learned nothing."

I didn't like where this was headed. "What do you suggest?"

"I gave you my suggestion last night. Did you think about it? This is the perfect opportunity to get away."

After everything that had happened last night and today, my mind was overwhelmed. I couldn't make a decision to save my life.

"That's what I thought." Had he read my thoughts or my blank stare? "Since we're here free from Rhiannon's eyes, let's go to that address and see what we find." His gaze flicked back and forth as he studied me. "You're in danger. If I'm to protect you, I need to know who is threatening you and why."

"You're going to deliver me to those who intend to harm me?"

"I won't let them hurt you." His eyes sparked as his hand flexed on his pistol. "Besides, we're in no more danger here than we are in the castle. Here we have the upper hand. They won't expect us to arrive with weapons."

"You saw what happened." I pointed back to the way our caravan had come. "Where can we go where we're not in danger?"

"I swear on my life. Nothing bad will happen to you."

"You can't guarantee that."

"No. But I seem to have an advantage as a human, and my pistol seems handy too." Again, he studied my face. "Think about it. If we go back, we won't learn anything. You're likely to fall into the next trap once they consider me and my weapons in their plans. But right now, we have the advantage."

He was right. Oh, but I hated that he was right. *God, what do I do?*

No answer came. I was in yet another foreign world where the rules eluded me. Nor did I have any concept of what was happening or who I could trust... except Liam. And Hiisi.

Hiisi.

"What should we do, Hiisi?"

His lower lip trembled, and he looked on the verge of wailing. He pressed his mouth closed.

"Should we do as Liam suggests?"

Hiisi swiped the budding tears away, releasing them down his rounded cheek. "Me no want you to go."

"Are you still my guide, Hiisi? Even here?"

With a deep frown, he nodded. His obsidian eyes shone.

"And you don't think I should go?"

He shook his head. "No. No, no, no. But me no say. God say."

I didn't understand him. Sometimes he was so brave he appeared bigger than life. Other times, like now, he was a cowardly thing. "And what is God saying?"

He gave a small shrug, then dissolved into tears, wailing.

"What is it Hiisi? Why are you so sad?"

He swiped an arm to wipe his tears and gazed up at me. "God no say. Me know what to do when God say. But when God no say—" His voice cracked, and he resumed his wails.

For such a little being, he had big feelings. But I could identify. How much easier it is when God tells us what to do. But having to make tough decisions while He remained silent? That was awful. I squeezed him. "I don't like making choices without God, either. But He hasn't given us a spirit of fear. And if there's a plot against me, shouldn't I find out what it is to prepare myself?"

My bobblehead shivered as he nodded at me.

"Then you agree? We should leave?"

After he gave me a few weak nods, I eyed my frozen lady-in-waiting. "What about Ruuta? We have to take her with us."

"Grab the royal dog's arm." The prisoner offered. "She'll walk with you."

Should it make me nervous that he agreed to our plan? Then again, following us meant a delay in turning him over to the queen and, therefore, more chances to escape. This was his turf. His people. He understood how fae magic worked. How many ways might he turn this around on us? Despite his binds, he had the advantage. But what choice did we have?

"Fine." I picked up Hiisi and tugged Ruuta's arm. Sure enough, she walked along. "Let's put some distance between us and this place until she wakes. Then we'll decide what to do."

TWENTY-ONE

With Hiisi on my hip, clinging to one side, I guided the sleepwalking Ruuta. Leading her was more difficult than I expected. We were far from the road where fae rarely traveled. Or so I assumed. There was nothing here except trees. No fae, no buildings, no gardens, no glamors... unless the local fae preferred rough terrain, which I doubted. My long, fluffy skirt and dainty shoes a hindrance, I steered her around shrubs, felled leaves, roots, and uneven ground. She couldn't correct her steps to keep herself from stumbling, which she did. Several times.

Liam had his hands full too, with the prisoner in one and his ready weapon in the other. He searched the woods. "We should be far enough from the caravan. Let's go a little further and find a spot to lie low until Ruuta comes to. We're in unfamiliar territory. We need her."

Wow. He'd found some value in her. If only it hadn't taken such a terrible situation to bring it about. I felt the surrounding air. Something lifted as we ventured further from the caravan. "I think I can cover us in a veil."

No one raised any arguments, not that our prisoner was likely to help me. I reached out, feeling the air, then peeled sections to wrap us in.

"Did you do it?" Liam asked. "Is it working?"

I shrugged.

"It is." Our prisoner scrutinized me. "What fae can't tell if their own veil works or not?"

I opened my mouth to say that a half elf-half fae who didn't grow up in this world wouldn't know, but Liam stopped me.

"It's not worth it."

"It's not, huh? When you want to retort to Ruuta, it's fine, but when I want to defend myself to some random fae, it's not?"

"Random?" The fae looked insulted by that, of all things.

Liam shoved him forward. "Have at him, then. Say what you want."

I lost my words. So we continued through the woods in silence. The air seemed to lighten. Perhaps because it wasn't weighed down with glamors and wards... other than the veil, I hoped surrounded us.

"Where are we?" Liam asked our bound guest.

"Fae don't wander about in the woods. We teleport."

Ruuta fell from my grip, landing at my feet. With my forward momentum, I tripped. My feet did their own thing while I clung to Hiisi. Somehow, I recovered and kept him from falling.

Liam jerked the prisoner to turn around. "She trip again?"

"She's coming out of the spell." What made me believe that, I wasn't sure. But I was right.

Ruuta hopped to her feet, gaze darting every which way as if she'd woken from a nightmare and feared it might be real. "Where am I? What's happened?"

"We're trapped in the Divide. The witch would've killed you if we hadn't rescued you." Nothing in Liam's countenance gave away his lie.

"Stop messing with her." I gripped her face to force her eyes to stop scanning and focus on me. "You were under a spell."

"A spell?"

As I stared into her eyes, something seemed... off.

"What spell?" She checked, perhaps expecting to find herself in someone else's body.

"I—" She caught sight of the prisoner and wheeled me away. "Princess, watch out!"

"It's okay." Liam lifted the fae's arm to show his limited movement. "He's bound."

Ruuta crouched with her hands up like she was ready to get into a fist-fight. "What's that matter? Do you even know what his talent is?"

"Uh, no. That's why we didn't leave you behind." Liam waved his weapon. "But I have this. It seems to work."

"Where is everyone? The caravan?"

"Probably where we left them, waking up about now. Same as you."

"We have to go back." She started off in the wrong direction.

"Wrong way, genius." Liam motioned toward me. "I don't have any free hands. Please bring her back?"

She turned on her own and clenched her fists. "What are you fools plotting? You know nothing about this place."

"Neither do you, apparently."

"Not helpful, Liam." I shook my head. "We don't know who came after me and why. This is our chance to find out. We were putting distance between us and the knights to ensure we'd be long gone by the time they woke, so you can help us find the place this guy planned to bring me."

"What place is that?" She assessed the criminal.

"Vihreä 20 in Laaksoon," Liam said.

"Laaksoon? No. We can't make it that far. That's almost all the way to the—"

"Valley of Bones." The fae finished Ruuta's sentence. Assuming that's what she was going to say.

"Sounds ominous." Liam raised his eyebrows. "Whose bones?"

"Elves." The fae's eye sparked as if he was inviting a fight.

Elves? I brought a shaky hand to my thrumming temples. "What's he talking about?"

"Nothing." Ruuta squished her lips together, trembling like she was restraining herself from relieving him of his limbs. "The pakana couldn't tell the truth if he was compelled."

"Is there a Valley of Bones?" Liam motioned the pistol in the air as if encouraging her to speed up.

"Yes, but—"

"Whose bones?" His tone said he was not to be trifled with. As did the weapon.

"It's a misnomer. There are no bones there."

"Oh, but there are. I've seen it. Elves' bones. Dragons' too."

For once, I was glad Sakki wasn't here. Was the fae telling the truth or trying to get a rise out of me? "The elves died in Talamh Sí. The humans killed them."

"Oh, the humans killed *some* of them. With the curse unleashed on the city, it seemed possible in all the chaos. But what was the death count? Where did the bodies go? Why did the Divide darken at the same time? Do you think donkeys could kill all the elves and their *dragons*? And don't you think the elves wouldn't have rushed to protect the Divide?"

Ruuta scoffed.

I held my breath as I tried to process the annoyingly talkative fae's words. Something in them rang true. "How do you know so much?"

"He doesn't! He's making it all up. The question is, why?"

"And what makes you say that, royal hound? Did you see it for yourself? Or do you only believe what that demon-serving queen tells you?"

Ruuta's face twitched, her gaze murderous. "I'm not listening to another word of this nonsense."

The prisoner laughed.

"Demon serving?"

Was that what piqued Liam's interest in all he'd just said? Despite being called a donkey, would he bond with the fae who'd tried to kidnap me over their shared belief that the queen served a demon?

"We should go back and deliver him to the proper authorities."

"I know we have our differences, Ruuta. But if you want to prove you care about keeping Colleen safe, then help us now. Someone tried to kidnap her. According to this guy, the order came from within the castle walls. Whether it's spies or—"

"You're basing this on what he told you?" Ruuta's glamor blinked in and out, revealing a flushed face between blinks. "The pakana lies."

The prisoner's neck snapped toward Ruuta. His teeth bared like a fasgadair. "For all I know, the queen herself ordered your kidnaping. You think she cares about you, have another think. She doesn't care about any of us."

Ruuta raised curled fingers like claws as if ready to strangle the fae. Or scratch him. But she lowered her hands. "Let's let the law handle this pakana. Bring him back to the knights. They can drag him to the penitentiary to await sentencing. Since he attacked the princess, I'm sure the queen will decide banishment won't suffice and curse him with a lethal spell. A just punishment."

"For doing the queen's bidding?" The unseelie fae straightened and stared down his nose at her. "Think again, royal hound."

Ruuta's mouth worked, but no words came.

"This is ridiculous. I have a hard enough time dealing with you two." I jerked my thumb between Liam and Ruuta. "Now I have to deal with a hate triangle?"

The fae met my eyes, then broke, shrinking away from my stare.

"Liam's right. We may never get another opportunity to learn who's after me and why. Maybe I'm safe in the castle—maybe I'm not. Maybe the fae is lying—maybe he's telling the truth. Maybe Queen Rhiannon is behind all this—maybe Alpertti is. Maybe Noita the witch is my aunt—maybe she isn't—"

"She is."

"What?" We all jerked our gazes toward the fae.

"Princess Maija. Your aunt? She's Noita. The witch."

TWENTY-TWO

"L ies." Ruuta grasped the sides of her head like she was about to tear her hair out. Then she gripped her pendant. "If we're to do this, travel all the way to Laaksoon with this rat, I'd rather he can't speak."

"You want to compel him?" I gawked at the crazed version of my once levelheaded lady-in-waiting. "I thought it was illegal."

She dropped the stone to throw up her hands. "Everything we're doing is illegal! Running from the queen's knights with a criminal, venturing far from the castle to seek your would-be kidnapers? For what part of that *wouldn't* Queen Rhiannon dose me with a lethal curse?"

"Because I asked you to?" My voice climbed higher as my face pinched tighter.

"Your words might have some weight *if* you're alive to utter them. If you die, I'm as good as dead."

"Not if you escape to the Divide."

"I'd rather die." Darkness flared in her blue eyes. Then she closed them. When they reopened, they were pleading. "What about me, Colleen? Don't you care what happens to me?"

"Okay, now we're manipulating with guilt?" Liam stepped between us, arms splayed. "I, for one, would prefer it if you used your compulsion to get the truth from him. So"—he stepped aside, giving her full access to his captive—"by all means."

She hesitated. Why was she hesitating?

I wanted to hear what he had to say. "Don't you want the truth, Ruuta?"

She pressed her lips together and shook her head. "You don't understand. He'll tell us what he knows, but that doesn't make it true."

"But you can make him tell the truth, right? *His* truth?"

"Yes." She flicked her gaze to Liam and set her jaw. "But I'll only agree to question him if we keep that distinction in mind—all we'll know is that he's sharing what he believes to be true and not something that he knows for certain. He's too young to have witnessed the elves' massacre firsthand or to have met your aunt."

Liam clapped his hands, startling me, and kneaded them. "That's good enough for me."

We spent the next few moments coming up with pointed questions only to learn that he'd been honest this whole time and he was the lowliest of lowly grunts. The only thing he seemed to know for certain was that he was paid to assist the albino in my capture. Everything else was rumors and speculation.

"We're wasting time." Liam dragged a hand down his face. "Make him bring us someplace close to where he was to deliver her. Someplace safe."

Her eyes sparked as she stroked her compulsion stone, then dulled as she lowered her hand. "I can't do this. You're right. We *are* wasting time. The longer we wait to return to Queen Rhiannon, the more incriminating we appear. If I do anything more to assist you with this, she will end me."

My back ached from hunching over this kid, hoping for something valuable. I stretched out the pain. "I'm going with or without you. But consider, without your help, there's no telling where he'll deliver us or what kind of trouble we'll run into."

Her groan turned into a frustrated growl. Her pleading arms dropped in defeat. "You don't know what trouble you're running into either way."

"You'll let Colleen go without you? Come now. Compel the cretin, and let's be on our way."

With one last beseeching look, Ruuta fingered her stone and stared at the captive. "You will transport the princess, Hiisi, Liam, and me to a safe place near Vihreä 20 in Laaksoon. You will not betray us. Nor will you hand us over to those who arranged the kidnaping, and you won't speak unless the princess or I ask you a question. Then you may answer."

"Nice." Liam raised an eyebrow. "No questions for me, huh?"

Her compulsion impressed me and made me feel safer. Despite Liam's annoyance at not being able to ask questions, his shoulders relaxed, his face grew less pinched, and a calm came over his otherwise turbulent eyes.

When I'd seen her compel others, they'd repeated her instructions. But he couldn't speak. Why would she add that to his instructions and not others?

"If he's under a spell"—Liam lifted the captive's arm as far as it would go—"do I need to keep the cuffs on him?"

"Probably not. We have a long way to go. It's best if he has his hands. Go ahead." She waved her hands. "Free him."

As Liam removed the binds, I tested the compulsion. "What's your name?"

"Kohl." The fire in the fae's green eyes expressed higher functioning, and he wasn't happy about his situation. Freed from his binds. He yanked off my gloves, tossed them on the ground, and rubbed his wrists.

"Can you force him to be kinder?" I reached for my gloves. Though I wouldn't wear them after his nasty hands stretched them out, I didn't want to leave evidence behind. I stuffed them in my skirt pocket. If only I'd known we were going on a journey when I'd dressed this morning. I never would have worn this fluffy dress.

"Can I lower the veil?" Holding the air around us was tiring.

"Yes." His mouth worked as if he wanted to say more, but he heaved a heavy sigh instead.

"Good." I released the veil and relaxed. "What if he wants to expand on one of his answers?"

"He can't." Her tone left nothing to discuss. "I'm turned around in this forest. Which way is east?"

Liam pulled back his sleeve, revealing the timepiece with a compass on his wrist. He swiveled, consulting his compass as he went, then pointed to the right of the way we'd come. "That way."

"Wait. We're walking?" I ran a hand down at my inappropriate attire—a fancy dress and shoes. "Didn't you put a spell on him to transport us?"

"You're confusing transport with teleport. And yes, we're walking. Teleporting is too risky. The spell might interfere and break the compulsion."

She addressed Kohl. "Is this the right direction?"

"Yes." He pointed where Liam had but further right. Again, he worked his jaw and huffed his irritation. He took off, checking behind him to ensure we followed, pausing to wait for Hiisi to climb upon his perch on Liam's shoulders.

The others set off, and I hollered after them. "Wait! Can't you just compel him again when we arrive where we're going?"

Ruuta's eyes twitched as she pondered, then faced Kohl. "Is there someplace safe to teleport near Vihreä 20, where we won't be detected?"

"Yes."

She looked up, considering the sky. "A place to hide for the night if necessary?"

"Yes."

"What is your gifting?"

"Tracking."

"You're a hunter?"

"Yes."

Ruuta laughed. "That works out well for us."

"What?" I asked.

"His gift—tracking—won't allow him to manipulate us should the compulsion break or weaken, and it may come in handy in our investigation." Her finger jittered, her movements almost giddy with relief as she rooted through her pocket and retrieved her roll of potions. "Change of plans. We're teleporting."

"I thought we didn't need the potion again today," Liam said.

"He might need it." She opened the bottle, sipped, and passed it to me. "It's best to use potions in moderation, and the double portion may intensify the itching. But I'll not risk anything going wrong."

After we'd all taken our dose, we latched onto one another.

With her stone in hand, Ruuta peered into Kohl's eyes. "Okay, pakana. Teleport us to the safe place."

The itching I'd experienced before was nothing like what I felt now. I fought the urge to disconnect from the others to scratch my insides out, if that had been possible. The moment I thought I could bear it no longer, we materialized in a room—a kitchen.

Before Ruuta could give Kohl new instructions or ensure the compulsion spell remained intact, he turned to the bewildered woman standing at a stove.

TWENTY-THREE

A spoon slipped from the woman's hand into a bubbling pot. "Oh my." Her eyes widened down at Kohl, crinkling at the corners as a radiant smile graced her lips. They bore a resemblance with the same upturned nose and stunning green eyes. Was this his sister?

No glamors masked her features. She appeared... real. Her smooth complexion betrayed faint imperfections. Somehow, those minor imperfections disarmed me. Her golden hair pulled into a bun frizzed around her pale face from the wafting steam. "May the sun shine upon you, my lapsi."

While it was difficult to discern their ages, something told me they weren't siblings. "Uh-oh." This had to be his mother. Mothers tended to be protective.

Kohl grasped Ruuta's hands and yanked them behind her back. "Äiti, cover me!"

"Unhand her." In one blink, Liam's pistol was in hand and aimed at Kohl with Hiisi still on his shoulders.

Äiti clenched a stone around her neck and mumbled.

"What's she doing?" My heart hammered as my hands fumbled for what to do. "Stop her!"

The barrel of Liam's pistol jerked to Äiti, and Hiisi slammed his hand over his eyes and turned his head.

She dropped the stone and raised her hands. "I placed a protective ward upon my son. Nothing more."

"And I'm protecting us from her spells." Again, Kohl spoke of his own accord. Teleporting had, indeed, freed him. He kept his grip on Ruuta despite her struggle. "Her compulsion."

Äiti gasped.

"I said unhand her." Liam ignored the squirming gargoyle on his shoulders and returned the weapon's aim to Kohl. He adjusted his grip for emphasis.

Still gripping Ruuta's hands, Kohl positioned her between himself and the gun.

"Do not threaten my son." Äiti stepped between them with a firm stance and green flames in her eyes.

God, please help us. We'd awoken and poked a mama bear.

"I'll do whatever I must to protect the princess." Liam gave her a sheepish look—apologetic, like the little boy within him didn't want to disrespect a mother—yet his hand holding the weapon didn't shake in the slightest. "He tried to kidnap her."

"Tä?" She whirled on her son. "Is this true?"

"We need the coin, Äiti. What would you have me do? Let us starve?"

"If your only means of earning coin is by criminal means, then yes. I'd rather starve." Her face flushed. "Why bring her here?"

"She compelled me to bring them someplace safe. This was the only place I could think of where I might get some help." He glared at his mother. "Was I wrong?"

"Bah." She dismissed him with a wave and turned to me. "And you? Why bring him to me and not to the queen to speak for his crimes?"

"We want to find out who tried to kidnap me and why."

"You don't think the queen would conduct a thorough investigation?"

"According to your son"—Liam stared down the barrel at him—"the order came from within the castle walls."

"So you're not sure you can trust the queen."

We let the comment hang in the air and infiltrate our minds, but nothing changed. Liam still held Kohl at gunpoint, Kohl continued to use Ruuta as a barrier, and Kohl's mother remained fixed between them.

Äiti raised both hands, then flopped them down by her sides. "This is getting us nowhere. But it seems my son and I are in your debt. We promise no harm will come to you and we'll assist in your investigation. But, in return, we require your promise not to harm us."

Something in Kohl's eyes flickered. I couldn't trust him. But I did trust her, and he would do as she asked. At least, he'd do what she asked while in her presence.

"Put your gun away." I touched Liam's forearm and pressed, urging him to drop it.

Gaze on his opponent, he lowered his weapon and holstered it.

Kohl released Ruuta and stepped away.

"No niin, are you hungry? Let's get something to eat." His mother returned to the boiling water on the burner.

"You're going to share a table with the royal dog, Äiti?"

"Töykeä." She spun and flicked Kohl's pointy ear. "Did I raise you to speak that way?"

He jerked away and rubbed his ear, feigning hurt. "She's one of *them.*"

"I'm aware." She waved the wooden spoon, flinging water droplets before she stirred whatever was in the pot. It smelled like nothing. "Every being with God's breath deserves respect."

"Äiti! Do you *want* to be banished?"

I sucked in a breath. "You believe in God?"

She craned her neck to smile at me. "I do. And you?"

"I do!" Waves of relief crashed over me. *Thank You, God.*

"Me too." Hiisi bounced on Liam's shoulders, sending him rocking. "Me too!"

But then, God meant many things to many people. Some viewed the sun or the moon, even animals, as gods. "The One True God? The God the human Bible speaks of?"

Her laugh rang out, melodious and calming, like birds chirping on a spring morning. "The one and only."

"My defender, Liam." I squeezed his arm, feeling his energy through his shirt. "He's a new believer."

"The good Lord saw fit to deliver three believers to my humble home." She dropped the spoon in the pot and clasped both hands before her chin, eyes sparkling like the heavens. "All strangers except for you, the princess's lady-in-waiting. But you're no believer."

"My name is Ruuta." Ruuta raised her pointy chin. "And no. I'm not. Nor did I think any fae were, since it's a banishing offense."

My jaw hung open with a loud smacking sound. "You banish people for believing in God?"

Now that her features weren't worry-pinched, the slender woman had the warmest, most natural face I'd seen on a fae yet. "God isn't too popular on this side of the Divide. I'll tell you that. We don't announce our beliefs when it's unwise to do so, but I'll not deny Him." An emphatic headshake sent her frizzies bouncing. "No, I will not. Not if I don't want Him returning the betrayal."

Hiisi sucked in air and leaned forward, reaching for the woman. She laughed and snugged him in a hug. Then she settled him onto her hip while he gazed up at her with adoring eyes.

"Forgive me—my manners." She plopped Hiisi on a nearby chair and curtsied. "I haven't introduced myself. I'm Nedra, Kohl's äiti. But you may call me Äiti too, if that's not too forward. Sit. Sit. Sit! Let me get you something to drink. I've got nuudelit cooking and plenty to spare. Do you care for nuudelit?"

"What's that?" I slid out a wooden chair from the simple table and seated myself.

"You've never had—" She splayed a hand on her chest as if her heart might stop. "It's a traditional fae dish. You'll just have to try it for yourself."

"Peasant food." Ruuta dipped her head, speaking under her breath.

My heart skipped a beat. How could Ruuta be so rude? At least, no one else seemed to hear her. Äiti had already returned to cooking.

"Do you use glamors?" It didn't occur to me until after I'd asked that it might also be rude. She didn't embellish her face, not with striking colors anyway. And her home seemed—real.

"Glamors? Bah." Her waving spoon sent more splatters raining across the tiled floor. "I prefer to see things as they are, don't you?"

"Yes!" I replied, perhaps too emphatically.

Arms crossed, Ruuta turned to face the wall as if it made for better company than we did.

"You shouldn't be so nice, Äiti." Kohl stood beside his mom. "You don't know what they did to me."

Liam leaped from his chair. "Do you know what he did to the princess? What he planned to do?"

Äiti stopped stirring to scrutinize both boys, then returned to her chore. "You're here now. Perhaps we can discuss your differences over a nice meal."

"They compelled me, Äiti!"

"He was trying to kidnap the princess!"

She gasped and cuffed her son in the arm. "Sit. And stop pestering me. I'll hear you both out soon enough."

I laughed at the power a mother had over two grown men. More power than royalty. If I possessed a portion of what Kohl's äiti had, I might make a halfway-decent queen. If that was God's plan.

Äiti wouldn't accept my help. But as she dashed spices into the pot, filling the place with savory scents, we learned she had four more grown children. Kohl was the youngest. And her husband had passed when Kohl was a boy. She wouldn't allow the conversation to lag or tread dangerous waters until we were all seated and thanked God for the meal.

I dug into my bowl full of noodles, wrapping them around my fork like I did with spaghetti back home. In a very un-princess-like fashion, I shoved the mound in my mouth. It didn't taste like spaghetti at all. Some kind of oil and spices gave the otherwise flavorless noodles a sweet heat. I set to work on spinning my next mouthful. Liam had a hard time eating his, trying different tactics, but all his efforts resulted in flinging spiced oil. Ruuta was trying to cut hers into small bites. Hiisi managed just fine in his own Hiisi style. He shoveled a big scoop into his mouth, leaned over the bowl, and sucked up the strands.

"Just spin it around your fork, like this."

"I thought you'd never eaten nuudelit?" Äiti used her fork as I did, but better, like she'd been eating noodles daily her entire life. While I over-loaded my fork with too large a bite and several dangling noodles, hers seemed perfectly sized every time.

"I've never had this. This is so good. But I've had similar noodles—spaghetti. My mom used to get it from Ameri–ca." I didn't realize until I'd trailed off at the end that I was speaking of a world they didn't know.

"Where's Ameri Ca?"

"America. It's another realm."

"Is that where you grew up?"

"I grew up in Ariboslia. My aunt Stacy lived in America. My mom grew up there. Aunt Stacy would sometimes bring things from home, like spaghetti."

"Isn't Queen Delyth your mother?"

"Uh, yeah. But I don't know what happened to her. I don't remember her. I was an orphan. My mom, er, Fallon adopted me."

"Did you know you were a princess?"

"Not until I bonded with my dragon..." My voice wobbled. How I missed him! I swallowed, though nothing was in my mouth. "Then he brought me to Talamh Sí, and the Saors told me about my father."

Äiti whistled. "Grew up without your parents, in another world, not knowing who you are?"

"That's about the gist of it." I didn't mention the horrors I'd seen. No point in it.

She smacked her son's arm, making him choke on his mouthful. "You see, lapsi? Bah! You think you know everything... how terrible the royals are. You know nothing about her. What did you want with her? Why kidnap the poor creature?"

Kohl's face darkened. He swallowed his bite. "I was paid to do a job."

"Oh, come now. Aren't you part of this Kapinallis group?"

He struck his face with a loud thwack and dragged his hand down his face. "Really, Äiti?"

Ruuta stood, ready to hand him over to the authorities. "You're one of the rebels?"

TWENTY-FOUR

Äiti pressed the back of her palm to her forehead as if checking for a temperature. "Give me the truth, lapsi. Did you kidnap the princess for coin or for your cause?"

"Coin." To his mother's assessing stare, he hurried to add, "I swear it. The Kapinallis are only involved in this for the money. It's a job, nothing more."

"That you're aware of," Liam added.

Kohl glared at him, then pleaded to his äiti. "Don't you want to remove these demon worshipers from the throne?"

"First, I don't take into my hands and expect God to follow me. I follow Him, and I've received no such instruction. Second, how would kidnaping the princess aid you in your quest?"

"Argh!" Kohl's neck craned upward while the rest of his body sagged. "That was just a job. I don't know who ordered it, but it came from within the castle. She's not safe there."

"No niin, you think you've done her a favor? What do the Kapina plan to do with her?"

He threw his hands up. "All I know is she wouldn't be harmed. I'd bring home some coin, and the Kapina would have more funds to aid their plans. That's it. Wins all around."

Äiti clutched her fists to her chest as if holding a protruding knife hilt embedded there. She shook her head at her son. "What did you expect those Kapina would do once they got her? Return her safely to the castle? Thank God you were compelled to bring them here rather than to whatever tyhmiä you're working for." She leveled her gaze at me. "I apologize for my fool son's actions."

Kohl's limp body found new life as he shot upright in his seat, arms waving. "So now you approve of compulsion?"

"I said no such thing. We are called to follow the laws of the land. But I've no doubt the good Lord can use evil actions for His purposes." Her gaze softened. "And what were they to do? They couldn't trust you." She scrubbed her mouth as she studied us. "Please allow me to help you."

"Äiti, no!"

"And why not, lapsi? Seems to me God may have used you to deliver the princess here for this purpose. If anyone can help us, it's her. Can it be a coincidence that she's a believer?"

Kohl rolled his head in a dramatic teenage fashion as if he couldn't take his mother's ignorance any longer. How young was he? My age? Slightly younger?

"Please forgive my lapsi. He doesn't believe in God."

"How did *you* come to know Him?" I couldn't imagine anyone learning about God in this place. But with God, all things were possible.

"I learned of Him when I was a little girl from my family's orja—a human slave. My parents were wealthy courtiers. When my isä bought him, he was only a boy about my age, and my äiti took pity on him."

"A *boy* crossed the Divide?"

"This was before Noita the Witch controlled the Divide. God told his family to go, so they went, hoping to share their faith. But they were captured, and the authorities separated him from his parents."

Poor kid.

"The boy wouldn't stop talking about his God—no matter how much my äiti or I implored him—which resulted in harsh treatment, though he was an excellent servant. Nothing would make him deny his God or kneel to the court's god—Zorac."

Could I be so bold? So strong? I shuddered.

Äiti quirked her lips with a headshake. "My äiti and I couldn't understand how he continued to be kind. Nothing extinguished the light in his eyes. We tried and tried to get him to flee, but he refused. So, we seized every opportunity to learn from him and came to believe in his God too. The One True God of all creation."

"Is he still with your family?"

She chuckled. "No. Though it is unlawful to free an orja, my äiti freed him after my isä passed, but he stayed to teach her and gave her his hidden copy of God's Word. Then, one day, he told her it was time for him to leave. She helped him escape into the Divide where the seelie court couldn't reach him and came here, the furthest place she could flee before reaching the mountains. A family took us in. They, too, believed her message of the One True God, as have many others, particularly those who fled the courts. This is a refuge for many. Everyone here has rejected Zorac and wishes to rise against the queen. But, sadly, a rare few believe in God."

"And we *happened* to find you." Liam's voice was thick and breathy. "What are the chances?"

"This wasn't happenstance. This was God's plan." As I spoke, amazement washed over me, making me tingle. Tears sprang to my eyes.

Even Ruuta gawked. But she blinked back the awestruck gleam to its sharp edge. "We're here to determine if there is a threat to the princess and what that threat might be so we can better protect her."

"Do you know anything about muisti marja?" Liam, adopting Hiisi's style of eating the noodles but with a little less slurping and liquid flinging, shoved a forkful in his mouth.

Äiti choked her food down, covering her mouth. "Why would you ask after such a thing?"

"That's an illegal berry." Kohl narrowed his eyes at Liam.

He bit off the noodles dangling from his mouth and swallowed as much as he could before speaking. "Before the kidnaping"—he finished his mouthful and wiped his mouth—"we had reason to believe someone in the castle has been involved in illegal activity. Someone who may have been helping King Auberon."

"I know nothing about such things." She stared at her son, awaiting a response.

"Don't search me! I don't either."

I twirled the last noodles in my dish. "Do you know what happened to my aunt, Maija?"

Confusion puckered her thin eyebrows. "She died many years ago."

Kohl scoffed. "That's not what I heard."

The crease between her eyebrows deepened.

"I heard she left to rule the Divide. She's the witch."

Äiti cocked her head like a dog trying to understand. "Where did you hear that?"

"From some donkey."

She held up a hand. "Please refrain from referring to humans in such a vulgar way in my presence. And with a human present, at that."

"My apologies." He spoke in an obnoxious tone, hand splayed over his heart. "From a human smuggler." He pointed at me. "They suspect she's the witch too."

I nodded. "I met her. She looked exactly like Maija."

"But why?" Äiti's face puckered. "Where's the sense in that? Why would she betray her sister?" Her breath came in a slow hiss as understanding descended upon her. "Unless..."

"Unless what?" several of us asked at once.

She seemed to hold her breath as she spoke. "Unless she *didn't* betray her."

We all closed in, silently questioning her, urging her to continue.

She tapped the table before her son. "Give it a think."

"She got sick of being the lowly, unwed middle princess with no lands to rule?" Kohl suggested.

"That might be part of it. Or maybe—"

I sucked in a breath. "Queen Rhiannon placed her there to help get me on the throne." I gathered the blank and skeptical stares. "From what I can tell, that's all she wants—to make me queen to take down the Divide."

"To take control of all the lands." Kohl deflated.

Ruuta crossed her arms and scowled, making her glamor look more sinister. "That makes little sense... Noita didn't help. She was an obstacle."

"Maybe. Maybe not." Liam pushed his empty bowl away. "That's what we're investigating."

"Then let's figure that out first. Once we know who tried to kidnap the princess—"

A buzzing crackled the air, and two fae stood in our midst.

"Alajos." Kohl thwacked out of his chair, then scrambled from the men. "What are y–you—"

"You think we wouldn't put a tracking spell on you?" The thickest fae I'd ever seen with icy green eyes and a mop of blond hair stepped forward.

A smaller male fae, more put together with his dark hair in a partial bun, held an arm out, stopping the other from advancing. "I see you captured the princess. You miss the drop-off point, Kapina?"

"I can explain." Kohl raised his hands as if he were being held at gunpoint.

Liam jumped from his seat and aimed his weapon at them, flicking back and forth between them. "Stay away from her."

The smaller fae balked at Liam's threat. "Yeah, we saw what happened to Yaeger. Bullet wound. If only we'd known there was a human with barbaric weaponry." He craned his neck, golden eyes trained like weapons. "We're prepared this time."

Liam squeezed the trigger.

Bang!

I slammed my hands over my sensitive ears and slid from my chair to the floor. The casing pinged on the tile as the bullet clanged.

Ting. Ting. Clink. Clang.

The ammo rolled toward me until two tiles trapped it between them. The bullet was flattened, as if it had struck something solid, yet the intruders stood, uninjured. They must have a shield.

"I see you've all gotten quite cozy, so I'll leave you to it. But we'll be taking the princess." He clutched a stone and thrust an arm out, his hand twisting like turning a doorknob with straight fingers.

Something slammed into my chest where intense itching swelled, radiating throughout my body. "No, wait!"

Liam leaped across the table for me, but he was too late. Even as I crouched under the table, Äiti's kitchen fell away, replaced by an enormous cavern full of fae and the two intruders.

All my friends—even Kohl and Äiti—were gone.

TWENTY-FIVE

I jerked every which way, searching. *Please, please, please, don't tell me I was taken from my friends.* My throat plummeted to my knees. My legs wobbled as reality settled in. *Not again.*

I tried to stand on shaky legs and seek my escape seconds too late. Mophead and Slim rushed for me, catching my wrists. I squirmed, twisting my wrists. But the more I writhed, the tighter they squeezed, their gazes darting to the fae in the cavern.

These fae were nothing like those in the seelie court. Their only commonalities were their pointed ears, and many males wore the same partial bun. They wore tattered, plain clothes. Dingy with stains. No glamors. No bright colors. No sparkles. Some bustled about with their tasks as if nothing had happened. Others threw us a second look as they carried on. But some stopped, jaws dropping as they approached and gawked.

They circled like a pack of hungry wolves, starving for answers as opposed to food, but it made me no less uncomfortable. I shrank away. Would Kohl know where to search for me? Would he help the others? Could Hiisi find me here as he had in the belly of the giant worm? Or did that only work in the Divide?

What would they do now? Without me?

And what heinous crimes were these people planning to commit against me now that they'd gotten me alone?

"Princess?" questioned a high-pitched fae with hair jutting in every direction from a tall ponytail.

One by one, as others spotted me, they mimicked her question until the chamber was an echo of the fae greeting as they bowed. My kidnapers cringed as though the onlookers' scrutiny caused them physical pain. Their shoulders caved, and their knees bent as if to make themselves smaller.

"Why'd you bring us here?" Mophead asked in a hushed voice through gritted teeth.

The other fae ignored him, choosing instead to search the enveloping crowd. His Adam's apple bobbed. Hope bubbled in the deep recesses of my soul. Something had gone wrong—for them. That had to be good for me, right?

Whistling echoed in the cave, seeming to grow louder as the crowd hushed.

My captors' roaming gazes stopped, falling upon a tall fae with long white hair—some stacked on his head, the rest spilling down his shoulders in snowy waves. The tune came from his pursed lips. The onlookers parted for him. My captors shrank further, searching for an escape route, but the crowd blocked all other paths. They cowered behind me, leaving me exposed. My bubbling hope slowed to a simmer as the fae neared, casting me under his shadow.

There was something about that melody.

As his feet stopped, so did my heart. I ceased breathing when he quit whistling and assessed me. An unnatural quiet overtook the chamber in the absence of his song. But the faint melody I'd heard all along returned.

Tink-ah tink tink. Tink-ah tink tink.

It was the same melody as this fae's whistle!

"Alajos, Egon... Princess Eerika, may the sun shine upon you." The man gave a sweeping bow. "To what do we owe the honor of your presence?"

My heart resumed with a tentative thump as my breath dared to return.

"L—Ludek," said Slim, whom I assumed to be Alajos. "I can explain—"

"Have you come of your own accord?"

"N–nay," I stammered, unsure if I should shrink from this man too. Was he a friend... or an enemy? And how did he know that song?

"I see." He clasped his hands before him, speaking to me, but studying my captors. "And why is that?"

The two men who'd seemed so powerful moments before trembled like schoolboys awaiting punishment. The thinner one straightened his spine, daring to meet Ludek's eye. "It's a job, nothing more."

"A job? You're taking on jobs without going through me, Alajos? I'm sure I would have heard of a job involving the princess's capture because I would have turned down said job."

"But it's a lot of coin!" Mophead came to his aid with a voice two octaves too high, unbefitting his broad stature. "We need the money. Besides, she's safe. The order came from Alpertti. He planned to return her to Talamh Sí. No harm shall befall her."

I gasped. "Alpertti?" So he *had* betrayed me. "Was Queen Rhiannon in on it?"

"You accepted a job from the royals!" Ludek roared, and everyone inched away.

My kidnapers pushed into the mob, forcing them back, pulling me with them.

"Have you learned nothing? Do you not understand why we're here? What we're trying to accomplish? You've put us in a terrible position. We can't aid the royals in their plots to seize the realm, nor can we risk bringing about their wrath. They'll stop at nothing to retrieve her. You just put a target on our heads."

"Forgive us." The slim fae dropped to his knees and bowed.

Ludek's blue eyes flashed. "It's already done, but there will be an inquiry."

They shared dejected looks, then cast their gazes to the dirt.

He held a hand out to me. "Princess, please come with me."

He wanted me to take his hand? Willingly? He seemed like a better option than my captors, but he was a stranger too. And if my captors were afraid of him, how did that bode for me? I refused his hand.

Rather than take offense or grab me, he acted as though his hand were merely there to motion me forward, showing me the way. "Please follow me, Your Highness."

I walked with him through the parting witnesses outside the cave. As we exited, Ludek barked orders: "Bring the tyhmiä to my office! Check the wards! Find out how a royal broke through!"

When he'd finished issuing commands, he brought me to a cliff over-looking a dried valley full of lumpy sand, and the whistle reclaimed his lips.

The music resumed, louder here.

Tink-ah tink tink. Tink-ah tink tink.

If there was any question his tune and the melody plaguing me since my arrival in the fae realm were one and the same, there was no question now. Both played together in perfect harmony.

Tink-ah-dee tink-ah-dee tink.

TWENTY-SIX

Ludek stopped whistling, lowered himself to sit on the ledge, and motioned for me to do the same. Not the spot I'd expect a leader to bring me for a conversation, unless he intended to push me off. It was a long way down. I wasn't afraid of heights, but I had a healthy concern for my life. Something told me to listen to him, so I sat and dangled my legs, dust puffing around my once-white dress.

I wanted to ask about the song, but I needed to feel him out first and determine if it was safe to do so.

"Forgive my misguided youths. It's difficult to oversee all their doings. Alajos is headstrong, always in search of coin, and Egon doesn't think for himself, just goes along with anything Alajos says. They shouldn't have brought you here or wherever they intended to bring you." He then spoke under his breath. "I'm sure coming here was accidental."

How could I forgive anyone during my kidnaping? They hadn't set me free. "What do you plan to do with me?"

His thin, gray eyebrows pinched together, twitching. "That depends on you. I can't return you to the queen without understanding her plans. Not that it matters if you give away our location—no members of the seelie court can enter, which is why I'm uncertain how you, a royal, got through our wards." He scratched his bare chin and sharpened his gaze.

"What about my friends?" I moved to stand, my billowy skirt twisting around my legs. "I must return to them."

He pressed a hand on my shoulder, staying me. "What friends?"

"Liam and Ruuta."

He sucked air through his teeth. "Ruuta of the royal court?"

"My lady-in-waiting."

"I'm afraid we can't go back for them." He worked his jawline, seeming to fight an internal argument. "It's too risky." He turned his intense blue gaze from the valley to me, making me squirm.

I jumped to my feet and shuffled a safe distance from the ledge. "Why am I here?"

Ludek groaned and stood to face me. "Because my helpers are fools."

"What do you want with me?" I jammed my hands on my hips.

"I'd love nothing more than to return you from whence you came." He scowled. "Your presence here is an unfortunate accident. Returning you or searching for your friends—particularly one of the royal court—is a risk we cannot afford. Not now. Not when we're so close."

I wanted to bite the bait and ask what he was close to, but I had to focus. "So, you're kidnaping me."

"I'm doing nothing of the sort, I—"

"Are you letting me return home?"

"Well, no—"

"So, you're kidnaping me," I repeated.

His shoulders sagged, and he hung his head. "I'm afraid I cannot allow you to leave." He eyed me askance with the grimace of someone expecting a face slap.

"So, you plan to hold me against my will and refuse to help me find my friends?" My hands slipped from my hips as hopelessness weighed down my arms. "My friend, Liam... he's a human."

Ludek flattened his lips into a grim line. "If I send someone to inquire after your friends, will that satisfy you?"

His request evoked a memory of my father. He'd asked something similar when I'd lost Liam before and assured me he'd locate him. And he was true to his word, but then he erased his memory. If my father could do something like that, what was this man capable of? A fae, no less.

Then Fergus's words rang in my mind. A "shifty lot," he'd called the fae. He hadn't trusted them. I didn't know if I could either, but now, with the fae pitted against each other, which side should I trust? Was either side trustworthy?

Ludek seemed to sense the war waging in my mind. "I shall send someone to glean what they can of your friends' current status and report back to me. If we find them in favorable accommodations and deem it safe to do so, I will get word to your human. Bring him here, if possible. But I'll not risk revealing our location to the seelie court by exposing it to anyone in Rhiannon's employ. Do you accept my terms?"

I studied him. While my naked eye couldn't find anything dishonorable in him, I'd learned not to believe what I saw. But then, when my father had said he'd find Liam, he'd made promises with no caveats. That should have clued me in to his deception. Perhaps I'd just wanted to believe him. But Ludek didn't make such lofty promises. And his concessions came with caveats. That should make them more believable, shouldn't it?

What would happen if I refused? I was still trapped here. It would be better to see if he would search for Liam and take a chance at being reunited than not.

I leveled my gaze at him. "Aye. I accept your terms."

His eyebrows lowered as the muscles in his face relaxed. "I'll speak with Alajos. I'm sure the tyhmiä will want to make amends, and he has questionable contacts to aid him in this task."

Ludek walked away, his whistling disappeared with him inside the cavern, and I returned to my seat on the ledge. The sun sank over the mountains, casting a shadow over the lumpy sand on the valley floor. It reminded me of Noita's desert, and I shuddered. Some kind of lizard skittered across the rocks beside me. It came to a quick stop and angled its head while its protruding eyes shifted to get a better look at me. Then it scurried away. A large carrion scavenger squawked overhead. It flew in lazy circles

over the valley as if it had found a carcass. If it had, its vision was far supe-
rior to mine. I saw nothing on the sand—alive or dead.

Feet scuffed behind me, and my hands scraped the gritty ground,
searching for purchase.

"Didn't mean to startle you." Ludek settled beside me, his white hair
aglow in the waning light. "I've spoken with Alajos. He's returning to
Kohl's house to see after Liam and report to me."

"Thank you." Though unsure I could count on him, I couldn't squelch
my relief.

"It's beautiful, don't you agree?" He waved a graceful arm toward the
valley. "Though it's barren, it's real. No glamors make it appear to be something it's not."

I had great appreciation for that. And his like-minded opinion softened
me somewhat. He leaned back on his palms and whistled the tune.

"What song is that?"

He squinted at me. "Have you heard it?"

"Only every waking moment since I crossed the Divide."

Ludek straightened, his neck elongated as he leveled his shoulders. "It's
what led me here."

I sucked in a breath. "You hear it too?"

Though his gaze fixed on me as he nodded, he didn't seem to see me.

"And it led you here?"

He continued nodding with a faraway look.

"What is this place?"

My question seemed to rip him from his thoughts. "This is the Valley of
Bones."

The place Kohl mentioned. "Why is it called that? Are there bones
down there?"

"There are indeed." He set his jaw and squinted at me. "I've never
understood why I sometimes hear that song or why it led me here, but I've
never met anyone else who's heard it. I believe that connects us and we can
be honest with one another. Am I correct? Can I be honest with you?"

"Aye."

His eyes twitched as he scrutinized me further. Then he nodded as if he'd consulted himself and both parties agreed. "I don't know what strange turn of events brought you to me, but I trust there's a reason for it and you won't turn on us."

"O–kay." I drew out the word. Could I promise such a thing after two kidnaping attempts in one day and no one had returned me to the castle? I had no reason to trust him.

He narrowed his eyes, seeming to calculate his next words. "Where do you stand with the queen?"

What did he even mean by that? "Uh, she's my aunt."

"I'm aware of your lineage. But how do you feel about her, about her practices, her beliefs?"

"You mean her belief in Zorac?"

"Precisely."

How should I answer this without getting myself killed? He seemed on the outs with the royals, hiding in a cave. It should be safe to tell him the truth. "If he's real, I won't serve him."

"Even though Queen Rhiannon does? Do you not wish to please her and do as she wishes?"

"Nay. I won't go against God. If what she wants to do opposes God's plans, I won't follow her."

Ludek puffed a relieved breath, and the tension in his shoulders left him. "You don't know how glad I am to hear that." He closed his eyes and took a few more deep breaths. "Seems you were brought here for a reason, after all. God saw fit to use those boys' folly to bring about His plans."

My muscles released tension I hadn't realized they'd trapped until I relaxed. "You're a believer." The way he spoke about God, his complete faith, set me at ease.

"I am." He smiled. As he shifted his gaze to the valley below, his smile disappeared. "Those bones belong to the elves and their dragons. And I believe, the tune I keep hearing, is their bones crying out to me."

I snapped my gaze to the lumpy sand, half-expecting them to start talking to me. But that was absurd. Wasn't it? Bones couldn't cry out. There had to be another explanation. It was more likely that God used that song to bring us here.

Aye, that made much more sense.

The mounds shifted in my mind's eye, and I could almost see the fallen dragons beneath the grainy surface. My spirit squeezed with sorrow for all the stolen souls. Not only were their lives cut short—they'd gone extinct. I was the only elf who remained, and I was only half. And Sakki was the only dragon. There was no way to replenish our races. "How did they get here?"

"Queen Rhiannon. She's responsible for it all."

TWENTY-SEVEN

My head swooned as I tried to focus. Everything seemed surreal, like my body wasn't mine and I was observing him through someone else's eyes. "How can that be? The humans killed the elves. How could she have been involved?"

"She plotted the entire thing with her sisters... all the way back to your mother's marriage to King Auberon. The royal family serves Zorac. They always have. You're his last opportunity to get his descendants on both thrones, and he knows it. Queen Rhiannon and Princess Maija are both barren. You're the last descendant, and Zorac has been plotting this since before your birth."

"He planned my mother's marriage?"

The breeze teased his long white hair, lifting tufts off his shoulders like milkweed seeds straining to detach from the plant. He raised a hand and tilted his head away. "I don't know the extent of Zorac's involvement. Or if he's real. If he is, he's using Rhiannon. If he's not, she's using him. Either way, she orchestrated it all. She arranged for the marriage. Though her sister would be the queen consort, her child would be the true heir to the throne. Once that child"—he motioned to me—"you, took the throne while

Queen Rhiannon occupied hers, the Divide would fall, freeing Zorac to rule the entire realm." He rubbed his chin. "That was the plan, anyway."

"What went wrong?"

"After your mother moved to Talamh Sí, she fell in love with your father and the people. And their God." He cocked his head at me, blue eyes intense as if awaiting a response.

I had none. "Then what happened?"

"I must add another caveat. We've gathered all this information over the years from former royal servants and disgruntled family, but this is the truth as I know it. Understood?"

At my nod, he continued. "Your mother began to believe they were wrong in serving Zorac, and she made the mistake of telling her sisters. Then, while you were a small child, she uncovered a plot to have her and your father assassinated, thereby making you a child queen. So, she fled with you, expecting to save Auberon and the kingdom. If neither of you were there to rule, no harm would come to him."

A longing I hadn't realized I'd had, buried somewhere deep within me was filled, and I choked back relieved tears. "My mother wasn't escaping my father. She loved him."

"So it would seem."

"And he wasn't the one to blame for the elves and the dragons' death."

"No, but they had the elves and dragons to contend with. They were a threat to your rule. Part of Rhiannon and Maija's plot included a way to annihilate them. Maija unleashed a curse to make the humans kill the elves. By placing the blame on Auberon, they expected the humans to kill him."

"But they didn't."

"Because he fled to the Divide and found Maija."

"And she gave him a new curse."

"Precisely. It's uncertain if Maija had already planned to betray Rhiannon once the last dragons died and she secured her place in Rotko, or if Auberon had something on Rhiannon, something that turned Maija against her. Whatever it was, Maija stopped working with Rhiannon, gave

Auberon the curse to control his people, and conquered the Divide for herself."

"Why didn't Queen Rhiannon kill him herself?"

"She couldn't risk the humans forming their own government while she searched for you. Auberon needed to maintain control, holding your place. Though she'd already gained Talamh Sí's dependence upon her for aether, she needed his dependence too. So she replicated Maija's curse to ensure he'd forever depend on her to continue cursing future generations."

"You mean keino?"

He cocked his head at me. "Pardon?"

"You said aether. That she ensured Talamh Sí would need her aether, but you meant keino."

He scoffed. "There is no keino. Queen Rhiannon never invented a synthetic form of aether. She uses the real thing."

Jolts ran through me, jerking my spine as tall as it could stretch. "But doesn't that require killing a living thing?"

His hand swept across the valley below. "Her supply came from them."

"But how?"

"Elves, and especially their dragons, have an incredible amount of aether. When Rhiannon killed them, she collected it all. She's been feeding Auberon from her stockpile."

My overloaded brain couldn't process this. "But how'd she kill them?"

"With the help of her sister. Maija unleashed the curse and attacked the Divide—"

"But how'd the witch enter the Divide? Shouldn't it have burned her up? She was evil."

"There are a couple of theories about that." Ludek raised his pointer finger. "One is that the Divide only burned up those God didn't allow to enter before it fell. Once the dragons were gone, the Divide wasn't so selective." He held up another finger. "Another is that Maija is half human. There are rumors her mother had affairs with her servants. But no matter how it happened, Maija got in, and God allowed it."

"Why would He do that?"

"It is not for us to question His reasons. But let me ask you this: Do you grow closer to God when things are easy or during tough times?"

Ouch. I'd like to think I'd be close to God when things were easy. But when things were easy, I didn't need God much. I cried out to God more and felt His presence most in my darkest times. And in my toughest time, trapped in the Divide, wallowing in my past, I'd met God face-to-face. The more difficult things became, the more I sought Him, the closer I grew to Him. "I see your point."

"The elves who survived the humans aided in the attack on the Divide. But they were too late. Once they destroyed the last egg, the Divide darkened."

"But the last egg *wasn't* destroyed." Clearly, Ludek didn't know everything. "It hatched for me."

"You have a dragon?"

"Sakki." My dangling legs went limp, and a profound sadness weighed on me. We'd been apart too long. "He's still in the Divide. Our bond broke."

He gave me a sad smile.

"As the only dragon left, he felt obliged to protect it, so he stayed behind while I sought help." Which begged the question—would he remain even if we restored our bond? I shook off the terrible thought, returning to the conversation at hand. "So how did the Divide go dark?"

"The egg must've left the Divide."

"And Maija took control."

With a wink, he clicked through the side of his mouth, like coaxing a horse to walk.

Again, the horrific idea infiltrated my mind and soured my stomach— Sakki would never leave the Divide unprotected. I looked over the edge. Nobody better be down there should I actually get sick. "What happened to the elves and their dragons?"

"Maija and Rhiannon unleashed a lethal curse upon them. Rhiannon gathered the aether upon their death. To my knowledge, she tried to destroy their bones with fire, but they wouldn't burn. So she teleported them here."

I watched the lumps, expecting a wind to sweep through, exposing the hidden remains. I shuddered. "And the song led you here?"

"Yes. I still don't know what it means." He touched my arm, something fatherly in his tender expression. "But it seems to have done more than bring me here, it brought us together. This is the safest place in all these cursed lands. The queen and her minions can't come here. Something repels them. We've enacted additional wards as a safeguard, but before putting them in place, we've seen the wrong sort try to follow us here and fail. I've heard of fae getting confused, forgetting where they were going, or being teleported back to their homes or other random places."

"And what... now you have a rebel group that opposes the queen?"

"I was called to bring this group together some years ago, not that we've accomplished much." He clutched the ledge and leaned back, observing the skies. "Rhiannon's army learned of our location and searched for this place. When they got close, they wound up in Järvi—the south lake—with no idea how they got there or what they'd been doing. This is how I can trust my people, misguided though some may be. Anyone who makes it here is here because God willed it."

Lumpy sand stretched out below me for millions of cubits, and I breathed in the wonder of it all. I was here—we were all here—under God's approval. "What do we do now? As you said, Queen Rhiannon will come looking for me." That reminded me of the earlier questions. We'd resolved the mystery of Noita the Witch, but what of my kidnaping? "Why do you think she'd order for me to be kidnaped?"

"If the request came from her, it makes sense she would return you to Talamh Sí to take the throne. She must be growing impatient."

"But why didn't she just return me the moment I arrived? Why pretend to help me restore my bond with my dragon and teach me the ways of the fae?"

"Queen Rhiannon isn't a forthcoming person. And what would happen if she had returned you and put you on the throne without considering your request?"

I shrugged. "I wouldn't go. Not without Sakki."

"Precisely. In order to control you, she needs to gain your trust. She will want to maintain relations once Zorac is freed. Better gain your loyalty by hiring people to kidnap you and appearing as a hero coming to your rescue."

Though my foot dangled over a ledge, I stamped it down in my mind. "I won't let that happen."

"It relieves me to hear that." He relaxed more, as if I'd removed a great weight from his shoulders.

"What now?"

"I don't know. But I'm grateful to God for the mix-up. Those tyhmiä boys didn't know what they were doing, but God did. All will be well." He smiled down at me.

Shuffling feet approached, and my kidnapers appeared, Alajos in the lead.

"Speaking of the tyhmiäs." Ludek stood, clasping his hands behind him, looking down on the cringing fae. "I can see in your faces you haven't brought good news."

"We returned to Kohl's, l–like you asked."

"And?" Impatience deepened Ludek's voice.

"They're gone."

Twenty-Eight

L udek had given me a private nook of their cavern with a pallet and somewhat comfortable bedding. Still, I'd never fall asleep here. It was dark. Too dark. Snores surrounded me, echoing off the cavernous walls. I imagined myself surrounded by mounds of hibernating bears.

Bears. Rebel fae. Either was just as unnerving. The nook offered three walls of protection, but one remained exposed. How could I sleep and put myself in a vulnerable position amid kidnapers? I didn't care what Ludek said about this place or how much he trusted his people.

And the incessant tinkling music was louder than ever. It snaked through the echoing snores and plagued my ears.

Tink-ah tink tink. Tink-ah tink tink.

It was for the best that I not sleep surrounded by prowling marauders.

Tink-ah-dee tink-ah-dee tink.

On my side, facing the one direction I might be attacked, I listened for movement, wishing I had a weapon. Or my friends to take turns keeping watch.

Where were they right now? Their location didn't change my situation, but knowing they were no longer at Kohl's mother's deepened my sorrow and pressed a sense of hopelessness upon me. Where had they gone? Did Queen Rhiannon find and capture them? Or had Ruuta betrayed us and turned them over herself? What were they doing? Were they sleeping? Searching for me? They must be off their heads. So many unpleasant scenarios played out in my mind. In one, Ruuta had turned them in. Liam paced a jail cell while Hiisi wailed. In another, Ruuta hadn't betrayed us. They all hunkered down in the woods, hiding— Ruuta fuming and Liam, with his face creased with worry, trying to calm Hiisi.

I flopped onto my stomach and ground my teeth as if I could squeeze the images from my mind. There must be a way to find them.

Should I trust Ludek or his promises to return me once he came up with a plan? I flung myself onto my back, twisting my blanket and dress. Suppressing a frustrated growl, I yanked both out from underneath me, taking my annoyance out on the innocent fibers.

I didn't know him from a crab in the sand. He might be lying to get me on his side. Was I playing into his hands? What if he was stalling me? What if he had no intention of reuniting me with my friends?

Should I try to escape?

Even if I did, how would I find my way back? I had no teleportation spells, nor did I understand how they worked. Nor did I have any idea where Äiti lived. I'd never find her house by spell or by foot.

I hated this darkness. So complete I couldn't see my hand in front of my face. It reminded me of being trapped in Noita's closet and the giant wormy thing. I shuddered at both memories. Both times, Hiisi had appeared. If only he'd appear now.

Creeping crabs! How many times had I been kidnaped? How could I be so stupid as to let it happen again? I kicked the pallet. Coughs came from someone not too far away.

Tink-ah-dee tink-ah-dee tink.

The song. Ludek had known the song. That had to mean something, right?

How had it come to this? I was trapped, yet again, in another place I didn't understand. Without my friends. Alone.

God, why do You keep allowing me to go through these things? What have I left to learn? Please... teach me already so I can get this over with.

No answer. No dragony sarcastic retort. No gentle pats from Hiisi. Nothing.

This cave amplified every sound, so I squashed my sobs. Tears leaked through my closed lids and slipped across my temples into my hair, and I hiccuped.

Light in, dark out.

Light in, dark out.

Breathe, just breathe.

I pressed my hands to my chest, feeling it expand and contract with measured beats.

God, forgive me. I'm failing to trust You again. I'm not alone. I'm not in Bandia. I'll never go back there again. Thank You for freeing me from that nightmare. You freed me from my father and Noita. You delivered me to Ludek, a believer. You must have a plan for this place too. I trust You, God. Help me trust You more.

I felt a familiar presence. Something touched my leg. My heart took off at a gallop as I scrambled to sit, rooting around for whatever it was.

"You okay?"

"Hiisi? Is that you?" But even as I whispered the words, I knew it was him.

"Hiisi guide. You need me? Me guide."

All the anxiety sickening my bones dissipated. I reached out for his little body. When I found it, I pulled him into a hug. "I'm so glad you're here."

"Me too." Though he whispered, a wail quavered his voice. "Me so scared. Liam and Ruuta mad. Very mad."

"I bet." I bit the inside of my cheek. "Were they captured? Why weren't they at Äiti's?"

"Äiti bring friends to church."

"Church?"

"Äiti fear home not safe."

"Can you bring us to them?"

"No." He sighed. "Only you."

"You can only miraculously appear to me?"

He gave me a sad nod. "Who snore?" He narrowed his eyes and peered into the darkness.

"The rebel fae. The Kapina. They live here."

The bedding rustled as Hiisi moved to the edge.

"Ludek, their leader, might help us. But he's afraid of Ruuta, so he might not." With Hiisi by my side, calm and a profound exhaustion washed over me. "We should sleep."

Hiisi curled into me, his arm draped over my waist.

I rubbed my hand on his back. Then, despite the snores and unearthly music, I fell into a deep, comfortable sleep.

Tink-ah-dee tink-ah-dee tink.

TWENTY-NINE

Hushed voices and bustling stirred me. I eased my eyes open, blinking to adjust. Tucked away in my corner, I couldn't see anyone though I sensed their activity in the cave. I peeled myself up to sit, rousing Hiisi. Yawning, he rubbed his eyes and stretched.

We stood, and I folded the blanket, laying it at the end of my bedding. My stomach rumbled. "Let's go see if there's food."

We passed many fae gawking at us as they went about their morning routines. When I spotted Ludek, I hurried toward him.

"Ah, Your Majesty." He bowed. His lowered gaze fell on Hiisi, and he jerked in surprise. "Who's your friend?"

How strange to have him treat me like royalty. I'd never get used to that, but it was one thing in the castle or accompanied by Ruuta. It was another with Hiisi in a cave. "This is Hiisi."

"How'd he get in here?" Ludek spun around, looking as if he expected to find a portal hovering behind him.

"I don't know. He's connected to me somehow. He always finds me when I'm in trouble."

"You're not in trouble—"

"Didn't you say you trusted everyone who entered this place? That God must've allowed it?"

"Yes, I—" He smiled, a series of small laughs escaping his nose. "Of course. Would you and, uh, your friend like breakfast?"

"Hiisi," I reminded him. "Aye. I mean, yes, please."

"Come with me."

We followed him through a sea of glamorless fae in tattered clothes. They didn't smile or frown. Nor did they avert their eyes like all the other fae I'd encountered. That was good, right? If Ludek spoke the truth, they must be trustworthy. It gave me a sense of security, false or not. I'd rather someone look me in the eye than not, but it still unnerved me. If only I could see their auras. They must be stifling them here too.

Ludek brought us to a line where people waited for their food. "If you don't mind, I've got things to attend to, including figuring out what to do to get you back to where you belong without setting off the royal army. I'll be with you as soon as I can. Please forgive me."

After Ludek bowed and strode away, a stern-looking fae with fierce eyes and sharp angles slopped something into a bowl for me.

"Can I have one for him too?"

The fae leaned over his tureen to find Hiisi. His eyebrows twitched, and he slopped more gruel and thrust the second bowl at me. I moved along and filled two cups with water before Hiisi climbed the table to get his. After handing Hiisi his cup, I plucked a roll from a basket. Hiisi snatched one that had fallen onto the table, and we left the cavern for the ledge where Ludek had brought me the day before.

Hiisi sucked air through his teeth and backed away from the edge. "Bones."

"So he was telling the truth?" I studied the mounds with fresh eyes. "There are bones underneath that sand?"

"Me no like bones."

"Do you want to go eat somewhere else?" He wouldn't want to descend toward the bones, and I didn't want to get closer to the fae. Now that it was daytime, my quiet place with Ludek wasn't quite so peaceful with fae mucking about. But I didn't know where else to go. "Will you be okay to sit here to eat?"

He nodded but eyed the valley as if the bones might jump up and attack him as he sat. He slurped his water and tore into his bread. The food was bland. It reminded me of porridge back home, but it needed more salt. And the one time fae magic might've helped make the food more appetizing... a little less... gray, they don't use it?

Hiisi leaped to his feet and pounded his chest, making horrible guttural noises.

"Are you okay?" I jumped to face him, hovering. "Are you choking?" What was that maneuver Fallon had taught us? Should I press his chest?

A fae ran over in a blur and turned Hiisi upside-down. He shook the poor little gargoyle until a piece of bread popped out of his mouth and landed with a squishy thud. Hiisi coughed as the fae righted him. He slammed himself into me, latching onto my leg as he gulped air.

"Chew your food, you little monster." The fae disappeared into a group of onlookers.

I was grateful to the fae for saving Hiisi's life, but why bother? He cared nothing about him.

I peeled Hiisi off my leg and knelt to inspect him. "Are you okay?"

"Me okay. God startle me."

I backed up. "God startled you? How?"

"He show me you." The gray color had drained from his gargoyle skin as he pointed down into the valley, then at me. "Go there. Wear ring."

I sucked in a disbelieving breath. "God told you this?"

Hiisi gulped at the bones. Then something came over him. His color returned to normal. He stood tall and gripped my shoulders to stare into my eyes. "God never more clear."

"I have to go down there?"

Hiisi screwed up his face and nodded.

Put on the ring.

I drew in another sharp breath. But this one wasn't so disbelieving. God had said He'd tell me when to wear the ring. And the last time I hesitated, my bond with Sakki broke. With fumbling fingers, I hurried to remove my ring from my necklace and slide it on my finger. The moment it slipped into place, a headache I hadn't noticed before disappeared.

The tinkling music strengthened.

Tink-ah tink tink. Tink-ah tink tink.

The breeze stopped, and I felt as if I might float away. I reached for Hiisi, but my hand slipped through his.

Creeping crabs! I needed to rip a hole in the atmosphere to pull him inside. How did I do that before?

I scanned the fae. The onlookers had dispersed, and we seemed forgotten. Everyone was eating their breakfast or engrossed in their tasks. Still, I couldn't risk them trying to stop us. So I wrapped us in a cloak. At least, I hoped the veil worked. Whatever happened, it was best if there were no witnesses.

With the veil in place, I stretched the atmosphere, ripping it until a sizable hole emerged. I reached through to connect with Hiisi. His solid hand responded to mine, squeezing tight.

"Woooooooo..." He studied his free hand and fingers as if amazed to find that they still worked.

Go to my elves.

"God spoke! You hear?" Hiisi danced in place, free arm pumping. "You hear God speak?"

"Aye. You heard Him too?"

My little bobblehead nodded with new abandon, his teeth hooking his nose as he smiled.

We were in the spiritual realm. It made sense that it would be easier to hear God speak. Did everything in the entire realm hear Him? "You're not scared to go into the valley?"

He stood proud, jabbing his free thumb to his chest. "Me scared of nothing now."

I decided not to tell him that demons roamed this realm too. I'd never seen any. But that was why we weren't allowed to use Turas, the enormous megalith that traveled through space and time, because it tapped into the spiritual realm where demons lay in wait.

But I wasn't scared. Demons knew to wait near Turas. With this ring, they wouldn't know when or where I'd tear into their realm. And I was following God's instructions. He wouldn't lead me to demons, would He?

I saw nothing—no angels or demons. If God kept this place safe in the physical realm, maybe He did in the spiritual realm too.

Hiisi yanked me forward, pulling me from my thoughts. "Me and you go."

We walked along the ledge, looking for a safe way down, but our feet weren't connecting with the ground. Hiisi stopped and shook his head. "No. You and me fly."

"Huh?" I stared at him like I could siphon the reasons from his mind.

Tink-ah-dee.

"You know." He flapped his free arm. "Fly." Though he was no longer flapping, he lifted off the ground. Even he didn't seem to expect such results. His eyes grew wide as his jaw hung open. He laughed. As he laughed, he flipped through the air as much as possible while still connected to me.

"We can fly?" When I'd been in the water, the physical laws no longer seemed to apply. I breathed and didn't need to kick or tread water. Somehow, without swimming, I moved where I wanted to go. Why wouldn't the air be similar? Rather than jump, I thought about lifting. The ground moved further away as Hiisi and I rose. My heart seemed to soar higher than the rest of me as I joined Hiisi in his laughing.

The fae outside the cavern were oblivious to us. My veil must be working.

TINK-AH-DEE.

The music was growing louder. I spun, searching for its source.

TINK!

"Come with me."

We whirled toward the commanding voice. A radiant being stood in the air—all in white with a gold rope tied around his waist. Or hers. It was hard to determine its gender. But it had to be an angel.

Now I understood why they always had to warn people not to be afraid. If I weren't in the spiritual realm and calm, I'd be afraid. Instead, I followed his glowing body through the air to the valley below. We stood at a narrow point before the lumpy sand.

"The bones cry out." The light illuminating the angel brightened as it spoke. "Remove your ring and tell them to wake."

THIRTY

With one last surge of light, the angel blinked out. Gone. Leaving a lingering shadow in its place. As the shadow faded, my disappointment grew. But now I understood another thing— why people never asked angels many questions. Shock and awe overwhelmed my mind, blowing reason away along with the plethora of questions. That, and the angel gave little time for processing before it vanished.

"You hear?" Hiisi cocked his head at me, then tapped my ring. "Remove you ring."

I released him, and he fell on his butt. Oops. He mustn't have been all the way on the ground.

I tugged the ring from my finger. The moment it slipped off, the heaviness of life pressed me to the earth, compacting my spine. Wind resumed along with the ache in my head and my cares of this world.

Tink-ah tink tink.

Curse that incessant music! Wait. The angel said the bones cried out. Could it be...?

Hiisi flung his arm out at the lumpy sand. "Tell them."

I restrung the ring on its chain, clasped it around my neck, and tucked it into my dress's neckline. Then I lifted my empty palms to Hiisi. "What do I say? 'Rise in the name of the Lord?'"

The music stopped, and the earth rumbled and quaked. I splayed my arms and feet to keep my balance as an earthquake swept through the valley. Screams poured from the fae on the ledge above, echoing around me. While the others fled, Ludek plodded toward the ledge as if in a trance. I feared he might keep walking right over the edge. But he lurched to a stop, backing up as part of the ledge crumbled away.

The lumps rose. Sand rained down, revealing bones underneath. The bones pieced together in clicks and clangs. Ludek shouted, drawing the fae to watch the bones form elf and dragon skeletons. Once a skeleton was complete, some taking longer than others, squishy sounds rang out as flesh regenerated, covering the elves and dragons in sinewy muscle. Webbing stretched across bones, forming wings, and dragons flapped, testing their revived appendages. They continued regenerating, and skin slithered over their vomit-inducing forms. Hair erupted from the elves' heads. Scales slid over the dragons in a wave, fanning out from their heads across their rotund middles to their feet and tails.

The elves and their dragons stilled, staring straight at me, not speaking a word. Although similar to the fae, everything about them seemed longer— their ears, torsos, arms, legs, even their faces. None wore facial glamors.

I stepped back from the army of elves and dragons. And then, miracle upon miracles, cloth covered the elves as if invisible machines stitched the material until they all wore the same clothing, in several layers with green fitted pants and white top. Silver armor slipped down their bodies like liquid metal conforming to each elf's unique shape, solidifying over their core, and spilling down their hips to form faulds that flowed like a skirt even after hardening. The pouring metal spread across their shoulders in over-layed pauldrons, then continued down their arms, forming a rerebrace. It trickled past the elbow and collected again to fashion a vambrace over the lower arm and wrist.

I gasped. If I hadn't witnessed the armor appear in such a supernatural way, I'd still think it otherworldly in its delicate design and intricate pattern.

I raised my face to the skies, searching for God among the clouds. *What now?*

The elves and dragons looked like living beings, but they stood unnaturally still. How would I get them to move, to speak, to *live?*

Gasps rained down from the ledge. The fae covered their mouths.

Desperate, yet petrified to see what had captured their awe, I turned. A great värikäs-colored cloud hovered above. A rush swept through me, into my lungs, pushing words out of my mouth. "God in heaven, breathe! Give them life."

The cloud careened toward the soulless beings, making my hair swirl as if a tornado passed above me. The cloud blasted the army, blowing their long hair straight back, pushing them onto their backs. Wisps disappeared into their mouths and noses. When the cloud reached the furthest elves, it disappeared. All used up.

The elves and dragons gulped air. Was I hearing their regenerated hearts pumping new life through them? On the ground, their hands searched their restored bodies. One by one, they stood, brushing sand from their clothes. As if they contained one collective brain giving them instructions, they stilled and focused on me, never uttering a word.

Was this real? I rubbed my eyes, expecting to find it was all a mirage. Once my vision cleared, the valley would return to sandy lumps.

But nay. No matter how many times I blinked, my vision remained the same.

An army of elves and dragons stared, waiting.

Command them.

God's voice struck me like a jolt of electricity, restoring my breath, jump-starting my mind. *Command them? With what?*

Silence reigned. No noise came from anyone up on the ledge or down in the valley. The wind didn't dare blow.

God didn't speak.

I squirmed under their expectant gaze. *Think. Think. Think!* "Who is the leader of this army?"

"You are." A stern elf with angular features stepped forward from the front line. He trained his sharp, iridescent-green eyes on me.

"Who's next in command?"

"I am." The same elf approached until he was an arm's length away. He placed a hand over his chest and knelt. His white hair spilled over his shoulders. "I am Niilo. Humble servant of Princess Eerika, daughter of Auberon, God's anointed—my rightful queen."

At his words, a wave of movement washed over the elves and dragons as they mimicked Niilo's humble posture, gave their name, and pledged their fealty.

Why would they pledge themselves to me? To *me*! I was a princess in title only. I'd received no training. And I barely knew my father—a king they'd be right to reject.

But God's anointed? Could it be? God Himself had breathed and given them renewed life. Who was I to tell Niilo he was wrong? *God, what do I do?*

Feed them.

Feed them? After what I'd just witnessed, I'd expected something grander. But, if they were alive now, like newborn babes, they must be hungry after all they went through. And if God said to feed them, I must. But where would I get the food?

As the helpless thought formed in my mind, a fae boy sprinted to us, carrying something. Once he was close enough, he stopped and leaned over, bracing himself on his legs as he caught his breath. He removed a satchel from his shoulder and handed it to me. "God told me to give you this."

I rooted around inside and came up with a roll and two hard-cooked eggs. What was I supposed to do with this?

A fae girl appeared. She handed me a waterskin. "God told me to give you this."

How odd that they should both appear with so little, saying the same thing, after God told me to feed them. Would a hundred more kids appear with their provisions? Then I remembered a story from Fallon's Bible. Was it possible...?

Nay. I wasn't Jesus.

But He did miracles through His people, didn't He? Couldn't He use me too?

I replaced the eggs and bread into the satchel and held it closed with the water. "God, please bless this food. I pray there is enough to feed everyone."

I opened the satchel. It was full.

THIRTY-ONE

My disbelieving eyes stared into the satchel full of bread and hard-cooked eggs. My heart thrummed in my chest as the world fell still and hushed. It wasn't enough for everyone, but God wouldn't feed only some of His resurrected elves and dragons. He would see that they were all fed.

A myriad of emotions bloomed like flowers breaking ground after a harsh winter, unfolding their petals, drinking in the sun's rays for the first time. Eager anticipation, hope, joy, and countless variations therein blossomed and multiplied as the realization of what I already knew settled into my heart with renewed confidence—There was nothing God couldn't do.

Rather than force His hand to fulfill my will—a futile and destructive task—I need only be a willing participant in His.

Overwhelmed by the uncontainable garden of gratefulness destroying the barriers within, I broke. Tears gushed, and my legs liquefied as I fell to my knees, dropping the stuffed bag and bloated waterskin. "Thank You, God!"

Hiisi gasped and caught the bag before the food spilled. His eyes grew as wide as his fist and blurred with unshed tears. An enormous smile took over his face as he wailed and flung an arm over my shoulder, still holding the bag while collapsing into me.

Niilo touched my shoulder. I smiled up at him and wiped my tears. Then I rose with renewed strength, aware of the army of eyes upon me. But there was no shame, no embarrassment, nor did I sense condemnation in their gazes. Rather, the entire valley seemed to resonate with my awe and gratitude.

I collected the waterskin and held it out to Niilo. He accepted it with a bow and drank. A lot. His Adam's apple dipped and dipped until I was certain he'd drained the bag, but it remained as swollen as ever. A line formed behind him, and he passed the water off to the next person. Hiisi held the bag open, and I reached in for two eggs and a roll and handed it to Niilo.

His smile grateful and eyes wide, he raised his face heavenward with silent thanks on his lips.

The line carried on—the next elf in line drinking their fill and passing the water along. Hiisi handled the bag, and I doled out the food. No matter how much I gave, there was never a decrease. Rather than tire with all the bending and receiving thanks, I energized. More miracles upon miracles. Hiisi and I shared a glance, and our smiles grew anew. This was the most fantastic thing I'd ever experienced, and with every thanks I received, I thanked God.

I kept thinking I'd reached my maximum capacity for thankfulness. And yet, with each face that passed me by—every smile, teary eye, and kind word—another cropping of gratitude bloomed anew. How was it possible to contain such emotion? Yet it never became too much for me to carry, nor did it ebb away. And I didn't tire from the repetitive motions. No matter how many people passed before me, they received the same beaming smile, and I felt the same sensations for each. Yet one emotion reigned supreme —love.

As dragons approached, their bonded elves popped their rations into their mouths like candies. Why didn't they shift into something smaller? Then I noticed their saddles. It would be a pain to harness them again unless the saddles came and went with them as Rhys's clothes had.

A pang struck me at his memory.

It probably wasn't the same for dragons. Otherwise, Sakki would have appeared wearing clothes when he shifted into my father. Maybe.

Another pang hit me. As eager as I was to return to him, I didn't want to rush this. I didn't want my awe of God to fade. God had plans for these elves and dragons no one could have predicted. He had plans for me and Sakki too. I just had to trust Him.

At least the dragons seemed satisfied with their meager rations. God might've multiplied the food in their stomachs, supplying them with all the nutrients they needed.

I should have kept count of everyone who passed, but I had been too emotional to consider it. There had to be thousands. Might Samu be among them? Nay. Queen Rhiannon hadn't killed him, her sister had. He wasn't buried here.

Another twinge tweaked my heart. So many losses. But what would Samu think if he saw this? He'd be glad. Perhaps more overcome with emotion than even I was. His sacrifice hadn't been in vain. And God would make sure he knew of it—somehow.

Someone tapped my shoulder, pulling me from my thoughts. A roll flew from my hand, landing at Hiisi's feet.

"Ludek!" I splayed a hand over my thudding heart.

"Forgive me." He bowed. "I didn't mean to startle you." He addressed the two fae who had kidnaped me, Alajos and Egon, standing behind him. "Please allow them to take over if only for a few moments, so you may eat and rest."

Egon took over for Hiisi holding the satchel open but raised so Alajos wouldn't have to lean while handing out rolls.

"It's a good lesson, I think. To serve the one considered so inconsequential as to kidnap her for coin." He motioned toward the miracle still unfolding before us. "Be careful who you judge and how. For you will be judged likewise."

They shied away from Ludek's hard stare and focused on their job.

I wanted to keep serving, but now that I'd stopped, aches from the repetitive movements settled in. I stretched my back, rolled my shoulders, and pressed my head from side to side. Perhaps a break was wise. My stomach cried for food too.

Hiisi and I helped ourselves to our portions and sat a little way off, away from the sand, to watch the procession. Ludek joined us. Hiisi climbed on a rock between us, kicking his dangling feet and wiggling as he ate with a big smile. If he were a puppy, his tail would be wagging.

I missed Sakki.

With a sigh, I bit into the dense roll. It tasted amazing. Like nothing I'd eaten before. Sweeter than honey with a doughy center and flaky crust. But what should I expect from miracle bread? It seemed to heal my body as I ate. Was this the same bread the child had offered? Or had God reconstructed it when He multiplied it? If it was a replica of what the kid offered, I wanted the recipe.

"Are you the commander of this army?" Ludek asked between bites.

"That's what they tell me." The weight of it compounded on me anew. "I know God has a plan for all of this, but He's not sharing. I don't know what to do with them."

Ludek laughed, the corners of his eyes crinkling. Judging from what my father told me about how fae age, he must be over one hundred years old. "I have an idea if you're willing to listen."

"Of course." I nibbled the roll, eager for some wisdom, hoping I was right to trust him.

"We should return to the Divide for your dragon."

"What?" That was the last thing I expected to hear. And yet, what I'd hoped to hear most. "Why?"

"Your dragon remained behind to protect the Divide, to ensure it didn't fall into the wrong hands. But look"—he waved toward the supernatural phenomenon—"you have an entire army of elves and dragons. Bring some to replace Sakki in defending the Divide. Then, with the help of the elves and the fae, we can work to restore your bond."

I liked that idea. I *really* liked that idea. Hope soared within me at the possibility. But it sounded wrong. Selfish. "Shouldn't I use the army to do something for my father's people? For the fae?"

"In time. But first things first. Think of it. With a dragon of your own, you'll be a true commander for this army."

Is that Your plan, God? It makes sense, but I don't want to do anything without You.

I didn't sense an answer.

"Also, the queen doesn't know what's happened to you yet. Right now, since one of your kidnapers survived and you're missing, she likely expects her plan prevailed."

"Unless they were to deliver me to her straightaway."

Ludek shook his head. "I interviewed the boys this morn. They were instructed to hold you for three days. Then the royal soldiers were to rescue you. This confirms my suspicion that the queen is manipulating you to agree to anything she says."

"Are you sure? We've only implicated Alpertti. Is it possible he acted on his own?"

Ludek scrunched his thin eyebrows. "It's possible. Though I can't fathom what's in it for him. What purpose would it serve him to hatch such schemes other than to scare you into returning to Talamh Sí to take the throne? That is Rhiannon's desire as well. Unless Alpertti is acting on his own to hasten your return, but no." He pressed his lips into a grim line. "The queen isn't above kidnaping to get what she wants. Anything to free Zorac."

"I keep hearing that said—that my taking the throne will free Zorac. I've also been told it will tear down the Divide. What does that mean? Which is correct?"

"Both." He rubbed his temple and grimaced. "If you become queen, the light protecting the Divide will collapse. Nothing will stop anyone or anything from walking through. And Zorac will be free to roam the entire realm."

"Where is he now?" I glanced over my shoulder, half-expecting to find him there.

"He's trapped in the spiritual realm within the borders of Seelie Clós. According to legend, he walked in the physical realm. All the fallen angels could. But these were angels who'd chosen to disobey God—to go their own way. They turned elfin hearts from God and wedded their women. But these were unholy unions resulting in offspring with tainted blood and hardened hearts. So God constructed the Divide to stop the spread and banished the demons to the spiritual realm to lessen their influence on the corrupted elves and fae. They've been scheming against God ever since. But their leader, Zorac, has devised a way to return through his offspring's rule."

He motioned to me, and I cringed.

I hated being in a demon's bloodline. "But how is he accomplishing anything if he's trapped?"

Ludek widened his blue eyes and blinked a slow blink, as if struggling to comprehend what I failed to understand. "Do you do the right thing all the time? Follow God's every command?"

I huffed a bitter laugh. "I wish."

"Me as well." He laughed too, then grew somber. He frowned, and his white brows furrowed, puckering his forehead. "Our nature opposes God. We don't need help to fail to do as He wants—to go our own way. Demons could sit back and watch us mess up our lives on our own with no help. But that's not good enough for them. They hate God, and because He loves us, they hate us too and seek to destroy us."

His milkweed seed hair rustled across his shoulders with his slow headshake. "Sadly, we require little prompting. All they need to do is whisper a suggestion in our ears, something we want anyway, and we spiral farther away from God. They can slip about, unseen, whispering damaging suggestions in unsuspecting ears and witness God's creation implode."

His words spoiled the food in my belly.

"They can also cause damage by entering the physical realm using fae as hosts."

"Like demonic possession?" Now even my mouth soured.

"Precisely. But if you claim the throne, his fallen angelic body will be able to materialize once more, only this time, nothing will hold him back. He will travel the realms as he chooses." Ludek shrugged. "Or so the prophecy goes to the best of my understanding. However things play out, we must do all we can to prevent his release, particularly while we have the element of surprise."

As much as I hated to miss even a moment of God's work in action by watching the stream of elves continuing before me, I jumped to my feet. "Let's go get my dragon."

Thirty-Two

We drew near the trail of resurrected elves still waiting for food. Alajos and Egon both seemed into their work. Smiles I wouldn't have thought them capable of transformed their faces, softening my heart. I almost saw them for the misguided youths Ludek cared for and not my kidnapers.

A young fae girl ran toward them, interrupting their rhythm. Egon abandoned the satchel as Alajos rooted around for food while staring at the girl. Their jaws slackened over whatever she was saying.

"Princess?" Ludek waved me to follow.

I lurched, wanting to know what they were saying, but followed Ludek instead. We approached Niilo leaning on his dragon's shoulder with contented contemplation. He spotted us and launched himself upright as if expecting me to be a harsh leader. He lowered to his knee and bowed his head. He'd secured his white hair in a queue, putting his angular features into sharper prominence. "Your Highness."

I wasn't comfortable being a leader at all yet, so his reaction bothered me. But what could I do to make him relax? "Please stand."

He obeyed, but every muscle in his body seemed taut, waiting for a command.

"Please." I pumped a hand in the air. "I want you to be comfortable with me."

His shoulders relaxed, but otherwise, he remained the same. "I will do as my queen wishes."

My insides tightened. "I'm not a queen. I've no country. No people."

"You are the rightful heir to the throne in Talamh Sí. I served your father and his father before him. You serve the True King and saved us from the brink of extinction." He splayed a hand over his heart. "You are our queen. We are your people."

Wow. How could I argue with that? And yet, a niggling gremlin in the back of my mind tempted me to do just that. I squashed it down and smiled. "God resurrected you."

His mouth twitched, like he wanted to speak, but thought better of it.

"We're planning to return to the Divide to retrieve my dragon, Sakki. He's there, alone, protecting it. Are there dragons and elves you can appoint to protect it in his place?"

"Of course, Your Highness." He bowed.

Ludek stepped forward. "We will need the rest to aid us should we face war with Queen Rhiannon and those who've claimed Talamh Sí. How many dragons do you think we can do without and sufficiently protect the Divide?"

Niilo closed his eyes. When they reopened, he said, "Forty."

"That's all?" Ludek's gaze flicked to me.

Creeping crabs, was I supposed to act queenly and give commands? "Is there a reason for only forty? We have thousands."

"That is the number God gave me. We will need our dragons for what's to come."

Why didn't I receive God's answers so easily? That didn't seem fair. But at least someone knew what to do. "Very well. Please appoint forty elves and their dragons to accompany us to take Sakki's place defending the Divide." My words felt so clunky. I'd never get used to this.

But then, I may never become an official queen. I may not live long enough.

Niilo bowed, marched into the crowd, and disappeared. How was it possible these were lifeless bones mere hours ago? Though I'd witnessed the miracle, logic screamed it couldn't be true. And my memories were fading. Like when I wake from a dream and, in that instant between sleep and waking, it all feels so real. But as I waken, details slip away until I can scarcely remember them. By the end of the day—nay, by *midmorning*—it's forgotten.

Please, God, don't let this be like that. Don't let me forget one moment of what's happened here today. Help me remember Your awesome power by keeping every detail fresh.

An idea came to me, and I pivoted Ludek. "Do you have a glass vial? One you'd keep for potions? And a string?"

His brows scrunched, but he didn't ask. "Of course."

He closed in on Alajos and Egon. I couldn't hear what he said. But he motioned a lot, pointing to two nearby elves who came and took over serving the food. Alajos reached into his pocket and handed something to Ludek. He returned to me with them in tow. Neither would meet my eye.

"Alajos had a vial." He handed it to me. "We'll find string later unless it's imperative you receive it now."

"Nay." I uncorked the vial, scooped some sand, and shook it out into the vial, watching it compact, leaving enough space at the top to replace the cork. "Later is fine." I placed my little reminder of this day in my dress pocket and patted it. I'd secure it around my neck with a string another time.

Niilo stepped up, gave a slight bow, and motioned to the convoy following him. "I've collected the forty dragons and riders you requested."

"Very good." Ludek patted Alajos's shoulder, jostling the slim fae. "He will teleport us to the Divide's boundary. It would be better if he could teleport us inside. But he's never been there before, and it will be safe. There are no patrols."

"Will you be able to bring all of us?" Could a fae possess such power?

Alajos shook his dark hair. "I wouldn't dare attempt more than ten dragons at a time. But I can come back for more until they're all at the Divide."

"That still seems like a lot. One dragon is like four horses or more. Can you transfer forty horses? And their riders? And the rest of us?" This tele-porting thing still unnerved me. Testing Alajos's maximum capacity didn't make me feel better. What if he scrambled us up en route? "What if they transformed into something smaller?"

"We could." Niilo squinted as if half his face hated the idea. "But we'd have to carry their saddles and harness them again later."

So I was right. Their accessories didn't come and go as Rhys's had. Which was better? Teleport them all at once—or at least, most of them—then take time with their saddles or move them in smaller quantities? Queenly decisions would be the death of me. "What's the most you've ever teleported?"

"Twenty adult male fae."

"And you think you can carry ten dragons?" I goggled at my kidnaper. If only I could gauge his capability and his trustworthiness from a glance. Or if I still could read auras. I pivoted. "Ludek, are you certain we can trust him not to teleport us to the wrong place or alert someone?"

He gave Alajos a hard stare. "Absolutely."

What choice did I have? Queens had to trust their subjects to a certain extent. "Keep the dragons saddled and move them in pairs. Send Ludek, Hiisi, Egon, Niilo and his dragon, and me first. Can you do that?"

Whatever evil I'd seen in Alajos before was gone. Now the fae nodding at me resembled a scared kid.

While he seemed susceptible, I had to ask. "Did you do everything you could to find Kohl? My friends?"

"Princess—"

"I need to find my friends," I said, hoping to quench Ludek's arguments.

If Alajos appeared scared moments before, he was petrified now. He and Egon shared horrified expressions.

"What are you afraid of? Did you lie?"

Alajos paled. His Adam's apple worked like a pelican's gullet stuffed with a flopping fish. "Your friends—"

My stomach recoiled and crawled up my throat, making my voice threatening. "What about them?"

"Th–they're back at the castle. Alpertti apprehended them this morning."

THIRTY-THREE

I must've misheard him. "How would you know they're at the castle unless—" As I was about to accuse him of being in on a conspiracy, I remembered. "That girl. She told you."

The blood drained from Alajos and Egon's skin, their faces turning cadaverous. Maybe they'd vomit their breakfast.

Still, I stepped closer and shot them with every question that came to mind: "Where were they? What happened to them? Are they all right? Are they prisoners, or did Ruuta convince him that they were kidnaped and—"

Alajos held out his palms to stop the rapid-fire questioning. "All I know is that Yaeger was shot with a human weapon and your friend is being held for questioning."

Liam was being "questioned"? Rational thought vacated. Fury and fear took charge. With shaking hands, I grabbed Alajos by the collar. "Did you know where they were all this time?"

"No!" He dropped to his knees, clasping his hands together in prayer. "They weren't at Kohl's. I couldn't search for them without rousing suspicion."

"Where'd Alpertti find them?" I tugged on the collar bunched in my fist.

"In Äiti's church."

"And you didn't think to look for them there?"

"I didn't know about it. Her church opposes Zorac. It's underground."

"If you didn't know of it, how did Alpertti find them?" My anger fizzled, along with any hopes I'd had of finding them.

"H–he has eyes and ears everywhere and plenty of coin."

Any queenly mindset vaporized. No longer pretending to know what I was doing, I spun on Ludek. "I need to rescue my friends."

He approached with an outstretched hand as if nearing a scorpion with its stinger poised and ready to strike. My body shook, ready to run, fight, anything I commanded. But no commands came. All reasoning abandoned me, and I came up blank. But I had to do something. Anything.

"We don't know that they're in trouble, and we can't do anything until we come up with a plan." His gentle hand warmed my shoulder.

"He's being held for questioning. What does that even mean?" My voice squealed like a violin in the hands of a novice player. "Will they hurt him?"

Egon cowered behind Alajos. "Your friend killed someone who was a threat to you. The queen might release him."

All the words in my brain exploded in a verbal eruption. "Release him? After he killed a fae? When she can use him as a pawn to get me to do whatever she wants?"

Ludek veered me from the others, shooing away everyone who drew too close. Then, his face inches from mine, he gripped my shoulders. "Get yourself together. These people are looking to you to lead us from the oppression we've been under." He released me, stepped back, and scrubbed a hand down his face. "What would you have us do? Attack the castle unprepared and you without your dragon?"

I wrung my hands together and swallowed down my desire to turn a weapon on Alajos and demand he deliver me to the castle to save Liam. Ruuta had better protect him. But what should I do? What would be better —to rescue Liam or Sakki first? *Think. Think. Think!*

"If I can give a bit of advice."

I'd almost forgotten Ludek was there. Useless thoughts kept cycling like an auto on a lift in a repair shop, failing to gain traction.

"Stick to the plan. Find Sakki. Once we have him and the Divide is secure, we'll make a plan to retrieve your friends."

"When? I can't wait. Liam's a human. He's not safe here. I can't trust Ruuta to protect him. And if Queen Rhiannon has them, we've lost the element of surprise, and she's gained the upper hand."

"Has she? Do you think she'll expect a resurrected elfin army?"

I released my hands. Thank God we had that going for us. "But she's so powerful. And if she threatens Liam, I don't know what I'll do." Visions of our battle with the witch assaulted me, reigniting my fears. We'd overcome one powerful adversary. Nay. Two, if you included my father. But at what cost? Rhys. Samu. My dragon bond. Pirkko. Taneli. Valtteri. My father's kingdom. What would I lose in a fight against Rhiannon? I couldn't afford any more powerful enemies. "I can't lose anyone else."

"Get your dragon." He drew near me to whisper. "Don't steal tomorrow's problems by worrying about them today. And don't look at everything that's to be done all at once. Focus on one thing at a time. Even with a broken bond, wouldn't you prefer to save your friends with Sakki at your side?"

My soul sighed, longing to be reunited. Having him at my side would ease my mind some, as long as I didn't lose him too. "I don't want to waste time."

"This"—he spun his pointer finger in a circle between us—"is wasting time."

He was right.

God, You saw us through once before. Please see us through again. Keep us safe. Alive. I can't handle losing anyone else.

With renewed energy, I spun toward the others. "Let's go."

Alajos fumbled to catch the stone around his neck. Once he had a good grip, determination removed the fear in his eyes. Telltale itching radiated within me, fanning outward and prickling my skin. The valley of restored dragons and elves fizzled out, replaced by a wall of rippling lights.

The Divide.

My heart skittered. The last time I'd neared Rotko, I sensed Noita's evil emanating from the wall. Now, with Noita gone, peace radiating from the lights abated my fears for Liam. Not entirely, but enough. And now that I was so close, my body vibrated with excitement. I would see Sakki. Soon.

Alajos gripped Egon's sleeve and retreated. "We'll go back for more." Before anyone responded, they blinked out.

"Back up." Ludek splayed his arms and guided us. "Give them room."

I snatched Hiisi and squeezed as close to the shimmering wall as possible without passing through.

More dragons and riders appeared, and their eyes gleamed at the sight of their safe place and the home of their holy temple.

Niilo's voice came from atop his dragon. "My guardians and I will await the others inside the Divide."

At Ludek's nod, the wonder frozen on the elves' faces thawed. With whoops and cheers, they commanded their dragons to rise. Wings flapped, billowing us with a gust of wind as they lifted into the skies. Their flickering shadows passed over us, and the barrier's brilliant lights surged, brightening to new levels, welcoming its guardians home.

More dragons and their riders arrived with as much enthusiasm. The same awe overcame them, rending them mute until they, too, buzzed us and vanished into the ever-brightening wall of lights.

By the time the last group left us, their zeal had infected me, and I was desperate to find my dragon and fly among them. But though Ludek stepped toward the light, Alajos and Egon hadn't moved.

"We don't have to go in there, right?" Egon swept blond hair from his eyes as he stared, his Adam's apple bobbed in his thick neck. "I heard it burns fae up."

"Not all of them." Alajos smacked Egon's muscular arm. "But if it doesn't kill you, you never escape again."

Sweat dripped from Egon's brow as if the lights were already warming him as he continued backing away. "Are we going to get trapped in there?"

"How did *you* escape?" Alajos asked me.

"She's only *part* fae, you tyhmiä." Egon took his turn smacking Alajos.

"I was trapped too. So was Ruuta. She's fae. He got us out." I pointed to Hiisi.

He beamed up at them as they stepped closer. They'd never let him out of their sight once they crossed. Good. They'd ensure his safety.

"You need to accompany us," Ludek said. "We need you to return us to the valley once we have Sakki."

"We can wait for you here." Egon's whine sounded unnatural coming from such a rugged elf.

"You're coming with us." Ludek's tone ended that conversation. Then he waved to the darkening sky. "Let's not linger. The longer we remain on this side of the Divide, the greater the chances of being found out." He stepped into the lights and disappeared.

"Did he burn up?" Egon asked.

"I don't think so." Alajos swept an arm, motioning for me to go before him. "After you."

Whether he was waiting to make sure Hiisi was there to ensure his escape or he planned to skip out on us, it didn't matter. Sakki was in there. So close. I grabbed Hiisi's hand and stepped through where Ludek, Niilo, and forty new guardians waited.

I searched the dragons for one without a rider. For a face with yellow scales and a green body to push through the lounge of winged lizards. Or a black-and-white dog to come charging through their legs. Or a gray-and-white cat to leap into my arms. But none came.

I shouldn't have expected him to be here. He had no reason to be. Still, disappointment weighed me down.

Ludek stared over my shoulder. "Are the other two com—"

The two mischievous fae appeared together, holding hands, making his question die on his lips. They gawked at one another. Then their splayed hands roamed their bodies, feeling to ensure everything was where it belonged.

"We didn't burn." Egon's breath whooshed with relief.

Alajos pushed his hand through the wall. "I can get out!"

Egon tested it too. "We're not trapped."

The two collapsed into one another, then faced us.

"How will I find Sakki? I can't reach out to him."

"Ulla reached out to him the moment we arrived." Niilo patted his dragon's neck as the beast swayed beneath him.

Ulla chuffed, reminding me of Sakki, making my heart ache for him all the more.

"She likes his name." Niilo laughed. Something beyond me captured his attention.

I craned for whatever he was seeing, but found nothing there. His expression changed. He must've been speaking with Ulla. Was that what I looked like when I talked to Sakki?

"She found him. He's at the temple. She says he's excited to see you." He beamed at me. "We'll meet him there. Another dragon will accompany us so we can fly you all there. The rest of the elves are going to spread out to guard the Divide."

She talked to him! While not being able to speak to him myself and missing out on flying with forty dragons disappointed me, I'd take it. Whatever it took to reunite with Sakki. My excitement grew as I pushed Hiisi onto Ulla's back and climbed up after him. I reached for Ludek to help pull him up.

Alajos didn't seem happy about his accommodations on the other dragon. A tinge of green spread from his pointy chin up to his overlarge eyes.

Once we were all situated with Hiisi clinging to me, the dragons took to the skies.

We're coming, Sakki!

THIRTY-FOUR

We swept through the cloudless sky on dragonback. The rhythmic sway from side to side while Ulla glided on the breeze lulled me into a calm, almost trancelike state. Normal sounds from the ground didn't reach us here, and their absence added another level of peace. But the dragons' wings whistled as they coasted with occasional creaks during their shifts to stay on course. Each time Ulla flapped her wings, the thunderous whoosh pulled me from my reverie.

The dragons made unusual vocalizations—melodious calls and clicks as though communicating with one another. Sakki had never been around other dragons to speak with. Could they communicate without talking in their minds? Everything about the creatures fascinated me. I longed to ride alone with Sakki, to lean forward and feel his power beneath me as we navigated the air as one, rather than sandwiched between so many others with a trembling Hiisi clinging to me.

I didn't recognize the terrain. There was no desert. No charred-looking nightmare trees. But I detected a light sulfuric scent. Perhaps it was my imagination—a phantom smell from my prior visit. Or the witch's curse had a lingering effect. Either way, flying to the temple was much nicer this time. I wasn't gritty from wormy gastric juices and sand. Nor was I on edge, awaiting an inevitable attack from the witch or one of her playthings. Nay. This time, the land below more closely resembled a tropical paradise—like home.

Aside from the slight odor, the air was clear and refreshing, blowing my hair into Ludek, who sat to the side to catch the view. It was too difficult to talk up here, but the brief snatches of his expression spoke volumes. His blue eyes sparked with renewed life.

Egon seemed to think so too. He released his grip with one hand to thrust it in the air and shout while Alajos clutched his waist, pressing his face into him and squeezing his eyes shut. Teleporting via spells seemed more to his liking. Why didn't he teleport us? Perhaps his abilities didn't work here. Or maybe he needed to have visited the temple before. Right. Hadn't Ludek said something like that?

As their dragon flew past, its eye trained on me. She caught me watching and opened her mouth, sending out a staccato roar, like an open-mouthed purr. I smiled. If only we could communicate. But that eye, alight with life and happiness, said it all. I nodded, and the magnificent creature burst ahead with a thunderous flap, undulating, making Alajos groan over the wind.

Before long, the temple came into view. These dragons knew what they were doing. Displaying extreme skill, they tucked into a dive. The whistling air morphed to a screech as they cut it. Hiisi squeezed me like an ever-tightening corset. Before we hit the wall facade, they billowed their wings to slow their momentum. The leathery membranes stretched and rippled, creating low-pitched, fluttering noises like a loose sail as we broke through.

Unlike my prior visit with Sakki, who slid to a stop, then transformed underneath us, making us drop to the floor, these dragons landed in a series of powerful thuds, bouncing us on their backs. Their wings rustled as they folded, and they let out low clicking growls.

The dragons crouched, allowing us to slip from them. The moment my feet touched the floor, Sakki came skidding down the hall. His puppy body contracted into his smaller cat self and leaped into my arms. He climbed partway up my shoulder and rubbed his face on my cheek. His whole body vibrated with his loud purr. Warmth radiated from my heart throughout my physical and spiritual being. Sakki filled the missing piece, making me whole again.

Sakki! I snuggled his furry little body, careful not to squeeze too hard. *I'm so happy to see you!*

He didn't respond. Or, I didn't hear it, and I remembered our broken connection. Regret sliced through my restored heart. While his presence made it whole, our broken bond was a sliver I had to mend. Until then, I'd have to speak to him aloud, so I repeated the words.

A hairy human strode down the hall into the cavern. "It's good to see you again."

"Hadwin!"

His beard started whitening in my short time away. What had caused that? His thick brown hair showed no signs of aging. He wrapped us both up in a furry hug, then stepped back, giving Hiisi space as he clawed at my leg. As Hadwin patted his back, I crouched for Hiisi to see Sakki too. He petted Sakki's back and beamed up at me. I almost felt the happiness radiating off them.

Niilo frowned. "I can't imagine losing my connection to Ulla."

The other elf who'd accompanied us pressed his lips into a grim line. "We'll do all we can to restore it."

"Between the elves and the fae, we should be able to come up with something," Ludek agreed.

"The witch broke your bond?" Niilo asked.

I nodded. "She hit me with some kind of potion."

"Well, let's hope Rhiannon isn't the only solution." Hadwin scraped the graying hairs on his lower lip with his teeth. It didn't annoy me as much as it had before.

Sakki dropped from my arms as if just realizing other dragons existed. He morphed into his natural state and faced Ulla. As they stared at each other, Ulla was more vocal and expressive with grumbling clicks, head-shakes, neck bends, wing ruffles, and tail slaps. She bared her teeth, angry eyes agleam, and chuffed, blowing smoke from her nose. Just how much of dragon communication included actual words, anyway?

I leaned into Niilo and whispered, "What is happening right now?"

"Ulla is telling Sakki all that has happened since our resurrection." He crossed an arm, using it as a brace for the other to rest his chin on his knuckles. "Now she's telling him he's free to leave. There are others to defend the Divide and oversee the temple."

Sakki's back sagged as though the weight of his burden got heavier when it lifted. His eyes caught mine and softened. Though we couldn't speak as we had before, I could still read the depths of his dragony gaze. Relief and gratitude. The poor beast. Carrying the weight of this place alone, thinking he was the last dragon and the Divide's only hope. Now, unencumbered... liberated from such responsibility, he looked like he could sleep for a week. He was free to return to me, and I'd do whatever it took to ensure we never parted ways again.

And fix what the witch had broken between us.

Until then, there was work to do. "What's the plan? Return to the other dragons and elves. Then what?"

"We'll devise a plan to attack Seelie Clós." Niilo's shimmering green eyes flashed.

"To rescue Liam and Ruuta?" Even as I spoke the words, I knew that wasn't his plan.

"We need to stop Rhiannon. We should have stopped her years ago. As long as she remains on the throne, she can find a way to free Zorac."

"What if I refuse the throne?"

"What if she put you under a spell?" Niilo closed his eyes and shook his head. "She's too powerful. Crafty. No telling what she might do. No, never underestimate her again."

"Are you sure you should face her? She killed you all before."

"Last time, she set a trap. She had the advantage of surprise. This time, we do."

THIRTY-FIVE

Hadwin tipped his head toward the new dragons. "Will you leave a dragon behind to guard the temple?"

"Aye." Since Niilo was a commander, he and Ulla couldn't stay. I motioned to the other elf and his dragon, whose names escaped me. "They'll take Sakki's place."

Ulla headed toward the chamber where Sakki had downloaded the memories of the dragons who'd entered before. Was she going to upload all that had happened in the Valley of Bones? I hoped that wouldn't make Niilo fall into a three-day sleep as it had me.

The new temple guard bowed, then tugged at his dragon's saddle straps. "You will need a seat should you see battle. Please accept ours."

"Don't you have need of it?" Something about his formality made me respond in kind.

"Send another when you can. In the meantime, you have more need of it than we."

Hadwin cleared his throat. "Might I join you and Sakki?"

Warning bells pinged in my gut. He was a human. I already feared for Liam. Did I want to burden myself with concern for another human? "The fae realm isn't safe for humans."

"I'm aware. I've been before."

That straightened my spine. "Are you a—"

"Slave?" He huffed. "I was once, but my master freed me."

"Then why would you want to return?"

He shrugged, teeth scraping his beard. "Why do anything? Because God wills it."

I'd argue that people did many things for many reasons, but if he felt God calling him to go, who was I to deny him? "Of course, you're welcome to join us."

The elf removed the leather cushion from his dragon and handed it to me. Its surprising weight slipped from my grasp, and I fumbled to right it. He explained how to attach it, correcting my botched attempts to follow his directions, climbing all over Sakki's colossal frame. Had he grown more since I saw him last? I had to loosen the straps to fit it around his girth. He was bigger than the other dragon? Was he increasing his size on purpose?

"Did you gain some weight, Sakki?" I chuckled.

He took a deep breath, inflating his chest as he rose onto his hind legs, sending me sliding down his back, catching at his hip. I slipped down his leg and away as he spread his wings. The half-fastened saddle dangled at a precarious angle. He seemed to grow more than his mere antics should have allowed.

Ulla chuffed, snapping her jaws on a plume of smoke, and Niilo laughed.

"What?" The others looked as confused as I was.

"He's joking about the extra scale weight adding to his majestic charm." Niilo raised an eyebrow at Sakki. "And we'll just leave out the bits about Colleen being fish bait."

I backhanded his leg, but the scaly beast didn't react. Try as I might to come up with a retort, I couldn't. That Niilo had to interpret squeezed my gut and held my tongue.

Sakki seemed to sense my mood change. He lowered himself with a dust-billowing thump, and I continued my task.

With the seat firmly in place, I gave the last strap a final tug. "How's that?"

Wings flailing and feet dancing, Sakki kicked up a dust storm. We scurried out of his way like mice protecting themselves from a spooked elephant. Sharp clacks echoed in the chamber as he twisted, snapping his teeth at the offending object as if it meant to kill him. The saddle twisted out of place.

The elf laughed. "It takes some getting used to—for the dragon wearing it and the elf to fasten it properly." He approached Sakki with palms out, waiting for the crazed creature to calm.

Sakki's wild eyes flared, but he stilled, his chest heaving with pulsing breaths. I took several deep breaths to calm myself too. Sakki had never acted like that before. I hated feeling so out of control... so disconnected.

The elf fixed the saddle and moved around Sakki, loosening and tightening the straps. When he finished, he admired his work, then stroked Sakki's cheek. "Better?"

Sakki wiggled, and the thing didn't budge. He settled on his haunches and huffed. Smoky wisps unfurled from his nose. He didn't seem to love it, but he'd learn to live with it—right?

"Perfect. Just keep the straps at this setting, and you shouldn't have any trouble in the future."

"Aye, if Sakki can pick a size and stick to it."

The elf chuckled as he unclipped bracelets from his wrists and held them out to me.

"Wha—?" I extended a tentative hand.

He grabbed my wrist, fastened one, and tugged a ring on the bracelet. "Snap this into Sakki's harness. I've adjusted the placement to allow room for your friend." He nodded at Hiisi. "But when you're flying solo, to get into a more crouched position, you can adjust the clip's placement. There are clips for your ankles too, but they're attached to my boots, which won't fit you. But be sure you get some..." He eyed my dress. "When you get appropriate riding clothes."

"I have some." No. The riding gear I had was destroyed from our journey to Queen Rhiannon and now remained in the castle if her servants hadn't burned it. Didn't matter. It would be unusable.

He made a grab for my other hand and secured the second bracelet. "I know you're used to riding him bareback without these things, but it's much safer with this, especially when engaging in evasive maneuvers."

"Those would have come in handy when we fought the witch." I heaved a heavy sigh, wishing I wouldn't need such a thing. But I would. And soon. "Thank you—" I couldn't remember his name.

His easy laugh rang like music through the chamber. "No thanks necessary, Your Highness. Thank you for the honor of becoming a temple guard. You've restored my people and our home."

"Not all of your home." I gave him a crooked frown. This entire realm had once been theirs. There was no fae or Seelie Clós. No humans or Talamh Sí. There was no need for the Divide to protect them. Now they were stuck, left with a sliver of their home. "All that's left for you is the Divide."

"Is that your doing?" He laid two gentle fingers under my chin and lifted it for me to look into his unearthly green eyes. "You cannot change the sins of the past. Nor can you restore what's wrong in so many hearts. You are doing what is within your control to do—following God, loving Him and others. For in so doing, you have restored a remnant. Love covers a multitude of sins."

My heart choked on itself, and my eyes welled, making him blurry. But those eyes. Those genuine eyes filled with love and gratitude amplified. I smiled, and tears dripped onto my cheeks. "Thank you."

"Thank *you*." He released my chin and stepped aside.

I swiped my wet cheeks, pushed Hiisi onto Sakki's spine, and followed, wiggling in the new seat, then stilled. If the contraption already irritated Sakki, my squirming would annoy him. So I turned my attention to the wrist clips. The slack allowed me to sit up, but I could see how to tighten them so I could almost lie flat when needed. I wrapped my hands around them and tugged. Sakki jerked his head forward, pulling me down, squishing Hiisi.

"Sorry." I cringed, expecting a barrage of complaints to assault my mind. But none came. I sensed the same sadness I felt at our broken bond emanating from Sakki, assuaging his ire. "I didn't realize the straps also affected your movement."

Ulla returned from the chamber and stood beside Sakki. With a new sheen radiating from her, she was almost glowing.

"You'll get used to it." Niilo strapped himself into his dragon, his white braid bouncing down his back with his swift movements. "It'll be much easier when your bond is restored and you can move as one."

I appreciated him saying when, not if.

Everyone scrambled into their places. Ludek and Hadwin squeezed to fit behind me and Hiisi on Sakki. I hoped it wasn't too much for Sakki. At least Hiisi was small. But if the weight bothered Sakki, he didn't show it. He'd ridden with more before and seemed full of energy, prancing as he waited, making Hiisi groan with each bounce. Was he impatient to go or agitated by the saddle? I hated not knowing. Only Alajos remained on the ground, the color draining from his already pale face. Niilo waited in silence, but Egon taunted him.

"Oh, come now. Where is the great and powerful Alajos now, O Wise One?"

Though my heart held no fondness for my kidnapers, I might've taken the kinder route. God used their evil plots to bring this about. But Egon's methods proved effective. Alajos screwed up his face in stubborn determination and climbed Mount Ulla.

As Sakki got into position, lining up behind Ulla, his nails clicked on the polished stone, and we swayed on his back. Wind blasted us while Ulla's powerful wings pumped. She ran, leaped through the temple wall, and disappeared. Thundering whooshes followed when Sakki prepared for flight. Hiisi trembled, clinging to me.

We broke through the facade after her, swooping over the lush greenery nothing like the witch's barren desert—the physical representation of her empty, grating soul. Was it my imagination, or did the landscape look fuller, more brilliant than before we landed?

An incomprehensible dread snaked into my heart and soul, choking out the peace I'd left the temple with. My gaze darted everywhere, searching the skies and the land. I expected the witch to intercept us. But that was impossible. She was dead. Where were these thoughts coming from?

Or was this like revisiting Bandia in my mind? I'd suffered there, and yet I'd kept returning as if I wanted to torture myself. Was I doing the same thing now? But God had healed me of that. Or so it seemed. I haven't returned there since. Though I preferred not to think about such a dreadful time, it didn't affect me as it had before. I didn't shake as I once had. There was no pressure in my chest, stealing my breath or making it come in rasping pants. I didn't break into a sweat.

So what was happening to me now? Had I replaced my torment from memories of Bandia with Noita?

Nay. I wouldn't let it. I breathed in the restored air, sensing no hint of sulfur.

We continued our peaceful flight. The dragons soared through the sky like a contented sigh, but my mind remained anything but content. Now that Sakki was with me, my thoughts turned to Liam. The time as a passenger allowed my mind to wander to a myriad of possibilities as to his fate. The border's wavering glow in my sights only increased my fears.

It was one thing to stop entertaining past trauma and quite another to thrust myself into a new battle. What would happen? How could we prepare to go up against a powerful fae with several giftings of fae magic? If Maija wasn't as powerful as the queen and yet we'd lost lives and I'd lost my connection with Sakki, what might Rhiannon do? No way could we prepare for all the possibilities of going against someone so powerful. And where was Liam? How could I rescue him? I didn't know where he was or what wards protected him.

Trapped in my thoughts, I barely noticed when we landed. I remained on Sakki's spine, keeping my wrists clipped in place, unsure where Hiisi's trembling ended and mine began.

"Before we go through the Divide, I want to test something," Alajos yelled from Ulla's back.

"By all means." Ludek circled his hand, urging him on.

"If this works and I'm not back in two minutes, come through the Divide." With a twist of his hand, a greenish Alajos disappeared with Ulla, Niilo, and Egon.

"What's he doing?" I twisted to catch Ludek's eye.

Before Ludek could respond, they returned only aiming in the opposite direction.

"It worked." Alajos's grin took over his narrow face. "I can teleport to the Valley of Bones from inside the Divide without your creepy little beast."

"He's not a creepy little beast." I turned to find Hiisi's face in mine. "Don't listen to him."

Hiisi closed his eyes and shook his head. Alajos's ignorance didn't seem to bother him.

With another spin of an invisible dial, Alajos teleported us to the Valley of Bones to plan our attack.

So far, we'd succeeded. And we were following God. Where was my faith? Things were going well. This was God's plan. He would see us through. Shouldn't I be at peace if I'd done everything according to God's plan? Did I do something wrong? Maybe we shouldn't have returned for Sakki first.

One thing was certain—something would go terribly wrong. It was just a matter of time.

THIRTY-SIX

Part of me hoped leaving the Divide might restore my bond with Sakki and the witch's magic only worked within its borders. But my more realist half knew better. And once reality proved my optimistic half wrong, a fracture sliced through the Sakki-sized hole in my heart that had seemed restored. The more time we spent together, the more I experienced the curse's effects. Having him with me was both a relief and a constant reminder of what we'd lost.

Ludek and Niilo had each appointed additional leaders from their ranks. And now, Ludek moved stones across a map of the castle in seemingly random patterns, voicing his strategy behind each move. Sakki perched beside two other dragons, all in cat forms. They seemed to communicate with rumbles, chirps, ear flicks, and tail swishes. Hiisi sat among them, laughing as if he understood everything they said. Maybe he did. Hadwin was our only human representative. Alajos and Egon were allowed to remain despite their past disloyalties.

I was an unnecessary addition. An imposter wearing the future queen's flesh.

The elect few tasked with strategizing our attack on Queen Rhiannon's castle interjected with what-ifs, sometimes stumping Ludek, sometimes offering countermaneuvers, sometimes speaking on behalf of their dragon counterparts. Niilo spoke for Sakki through Ulla.

I hated not speaking to him in our minds or communicating for him. That was my job. The one thing I could've done if I hadn't delayed and broken our bond.

Rather than retreat into myself, I felt outside myself... like someone else. I was in their midst, watching their plotting and planning, but my mind, separate from my body, floated outside myself. As if I watched from afar.

Ludek studied maps of the royal grounds, listening to his advisors' limited knowledge. Niilo offered insight as to dragons' abilities and warfare tactics, but he knew nothing of the castle and little about Rhiannon's abilities, other than there being many. The fae understood fae magic and some of Rhiannon's gifts, but little of the wards protecting her and the castle.

Even Egon and Alajos were more helpful than I was. They had connections with the seelie underground that Ludek wasn't privy to.

But I stood by, an unnecessary prop. I didn't know anything about fighting or strategic attacks. The castle remained a mystery. I didn't have specifications, nor did I understand the protective wards. Creeping crabs. I didn't even remember what the stones represented.

This was hopeless. I couldn't command an elfin army. Who was fool enough to appoint me?

If only Liam and Ruuta were here. Ruuta knew the castle inside and out. Liam was a soldier, not that he'd seen any wars. I'd been in wars, but only as a cowering victim and a bystander.

I had to get them back. No more losses. "What about Liam and Ruuta? What are your plans to rescue them?" My voice sounded like it came from far away.

All eyes shifted their gazes from the map to me.

Ludek cleared his throat. "Liam is the princess's human friend. And Ruuta is—"

"We know who Ruuta is." A dark-haired fae with chiseled features wrinkled his nose as if the most unappealing person paraded before him. "We have more to consider than Zorac's pawn and a donkey."

I slammed back into my body, flaming with indignation, and leaned over the table toward him. "Liam is no donkey." My low, menacing voice sounded foreign.

"Come, now." Ludek's calm carried a threatening undercurrent. "Is that a way to speak of her highness's defender?"

Hadwin, who had been hanging back, pushed up to the crowded table beside Ludek, facing the fae. "Look around this table." He waited for everyone to do as he said. "Fae, dragons, elves..." He motioned to each, then to me. "Our half-elf, half-fae queen." Then he pressed a hand against his chest. "And a human... a freed fae slave."

He let his words sink in. "We've all caused one another pain. And yet, God saw fit to bring us together. Do you not see His hand at work here? Do you not see the miracles that have gotten us to this place?"

The tense lines crossing each face around the table slackened with their posture. The dark-haired fae who'd offended both Liam and Ruuta offered a regretful frown.

Hadwin's shoulders swelled with a deep breath, his intense gaze daring each person to argue, then focused on the elves and dragons. "We have fought for far too long. Nearly two hundred years ago, King Eerikki, Colleen's grandfather, saved my people from extinction in our land in Ireland. We've been fighting until your extinction. Mere days ago, you were nearly extinct, with no hope of restoration. Did you think it was possible that you might be reborn?"

Sakki interjected with a growly meow. The other cat dragons responded by rubbing their faces on him.

Hadwin faced the fae. "You have been fighting the elves for centuries, enslaving humans, and working for Zorac until God opened your eyes to the truth."

Ludek swallowed hard, his eyes gleaming, while Alajos ducked his head and rubbed the back of his neck and Egon cracked his big knuckles.

Hadwin pounded a hairy fist, jostling the maps. "After centuries of division, could you ever, in your wildest imaginings, believe it possible for us to stand in a room, working of one accord?" He laughed, then skewered the elves with a hard stare. "You were bones mere hours ago." He sliced the air to motion to me. "My queen was lost to us. And now she's here, working with us." He jabbed his thick pointer finger on the table. "Each of us is here because God willed it. If He can bring us here, together, why would we doubt that He'd see us through? And if God, who brought us together, stands with us and fights for us, who are we to argue amongst ourselves? Who are we to look down upon any other?"

The air in the cave grew thick. I could almost hear their pierced hearts deflating, purging any animosity.

The dark-haired fae lowered his gaze. "Forgive my ignorance, Hadwin, Your Highness."

I struggled to hold my head up while bearing up against such incomprehensible emotions. Aye, God worked such miracles to bring about His plans and allowed me to take part, yet I felt more unqualified than ever. And after Hadwin's speech, the opposite should have been true. God had chosen *me* for reasons—perhaps I'd never understand why. But whatever was about to happen, the outcome didn't depend on me. And while I might be incapable, God wasn't. And wouldn't His mighty power appear all the stronger using such a weak vessel as me?

God wasn't putting pressure on me. I was putting it on myself.

And yet, despite all my doubts, all my weaknesses, all my fears, God *still* chose to use me.

A sob welled up, and I hurried from the cave before I could dissolve into a puddle amongst the leaders God had entrusted to me.

I sat on the ledge overlooking restored beings settling down to sleep under the bright moon. Their laughter formed a beautiful melody. An entire army—nay, two entire species—that hadn't existed two days ago now enlivened the barren wasteland.

Only You, God.

The stars above blurred, and I blinked my tears back, wiping away escapees. Something furry nudged my elbow.

"Sakki." I made room for him to wind his cat body around me and settle into my lap. Hiisi appeared behind him and snuggled against me.

Heavy footsteps scuffed the rocky floor. Then, with a groan and a cloud of dust, Hadwin sat, sandwiching Hiisi between us. "We thought you might like some company."

"Sorry I left. I—I appreciate what you said in there."

"No need to apologize or explain. You have a lot on your mind. Though it's wonderful to be used by God and at times is elating, like it must've been when those dry bones came to life, it's also difficult... and emotional."

"That's the truth." I petted Sakki's soft fur, his warm body and vibrating purr comforting. "I'm glad for it, but just because God works through us doesn't mean all will end as we want it to."

"No. God never makes such guarantees." Hadwin's teeth scraped against his wiry facial hairs. "In fact, He promises the opposite. That we will face many trials."

"I just... I wish it would be easier. I can't lose any more—" My voice broke.

Hiisi's face tipped up at me, his eyes welling. Then he hugged me tight. Hiisi understood. He was the last of his kind—like I had been this morning. But I had my adopted family. He'd lost everyone.

Hadwin draped an arm over my shoulder and pulled me into him, squishing Hiisi. "I understand. I lost my entire family in their attempts to share God's love with the fae. But remember, this life is but a breath—a wisp of smoke. Here today and gone tomorrow. And while God doesn't promise our brief lives will be trouble-free, He does promise this isn't the end. Those of us who believe in Him, who believe in the Son He sent— we'll all be together in paradise one day and for all eternity."

I kicked my feet against the ledge. While that was comforting and eased death's sting and I was grateful God allowed me to witness Rhys's wish to be accepted in heaven, it didn't ease my fears about losing Liam. Ruuta too. But Liam. Something was there, growing between us. I missed him. The more I thought about the danger he was in as a human in a hostile environment without me to protect him, the more I feared. At least he was a believer. He'd be in heaven. But—"I don't know what I'll do if anything happens to Liam. I don't want to wait for someday in paradise with him. I—I love him." My throat twisted as the confession escaped. My vision blurred with tears.

But the admission also emboldened me. More certain in my feelings, I forced myself to speak past the lump weakening my voice. "I–I want a life with him here. Now. A life free from all this turmoil and uncertainty. Is that wrong?"

"Of course not." He gave me a reassuring squeeze. "Nothing's wrong with appreciating, even wanting more of, what God offers us here in this life. We should be grateful for every good thing He gives. But we must trust Him in all things. We needn't fear, but love. Perfect love casts out fear."

"Aye. I guess I haven't arrived at that place yet."

"None of us has. Not while we're still in this place, in these bodies."

I leaned into him. His beard tickled my forehead. With Hiisi snuggling my side and Sakki in my lap, shouldn't I be content? God had returned Sakki to me and resurrected my race. He'd given me so much. More than I could ever ask for. Love surrounded me. I'd witnessed an incredible miracle —undeniable proof God was with us. Would it never be enough? Why did I have to have Liam too? Was I just being greedy?

Perhaps. But greedy or not, I'd do everything within my power to save him.

God, please. Please, please, please bring him back to me.

THIRTY-SEVEN

Navigating the passing days reminded me of riding turbulent waves. Nothing was as exciting as God providing for us all. He ensured we didn't want for food. For three days, the satchel replenished with all the nourishment we'd need for the day. Such confirmation kept our spirits up, carrying us atop the wave in triumph.

But despite God's provisions, I fretted over Liam. The waves seemingly overcame me, tossing me into the icy waters, pressing me down into the sand. I fell to my knees and asked God to watch over him, praying he was safe. All the while, the fae worked to gather whatever we needed for the coming attack while the elves and dragons practiced fighting, working their renewed bodies.

We delivered the Kapinallis' stockpile to the elves. Ludek and Niilo hauled a trunk full of swords while Hadwin and I carried another. When we were ready, Egon teleported us into the valley.

The heavy trunk threatened to pull my arms from their sockets as we lugged it to the line. "When the elves and dragons returned to life, they had their clothes. Some had sheaths. Why no weapons? It can't be because it's metal. God gave them armor."

"Set it here." Hadwin lowered his end and wiped his hairy hands.

"That's hard to say. Either they left their swords where they died or someone confiscated them."

The elves approached to inspect the weapons, balking at the trunks with fae wards and potions and perusing the guns with disgusted looks. When Hadwin threw back the lid, revealing swords, some with sheaths, several elves discarded their guns to collect a sword instead.

"They're not taking the guns." I pointed out.

"They will when we run out of swords." Niilo had long since discarded his cloak and armor in the heat of the day. Now, though night was falling and it would grow cold, he must be warm from his work. He tugged his silky sleeves, revealing hairless arms. "But they should've spared themselves the effort of carrying fae magic down here. The elves won't touch it."

Elves took turns inspecting our goods. One retrieved a sword, holding it as if it were a rare, invaluable gem. He balanced it across his palms, tested its weight, then held it close to stare down the blade.

"This is Aldemar's work." He spun to the elf beside him, showing her the hilt, pointing to the unsharpened metal. "Look at the ricasso."

The other elf swept silver hair from her face for a closer look, then raised her eyebrows and let out an appreciative whistle. "So it is."

I leaned in to see for myself, but I couldn't read the etching. "How did the elves come to learn to make swords? Did the humans teach you?"

Just why would the elves, who were peaceful, have weapons, or why would the humans, who possessed guns, teach the elves to forge weapons against them?

"Aldemar was a pech," said the elf, still admiring the blade.

"Did you say pech?" I couldn't have heard him right. "There are pech in Talamh Sí?"

"Pech are everywhere." The girl laughed. "They create portals that allow them to travel between realms."

My heart skipped like a three-year-old. "Do you know Pepin?"

The girl's silver hair flowed like a selkie ribbon blowing in the breeze as she shook her head. "I haven't heard of him."

The skipping child lost some enthusiasm. "He's a friend from Ariboslia.

I came here through a megalith. We had pech there, but I haven't seen any here."

"Oh, they're here." She rooted about the chest's contents, careful not to cut herself. "Well, not *here*. When the fae began encroaching on our lands, the pech kept to our side of the Divide. Later, when the humans arrived, they went underground."

"They hate fae magic more than we do." The elf with Aldemar's sword swung it in a practice arc. Something in his voice and youthful expressions made him seem young. My age maybe.

There were pech. Underground. Dare I hope? "Is there a way to reach them?"

"Once we return to Talamh Sí, yes." He held his claimed sword, thrusting it toward me like an offering, and bowed. "Thank you for the sword." With expert precision, he sheathed in the scabbard ready at his hip. "I shall use it wisely."

They studied the blade the next elf selected, admiring another pech's work. Their words faded into the background as they carried on their conversation without me. My mind whirred. If I could find the pech, might I reach Pepin? I couldn't see how the pech or their portals would aid us in our fight. They might be no match for fae magic. Perhaps that was why they hated it. But if I could send word back home that I was all right, that alone would bring incredible relief.

Our stock depleted, leaving the elves to consider whether they needed a weapon, many preferring not to use a gun. As they deliberated, we took our leave and returned to Ludek's lair above the valley.

Ludek clasped his hands behind his back, his long white hair grazing his fingertips. "God has blessed us with so many supplies to aid our attack, but we must move swiftly now. It's unlikely our stockpiling has gone unnoticed by the seelie court."

Seeing our supplies and our surprise army, it seemed we couldn't lose. But then, I considered Rhiannon. How powerful was she? Her strategic mind tricked my father with a long con and, when that failed, enacted another diabolical plan. How many fallback plans did she have? Had she accounted for every scenario? No telling what she might do with demonic help. One thing was certain—she was crafty. Shifty, as Fergus would say.

And she had Liam. She'd use that to her advantage, no doubt.

Despite my fears, I had to remember—God was on our side. No matter how powerful our enemy was, none was stronger than Him.

"How much time do you think we have?" Niilo asked Ludek where both overlooked the practicing elves. Elf and fae—with their white hair, wise countenances, and stern bearing they could've been brothers.

Singing metal rang from the valley as swords clashed.

Ludek sucked air with a hiss. "Two days, at most."

Hadwin's teeth scraped his beard. In the quiet contemplation, the scratchy sound was louder than ever. His gaze shifted back and forth, not landing on anything in particular. "I should go to Talamh Sí."

Ludek's attention snapped to him. "For what purpose?"

"To find the pech." At our blank stares, he raised both hands. "Whether Colleen takes the crown or not, she's going to need to return to Talamh Sí. People there want her dead, and Queen Rhiannon will only help if it serves her purpose. The pech might aid us, if only to get her back to Ariboslia."

"You know how to find the pech?" I barely breathed, enthralled by the idea of returning home.

"I know of one in the Divide." He nodded, and his gaze continued to shift. "A believer who remained to assist those in need, as I had. If I can find him, he may lead me to the pech to beg for their assistance."

"But you heard the elves"—Niilo pinched his angular chin, his sharp green eyes squinting at Hadwin—"the pech won't come to Seelie Clós."

"I'll leave that battle to you. But you came here for Queen Rhiannon's help to take your rightful place as queen of Talamh Sí, correct?"

"I came for her help with my dragon bond and because my life was in danger."

"Regardless," Hadwin continued, "if we attack Seelie Clós, it's safe to say Rhiannon won't help you."

Niilo and Ludek voiced begrudging agreement.

"Should our mission to subdue Seelie Clós find success, Colleen's help must come from another source."

Ludek whistled. "And you think the pech will help?"

Hadwin's dark eyes shone, even while his lips flattened. "It's possible. And we should be open to all possibilities."

"Egon can teleport you to the boundary," Ludek said.

"Will you be able to make it through the Divide to the pech on foot?" Niilo asked.

"I have friends in Rotko... and at least two days before you move out, correct?"

With stiff arms, Niilo gripped Hadwin's shoulders. "If there is a possibility for more aid, we will take it. Go. May God be with you."

"Come." Ludek started out of the cave. "We will find Egon and some supplies for your journey."

I caught Hadwin's wrist, pulling him around. "If you can, try to get a message to a pech named Pepin. He's a friend."

Hadwin bowed and followed Ludek outside.

God, please be with him. Help him find the pech. And Pepin.

I stepped out to watch the dragons and elves settle down for the night. Hiisi and Sakki, in his dog form, sat beside me on the ledge. The elves all slept the same way, curled beside their dragon, under their wing. Those without dragons nestled under blankets. From up here in the darkening sky, they looked like rocky terrain.

Other than the murmurs coming from within the cave, all was silent. Stars blazed like pinholes in black paper against a light. No birds sang. No insects chirped. No critters scurried. No trees existed here to rustle in the breeze. And no talking rose from the still mounds below. But how many conversations happened in their minds before they drifted off to sleep? How I missed that.

With my arm wrapped around Sakki, I stroked his chest. He leaned into me. At least he was here.

If this is all I ever get with Sakki again—even if we never speak as we used to—it's okay. I'm grateful to have him by my side. Thank You.

THIRTY-EIGHT

As time ticked by, I grew more anxious about our attack and Hadwin and Liam. It had only been a week since the Dry Bones Revival, as everyone now called the dragon and elf resurrection, but each day felt like a week. And while every day offered us more time to prepare, it did the same for Rhiannon.

What was she planning?

Though steady snores still echoed in the cave, the subtle rustling of the early risers had begun. Like the delicate whispers of nature, the sound carried a sense of gradual awakening. A symphony of soft movements heralded the new day I had no energy to face.

I'd barely slept—again—and my hazy brain and exhausted body refused to function. Sakki had opted for his dog form. He stretched against me with his butt in my armpit and his head resting on my shin. Hiisi flopped on my other side with an arm draped over me and his fingers embedded in Sakki's fur. They had me pinned. The stagnant dry air reeked of musty body odor. All these things inspired me to rise, and yet... there I lay, unmoving.

Instead, I opted to inflict self-torture with the same unanswerable questions... again. Where was Liam? Would he be in the castle when we attacked? Would we be able to free him? Or had Rhiannon hidden him somewhere to use against me later? Was Äiti with him? Had she gotten captured too? And Kohl? He deserved whatever befell him, but not Äiti. And what about Ruuta? Was she helping Liam or Rhiannon? Whose side was she on?

As much as I didn't want to fight Rhiannon, I wanted to get it over with. We needed to act before we lost our element of surprise.

A renewed sense of urgency made my innards itch. I had to get to them. Soon. I braced to slide myself upward, trying not to disturb Sakki and Hiisi. Sakki groaned and moved his blocky head onto the bed. Hiisi whined when his hand broke contact with Sakki. Once I was free, I placed his hand back on Sakki, and he calmed.

I tugged on my shoes and tiptoed across the uneven stone floor, past others still sleeping, avoiding those preparing for the day, to the planning corner. The lanterns' warm glow pushed back the darkness. Shadows danced on rugged walls adorned in stalactites, revealing a table littered with maps. Ludek hunched over the maps, his hair falling over his shoulders to conceal his expression.

"Are we almost ready to go?" Though I tried to whisper, my voice increased in pitch, teetering on the edge of a hopeful question to a desperate whine.

"Mm-hmm." Ludek rubbed his chin without looking up. Then he jerked his head up as if realizing I was there and had spoken. "Your Highness. My apologies. Did you say something?"

As I was about to repeat my question, he answered it. "We have the battle plan set. First, we'll cover ourselves with an everlasting spell to hide us in veils, teleport us, and protect us from as many spells as possible."

"Everlasting spells?" That sounded terrifying.

"They break when you receive the antidote."

"That sounds like a curse." I jittered foot to foot. Creeping crabs. This sounded like a *bad* idea. "The spell hides us from everyone until we receive a cure?"

"It'll wear off on its own eventually. And you won't be hidden from everyone. Anyone who receives the potion will see you."

It still seemed like a terrible idea. "Are you sure the elves will take it? They don't approve of fae magic."

"They will if they have any hopes of surviving Queen Rhiannon."

I'd have to leave that between him and the elves. "Go on."

He collected a bunch of stones and placed them near the lake north of the castle, the lantern light stretching their shadows across the table. "We'll fly in from the north to enter through the disposal gate where it won't be so heavily guarded. No one wants to go through there." He wrinkled his nose. "But it's our best chance. Tunnels there run underground to dispose of the waste within."

What would a waste disposal look like in a sparkling world of rainbows and sprinkles? They must need a lot of potent spells to mask its appearance. And its smell.

"Our perimeter teams, groups of elves, dragons, and fae gifted with counterspells, will bring down wards, guards, and secure the perimeters here, here, here, and here." With each "here," he moved a stone to another section outside the castle. A lock of his white hair fell over his forehead before he chuffed it away. "Once the perimeter is secure, we'll send in our infiltration teams. They'll enter the disposal gate and fan out, securing the castle from the inside." He switched maps to a rough sketch of the castle, moving stones to show their placements inside. "When the northern section is secure, we will enter."

"How will they know when it's safe to enter or to attack?"

"The spell cocktail we'll ingest allows us to communicate telepathically." He spoke as if that were a normal thing to say.

"Dragons can do that."

"Yes, but only among themselves. This will work better."

"Will it allow me to communicate with Sakki?" I might not love the idea of this spell concoction, but I longed to hear Sakki's voice.

Ludek's cheeks rounded in a rare smile as he nodded.

This all sounded too good to be true. "Will the seelie fae hear us? How will we know if one of Rhiannon's people sends a false message?"

"The potion blocks messages or compulsions from any fae who haven't ingested it."

"Creeping crabs! Is there anything this potion can't do?"

"We've tried to cover every possible scenario."

Though being able to talk to Sakki was tempting. Very tempting. I wasn't sure I was okay with this. "What is this magic? Why do the elves hate it?"

"Because they don't understand it. They don't have such abilities."

He made it sound so simple, but it wasn't. "Isn't there something more than that? Would God approve?"

"We're using our God-given abilities to bring down Queen Rhiannon and a demon—to free the people from their influence. Why wouldn't He approve?" Raising his head, he pushed his hair back from his face. "We're not doing what Noita did. We're not using our abilities for our personal gain, but for the greater good. Nor are we inciting energy from the spirit realm or tapping into evil things. Nothing so nefarious."

Though I was softening, I wasn't convinced. "I don't think the elves will accept this."

"If they want this to work, they will." He closed his eyes and steadied his breath. "I assure you. We've been over and over this. Praying about it. We have a solid plan."

That was what I needed to hear. He'd prayed. "So why the delay?"

"The potion is complex and has undergone vigorous testing. We're waiting on one last test for final approval. It should arrive at any moment." He stared off into the distance as if he expected someone to arrive with it now.

Shouts came from outside. Then a fae boy barged in. "The food's run out."

I spun back to Ludek. "Is that God telling us it's time?"

THIRTY-NINE

Ludek crossed his arms and rubbed his bare chin as his blue eyes focused on the map with renewed intensity. "You may be right, but I fear we're not quite ready."

"But you just said you had a solid plan."

"I know what I said."

His edgy tone made me soften mine. "Maybe we're not supposed to be. Ready, I mean." The words escaped me before I'd thought them through, but they felt right. As if God were speaking through me.

His twitchy eyes narrowed at me. "Is this the same person who just barraged me with questions, sounding so uncertain?" He nudged one of the stone markers like a child forced to sit at the table until his plate was clear prodding the unappealing food. "It's folly to engage in battle unprepared. Only tyhmiä do such things."

"Is anyone ever truly prepared... for *anything*? And if we were, what would we need God for?" As I tried to convince him, I convinced myself, building my confidence. "This is His timing, not ours. God has made that clear. We need Him to go before and behind us. He needs to be the One in control." I huffed a laugh and mumbled, "He is anyway."

"Perhaps you're right." He snatched his lantern and marched to a group of fae huddled together deeper in the shadows. "Is the spell ready? We need it now."

"Yes, sir." A fae sprang to his feet. His skin was so taut, scarcely moving as he spoke, it seemed he'd pulled some of his face with his brown hair into the slick bun piled atop his head. "We finalized the potion last night. The approval just came through, and we were about to notify you."

"That's it, then." He threw his arms up. "Ready the elves. We leave at dusk."

An elf approached carrying something leather with dangling straps clapping against his thigh as he walked. Golden hair poured over his shoulders like liquid gold as he bowed and offered me his bundle.

I held it out and adjusted the position to make sense of the strange strappy thing. "What is it?"

"When elf fly with their young, they put the fledgling in a sling like this." He repositioned it so it appeared like a satchel with two holes. "It should meet your... Hiisi's specifications."

"His legs go here?"

"Yes." He grasped two straps. "These go over your shoulders, and these"—he dropped those and picked up two more—"go around your waist. Until you grow accustomed to it, you'll require assistance to secure it in place."

"Will you help me test it?"

"I'd be honored." He followed me to where Hiisi and Sakki were stumbling from bed and helped Hiisi step into it. I squatted to make it easier as he adjusted the straps, tightening them so Hiisi was snug against my back and clasping them in place.

I craned to find Hiisi's face in mine. His breath, hot in my ear, smelled like eggs, which he hadn't eaten yet today. He smiled, then vibrated as he laughed, throwing off my balance. Being tied to me was hilarious, apparently. But his infectious laughter got me. "This is wonderful. Thank you."

The elf bowed again. "The straps over his shoulders will keep him secure should you need to pitch forward or upside down."

Hiisi's laughter stopped.

"Are you returning to the valley?" I knelt and undid the clasps.

The elf helped me remove Hiisi without dropping him. "I am."

"Join us." I held out the teleportation spell.

"Forgive me." He held up a hand. "I'd rather walk."

He spun in the dirt and loped down the cliffside with ease. Ludek was going to have a time of it, convincing the elves to ingest a magical fae cocktail. I teleported Sakki and Hiisi to the valley, spotted Niilo, and maneuvered through the crowd toward him.

"It's time." I was out of breath, though I'd expended little energy getting to him. "We must prepare for battle. We're leaving at sunset." Panic for Liam slammed my chest. "There is a human among them. A male with black hair and ocea—I mean, blue—eyes. Do not allow any harm to come to him."

"Does your dragon have his likeness to share with the others?"

After I nodded, the elf spun to his dragon. Unspoken words passed between them.

His dragon puffed smoke from his nostrils. Sakki straightened as if raising invisible antennae. All the dragons, including Sakki, froze, their faces alert. After a disturbing moment when I might've been driven mad at the idea that time had stopped, the elves resumed donning their armor.

Niilo half bowed to me. "Your dragon shared Liam's image with the others who shared it with their elves. We'll look out for him."

"Oh, good." I almost relaxed, appreciating how he used Liam's name, though I hadn't. While the news bolstered my confidence Liam might survive this, I wouldn't be at ease until this was over and he was at my side with Sakki.

I should be concerned about Ruuta too, but this was her world.

God, please protect Liam and Ruuta.

Clashing metal clanged with the elves' sword practice. Dragons and elves flooded the skies, performing aerobatics, twirling and diving, chasing one another. It all looked like great fun until you considered the reason.

Sakki's doggy nose prodded me. As soon as he had my attention, he dragged a saddle to me, then morphed into a dragon. I took the hint.

"Me fly?" Hiisi pointed to himself.

"You hate flying. And you won't love the maneuvers we need to practice."

He thrust out his lower lip in a pout.

"I'll bring you with me when we leave for the castle."

As he stomped away, kicking up sand, I saddled Sakki, then put on the armor Niilo had given me and took to the sky.

We were out of practice and not being able to communicate complicated things. When he engaged his evasive maneuvers, I was delayed in keeping up and threw him off-balance. But rather than try to use weaponry in the skies where we were unlikely to meet a battle, I clung to him, fusing myself to his spine so I remained in the same potion no matter what he did. He realized what I was doing and moved with more precision after he grew accustomed to the predictable weight on his back.

I loved being in the sky with him again, even if we were preparing for war. At this point, whatever we'd failed to achieve must not be necessary. God was ensuring we had all we needed. But then, whatever we were lacking, we'd more than make up for in Him.

FORTY

A fae spell lit the valley in a dull glow, darkening the sky beyond to an inky blackness, as the fae readied the diffusers. Elves without dragons doubled or tripled up so each elf was on dragonback, settled in, saddled up, and rearing to go. By some miracle, I wasn't hungry despite the day's exercise and lack of a physical meal. All we needed was the fae cocktail Ludek had conjured up to enact his plan.

Hiisi and I waited, strapped onto Sakki, overlooking the shadowy dragons and their passengers beside Niilo and Ludek on Ulla. I hadn't quite gotten used to my armor. Hiisi kept banging into me, responding with "oofs" and "ows."

I ran my hands along the wrist straps. The ingenious invention allowed me to tighten or release by clasps in my palms. I fiddled with them while I waited, my anxiety building.

Flick. Flick. Flick.

Sakki shook, starting with his head and ending in his tail, sending Hiisi and me swaying.

"Watch what you're doing, you scaly beast." I scooted forward, gripping his spines to still myself.

Sakki craned his neck, tilting Hiisi and me, and blasted us with smoke.

"What was that for?" I coughed and waved the pungent cloud away while Hiisi hacked in my ear.

Niilo leaned to me. "You're playing with your wrist clips. It's annoying him."

I sighed and clasped my hands together, focusing on the activity below rather than my insecurities. "How did you get the elves to agree to take the potion?"

"I didn't. God did."

I'd forgotten. Elves didn't have the sin nature fae and humans had. What would that be like? Did God talk to them? Or did they just inherently know what to do? There was so much I didn't understand, but my voice felt so loud in the silent night. The only sounds now came from the fae attaching the appointed dragons with diffusers. Were they done? The fae were climbing onto the dragons behind their elves.

The majestic creatures spread their sinewy wings, their wingspan the length of a small tree, and flapped, sending sharp gusts of wind and dust. Talons pierced the rocky ledge, crumbling the dirt crust. With powerful thrusts, their hind legs unfurled, launching the three into the sky. Two broke off to fly over the valley to the east and west, while one kept to the center. The fae flipped the switches on the diffusers. Wispy clouds of ethereal colors collected, forming an enchanting mist of iridescent swirls. The airborne dragons dispersed the fae concoction with purposeful wing flaps. The fae in the sky reached for the cloud, their hands twisting, pulling off sections of it and sending it soaring to every awaiting nose.

My portion rocketed at me and rammed itself up my nose. It burned my sinuses as it forced its way in. My eyes watered. I fought a sneeze. Though my mouth was closed, it tasted like tartberry mint.

My queen, can you hear me?

I jerked to Ludek. "Did you say something?"

I did. A playful smile twinkled in his blue eyes, but his lips hadn't moved.

This is the communication spell?

Among others. He nodded toward the waiting army. *Say something to inspire them.*

What would a queen say to inspire her army? *God, give me the words.* I faced the elves and dragons in the valley and opened my mouth.

Use your mind.

Like I did with Sakki before—Nay, I wouldn't do that to myself right now. *How do I know who I'm projecting to?*

Think of who you want to speak to, and they will hear it. Unless they're blocked, but that's another matter. If you want it to go to everyone, think that. It's helpful to address whomever you're speaking to.

Ludek was right. I needed to test this spell. *Sakki?*

It's been too long since Sakki heard Little One in Sakki's mind. He sounded as relieved as I felt.

Still calling me Little One, huh? I laughed. *I've missed you.*

Sakki and Little One can catch up later. Right now, Colleen needs to play queen.

You're right. Hearing his voice bolstered my spirits and renewed my confidence. Maybe, if we couldn't restore our bond, I could get more of this spell. But I'd deal with that later. Right now, I had a queen to stop, a castle to infiltrate, a human to rescue, and an army to command. *My army, mere days ago, you elves and dragons were nothing more than bones in these sands, killed by Queen Rhiannon's hand. Nearly extinct. But God has breathed new life into you.*

The elves raised their weapons or fists and whistled while their dragons blew fire into the sky, making the valley look like a maze of torches.

Kapina, your queen oppressed you, forcing you to subject yourselves to a demon, calling you unseelie and banishing you from your home if you dared rebel. God gave you solace and purpose here. I scanned the crowd. They were too far away to meet eyes, but I tried to catch as many faces as possible. *Do you not see? God has already given us victory. Queen Rhiannon couldn't snuff out your life forever.* I motioned to the elves, then to the fae. *Nor could she infiltrate your camp. You have already won. No mere mortal can stop God. Today, we will finish the battle begun so long ago. God is with us! He has assured our victory!*

Shouts thundered from all around me until I worried they'd cause an earthshake and send me toppling over the edge in a pile of rubble. I unclipped my wrist, unsheathed my sword, and thrust it into the air as if it were my enemy's belly. *Take to the skies!*

Dust kicked up as all the dragons flapped at once, soaring past me. I fumbled to sheath my weapon. While clumps of them disappeared in orange smoke, a cloud engulfed us, and my insides itched. In the next breath, we were hovering in the night sky. The castle's dark outline jutted in the distance. We blocked out the moon as a soft hum from flapping wings enlivened the quiet.

Ulla coasted to our back lower right to prevent her wings from colliding with Sakki's.

Were we too close to the castle? *Ludek, can the guards see us?*

The spell you inhaled is hiding us. I'll copy you on every command so you can stay apprised of the situation. Perimeter Team 1, enact Phase 1. Secure our entry.

Several dragons broke off, swooping low over a lake infested with the castle's waste. It looked beautiful from here, with the full moon reflecting on its mirrory surface. Or was that another seelie spell?

Like autobikes racing up a ramp, they flew up the cliffside. Some landed on the ledges flanking the waterfall of waste coming through the gate, while others continued to their positions surrounding the castle. The team's fae released shimmering blue spells from their designated places on the ground and in the air. The cloud fanned out, reached for its missing parts, then sealed shut as they connected until every part united, obscuring the castle in a glistening azure bubble.

Could the enemy see that? Or was it somehow covered in a veil too? Being inside the veil was comforting and infuriating, making it impossible to know what those on the outside saw.

Remaining perimeter teams and infiltration teams, prepare for Phase 2. Prep us to enter the disposal gate.

A detachment of dragons descended. Some landed in groups within sight while others disappeared around the sides. All was quiet but for the steady hum from so many dragons keeping us stationary as we pulsed up and down in opposition to their wings, waiting for our turn.

More shimmering blue clouds illuminated the night sky. Unfamiliar voices infiltrated my mind, alerting us that their section was secure.

Phase 1 is complete, came yet another voice. *Disposal gate is clear and ready for Phase 2.*

Ludek, his flowy white hair twisted into the typical fae bun in preparation for the battle, raised a fist, then aimed at the castle. *To the disposal gate!*

The dragons arranged themselves in clusters of their assigned teams. Some skimmed the questionable lake, dipping the tips of their wings, disrupting its smooth surface. I hoped no guards noticed the thin wakes, though we were still far away.

As we approached, the peaceful night exploded in organized chaos. Dragons swooped, breaching the barrier into the courtyard and onto the roofs. They got through! The counterspells must've worked. *Thank You, God.*

My relief didn't last long. Gunfire blasted with deafening shots.

Bang! Pop! Pop, pop, pop! Bang!

Unprepared for such an attack, the queen's fae guards fell.

Thumps reverberated through the night, followed by soft thuds as dragons landed and riders dismounted. Clashing metal rang out among the pops and bangs when elves joined the combat.

Sakki found a spot beside the waterfall and lurched to a stop. I unclipped myself and slid from him with Hiisi strapped to my back. Once we were clear, Sakki shot up into the sky, and I freed my gun from its holster, hoping I wouldn't need to use it but finding it preferable to shoot from a distance than to wield a heavy object up close.

Ludek found me. *This way, Your Highness.*

He led me to a breach in the gate blocking a large hole, the waterfall's source. A thin walkway ran alongside it on both sides. Weapons poised, Ludek squeezed through first, checking to ensure it was clear, then waving me in. Metal sang, and our footfalls echoed in the tunnel as we ran in heavy armor along the walkway beside the wastewater, leaping over and sidestepping felled court guards. A guard, facedown, floated by. Though I knew he must be dead, I held my gun ready, watching as he passed, just in case it was a clever ruse. It wasn't. I hated to think of him trapped at the end of the tunnel, stopping up the flow.

I followed Ludek to an open door leading to several flights of stairs—an endless maze meant to confuse the uninvited. He took every right, checking unlocked doors and backtracking at dead ends. Before a building scream erupted, by God's great mercy, we reached a door to a somewhat-familiar area. Everywhere we went, Rhiannon's guards were down. But none of ours. Could it be this easy? A suffocating fog of despair settled upon me. Nothing was this easy.

I raced through maddeningly similar corridors and found the banquet hall where we'd taken our meals. The familiar sight renewed my energy. I sprinted from there to the throne room. Empty. Not a soul in sight. Not one guard protected the door to Rhiannon's office.

Pervasive unease crept through the air. Liam had to be here somewhere. He just had to.

Even as I motioned for Ludek to follow me to Rhiannon's office, the fog obscured any lingering hope. With our guns cocked and ready, I eased the door open. Niilo blasted through. There was no one. Hiisi sucked in a loud breath and gripped my arms tight.

Where were they?

FORTY-ONE

Nay. Nay, nay, nay. I spun in a hopeless circle, half expecting forms covered in veils to reveal themselves if I looked hard enough. "Where is everyone?"

His features somehow different without his soft white hair surrounding them, Ludek screwed up his ageless face, one eye twitching. "Where are her chambers?"

"I don't know." I was such a fool. Why hadn't I studied this place when I'd had the chance? How didn't I know where Rhiannon slept?

I riffled through the papers on her desk and yanked drawers open, but found nothing helpful. I couldn't read a thing. Nothing was written in English or Ariboslian. "Is anything here important?"

"What are you hoping to find? She's not dense. She wouldn't leave hints for us." Despite his doubt, Ludek placed his weapon on the desk and leafed through the papers. He pulled open the drawers and pawed through their contents too. "Just pleas from subjects and receipts for goods. Nothing helpful."

"There has to be something." I darted past the waterfall to the exit we'd taken when we left for the school and kicked the door. It slammed open with a bang, startling no guards because none stood watch.

In the oppressive silence, the fog pressed in, pregnant with an ominous weight of something too sinister to conceive.

"Search the castle!" Ludek hollered to the fae I hadn't realized were behind us. "Find any living guards and bring them to me for questioning."

The fae darted off with stealthier footfalls than mine.

My hopes of finding Liam lay dead at my feet. "They're gone."

"We'll find them."

We'd messed up somehow. But what? And how badly? Did Queen Rhiannon suspect I was involved in this? Where was she? Frustration rose from my belly, erupted into a growl, and grew into an unqueenly roar.

"What happened?" I spun on Ludek. "Didn't the fae put a block on the castle to keep anyone from teleporting out?"

"Of course. Didn't I tell you Rhiannon was crafty?" He shook his head. "We knew this might not work. Rhiannon's abilities and knowledge are uncanny. Far greater than any I've encountered before."

"She knew we were coming." I wasn't asking. Still, I studied him for an answer.

He sucked air through his teeth in a hiss. "She did."

"What do we do now?"

He opened his mouth to speak, but footfalls caught his attention.

A fae came rushing toward us out of breath. "Sir, we've captured a guard. They were expecting us. Queen Rhiannon and her army left in an airship this morning."

My heart twisted into an incomprehensible mess of unanswered questions and dire expectations. "Was a human with them?"

"What was the airship's destination?" Ludek's voice dragged, like he didn't want an answer.

The fae flicked his gaze flicked between us, unsure who to respond to first. "Talamh Sí. And yes." He clasped his hands together. "Liam was with them. The guard wanted to make sure you knew that."

I collapsed, hands planted to keep me upright while I hung my head. Hiisi patted my arm, but I barely noticed. My heart shattered into useless shards. "She wants me to follow."

The fae continued. "They plan to unleash a curse. It seems they intend to bring down the Divide."

"And Liam is the bait." I jerked up to look at him. "They *need* me to follow."

The fae flattened his lips into a grim line. "That is our fear, yes."

My worst nightmare was coming true. She'd use Liam against me. And it would work.

WHILE THE FAE took control of Rhiannon's castle, the elves and dragons regrouped in the courtyard. I couldn't wait around until everyone collected themselves. If I was about to fly through the Divide to fight another battle, I'd need better clothes. I hurried to my quarters, double-checking Liam's annex and the balcony though the entire castle had been searched. Liam was Rhiannon's captive. I knew this all too painfully well. Yet, I had to look.

Remembering my mission, I rummaged through the clothes I'd arrived in. They were a torn mess. Something hard was in the skirt pocket. The cure. I might need that should I run into anyone under my father's curse in Talamh Sí. I fisted the vial, rushed to my closet, and found suitable riding attire by seelie fae standards. Tight purple leggings with a long slitted lavender skirt and a matching hooded cloak. It was sparkly, but it would do. I paired it with a comfortable-looking blouse and boots.

I dropped Hiisi onto my bed. He yanked off the carrier as if it were attacking him, then hopped onto the floor, and twisted into several interesting positions as he stretched.

"Stretch out there while I change." I pushed him out and closed the door on his grumpy face. After I dressed, I shoved the cure into my cloak pocket and permitted him into my room while I crammed more essentials into a pack. I snatched it and Hiisi's carrier. "Come on. Let's rescue Liam."

Hiisi huffed a yes and raced to keep up as I hoped I followed the right path. After a couple of frustrating wrong turns, I floundered my way to the courtyard. The dragons took up all the free space with two, sometimes three, elves on their back.

While I had seen a massive display of gathered dragons from afar and from the front lines, I had never walked among them. The dragons regarded me with curiosity, their intelligent eyes watching. Despite the potential danger, a strange sense of reverence and privilege enveloped me. A palpable energy pulsed in the air, along with the faint aroma of smoldering embers from the occasional exhale of fire. The hum of dragon conversations, a symphony of rumbles, clicks, and growls, echoed along the gardens and trellises, and their iridescent scales glistened in the moonlight.

I'd never felt so small.

God, I'm in awe of Your creation.

As I navigated through the majestic sea, I reached out for Ludek with my mind, then found him near the eastern wall with Niilo and Ulla.

Ludek turned to me, his jaw tense. "There's no convincing you not to go, is there?"

It didn't sound like a question. "I have to."

His brows knitted together. "You care about Liam and would do anything for him. But please, I beg of you—consider how your actions might affect us all."

My heart contorted as if it were being squeezed and ripped apart.

He placed a hand on my head and closed his eyes. "God, give Colleen wisdom. Protect her from the evil one and keep her from temptation."

I hadn't thought of rescuing Liam as a temptation. But, if rescuing him was giving in to my desires over the good of the majority and God's will, then it was. "Thanks. I need it."

Moonlight set his upswept white hair aglow like a crown and caught the sheen in his eyes. "I'm going too. I've commandeered a ship. My people are preparing it now."

He would join me? I choked back tears. "But what about the castle? You need to secure this place under your control."

His warm hands gripped my shoulders. "Rhiannon is gone. Her wards and her guards are disarmed. My people will handle it."

"I don't understand." My mind whirred, foiling my ability to make sense of my troublesome aunt. "She needs to be on this throne. Why would she leave?"

"This changes nothing. She is queen until she dies. All she needs is to get you on the throne. Her desertion reveals her desperation. That is good—dangerous, yet good."

If he wanted to help, no way would I stop him. I hugged him, grateful for his support. "Why take a ship? Why not fly with us?"

"Niilo and I have already discussed it. It's a long journey. The extra weight on the dragons will be too hard on them."

Aye, the last thing we needed was for our dragons to arrive exhausted. I stepped back from Ludek. "Niilo, how long will it take the dragons to fly to Talamh Sí?"

Standing at attention, the stern elf gave a sharp nod. "Three days if we don't make too many stops."

Too long. "Ludek, how long does it take a ship to travel through?"

"About the same."

Great. We'd need to stop and rest while Rhiannon and her guards rested well on a ship. "And there's no way a fae could teleport us?"

Ludek tugged his chin. "We can only teleport to places we've been before, and we can't go through the Divide."

My hopes deflated. "I was afraid of that. We'll have to allow the dragons to rest. Queen Rhiannon already has a head start. She'll have a firm grip on the castle before we arrive."

Ludek held up a finger. "But—"

I leaned in, eager for a better option. "But?"

"Fae can't teleport *through* the Divide, but now that we've visited the temple, we might be able to teleport there."

Niilo's weary face brightened, his stiff stance relaxing. "And the temple will restore the dragons' energy."

"It will take time to get them all in there." I jittered in place, excess energy urging me to get moving—*now*. "But if we travel in waves, not all of us will be too far behind."

"I'll find Alajos to test it." Ludek darted off into the castle.

Sakki?

Colleen?

Where are you? How good to hear his voice again, even if it was through an unseelie spell.

A familiar face peeked through the glimmering scales and forced a smaller dragon sideways as he squeezed past to us. He nuzzled my face with his gargantuan head, almost pushing me over. I laughed and rubbed his velvety ear. *We have to go to Talamh Sí to rescue Liam.*

Sakki knows.

But I might not be able to. Not if it means doing what Queen Rhiannon wants and setting Zorac free.

Sakki knows that too. Sakki will help Colleen.

I kissed his scaly face, then held open the carrier for Hiisi to step into.

He crossed his gangly arms and gazed at me like an obstinate toddler.

"Do you think I want to do this? It's not comfortable for me either." I pushed my hands into the small of my back and pressed my shoulders into a backbend to prepare for his weight again. "But it keeps you more secure. You don't want to fall off Sakki, right?"

He flopped his arms so his knuckles grazed the courtyard's marble paving stones, then stepped into the carrier. While I was hooking him up, Ludek returned with Alajos.

Ludek heaved Hiisi into place and flung the straps over my shoulder to clip him in. "Alajos is going to test the teleportation to the temple. Are there two dragons you'd like to appoint for the task?"

Niilo whistled, gaining his elves' attention, pointed to two, and motioned them to approach. "You are to accompany this fae to the temple."

Alajos twisted his hand, and they all blinked away.

I climbed into my seat and clipped in my wrists.

Alajos returned. Alone. "It worked. They're taking turns renewing their energy in the chamber now."

What a relief. Maybe there was a way to arrive in Talamh Sí before Rhiannon had too secure a hold on the castle. Before she unleashed whatever curse she planned. And before she set any traps.

Niilo formed another group to join Alajos. They vacated, and he began rounding up more elves, appointing them to ready more groups to teleport.

"It's not too late to stay behind," Ludek implored. "The best way to keep from giving in to temptation is to avoid it altogether."

"How could I do that? I have to stop her."

"Has anyone ever told you how stubborn you are?"

Sakki chuffed. Smoky tendrils steamed from his nose. *Colleen goes with the flow like a boulder in a stream.*

Ludek harrumphed while Hiisi's laugh tickled my ear. So, they heard his sarcastic retort too. There was something to be said about the bond being between us and not shared with others.

"I've heard comments about my stubbornness a time or two." If he was trying to stop me, that comment backfired and fueled me. I had to free Liam. Ruuta too, if she would come with me. "I have to go."

"Very well." Ludek bowed. "My people are nearly ready to ship out. I'll join them and meet you when I can." With that, he waded into the sea of dragons.

Ulla sidled up to us with Niilo. He bowed as deeply as his saddle would allow. "Your army is ready at your command."

"Then let's move out."

FORTY-TWO

At the temple, the dragons who had gone before us bathed in a renewed radiance. Their dimmed scales now pulsed with a vibrant luminosity. As the dragons moved, the glow cast intricate patterns on the surrounding landscape, illuminating the floor and pictorial tales on the walls. Residual energy crackled in the air, leaving a faint, enchanting hum.

I drew closer to the chamber with Sakki while he awaited his turn. I'd never seen dragons emerge from the chamber like that. Words failed to form as I gawked.

One elf seemed to understand. "It took less than a minute."

"Closer to thirty seconds," another elf interjected before greeting his restored dragon with another close behind.

"They're entering the chamber in pairs?" I asked aloud to no one in particular.

The elf in line before us shuffled closer. "I didn't know the chamber could hold more than one dragon at a time."

The heavenly glow held my eyes captive as the dragons paraded by. When it was Sakki's turn, he ambled inside, head bowed in humbled rever-

ence. A smaller purple dragon entered behind him with the same countenance. Sure enough, in less than a minute, they emerged as the others had.
His eyes, once tired and dim, now gleamed, their intensity almost fierce.
With each exhale, wisps of iridescent steam escaped his nostrils, adding to
the mystique of his reenergized being.

How do you feel? I asked. If only I was allowed entry too.

As if Sakki contains the boundless energy of the skies.

Thank You, God. Too bad it didn't restore our bond. But maybe we'd
arrive with a decent-sized army of renewed dragons without having to wait
too long.

Niilo and I stepped out into the night as more dragons arrived and
waited their turn.

The new temple guard wandered about, handing out flatbreads. "My
queen." He bowed, then retrieved two more doughy discs. "How is the
saddle serving you?"

"Perfectly." I accepted his offering. "Thank you for helping us. Have
you seen Hadwin?"

"Who?" He leaned in and cocked his head as if he hadn't heard me.

"Hadwin. The human who was here with my dragon and left with us."

"Ah." His face smoothed, then crinkled. "I'm afraid I haven't. Is he all
right?"

"I'm sure he's fine." I hoped. "Thank you for everything. Sorry for
disturbing your sleep."

"To save my realm, my sleep can handle a little disturbance." Eyes
twinkling, he wandered off to hand out more food.

"There was little chance of Hadwin coming here." Niilo bit off a piece
of his bread.

"I know. I had to check." Where was he? Had he found Pepin? *God, I
pray Hadwin is okay.*

Though the lush greenery surrounding the temple was difficult to
make out in the darkness, it was impossible to imagine it had ever been a
barren wasteland with nothing but sand. Dragons came and went,
entered dull, and exited with an ethereal glow that eased the darkness,
revealing more of the rich landscape growing more vibrant. The trees

had proliferated. Bright berries and flowers now weighed down the shrubs.

"This place is more beautiful every time I look at it. Do you think it's happening as the dragons are restored or as they return?" I nibbled the corner of my sweet bread.

Shrugging, Niilo swallowed his bite and wiped a tear from the corner of his eye. "Maybe both. Either way, it's returning to what it used to be."

"Did you see it when Noita was here?"

"Only after she'd first arrived and Rotko was darkening."

"Be glad you never saw it when it was under her control." I shuddered, remembering the hand reaching up from the ground and grabbing my foot. Thankfully, that was over. But I had Rhiannon to contend with now and needed a new plan. "We should fly out in packs of one hundred."

"Flights."

"What?"

"A large group of dragons is called a flight. We'll fly out in flights of one hundred."

"Okay." I formulated the plan as I spoke. "Let's see—two dragons every thirty seconds. That's four per minute. We could send out flights of one hundred whenever the full sum is gathered, every thirty minutes or less."

Niilo nodded. "I will speak with the temple guard to ensure he appoints a leader to each flight. What is the destination?"

That all depended on what Rhiannon was up to. "How far away does the communication spell work?"

"I fear we would need Ludek for such answers."

We should have kept him with us. "Well, if the seelie spell fails us, how far can a dragon cast a message to the others?"

"As long as they're in the same realm and on this side of the Divide, projecting is limitless. Though, the further the call, the more energy the dragon spends."

"We need a place close to the castle, but inconspicuous, with room enough for thousands of dragons. The castle is surrounded by a city." The woods surrounding the hideout were too thick, and it was too far from the castle. "Does such a place exist?"

"Castle Bay's north shore. Across the bay from the castle, there was a fishing village, but nothing to the north. It's a barren desert, so I can't imagine anyone has occupied it in the last fifteen years. There's plenty of room for all the dragons."

By teleporting to the temple, we'd shaved almost a day off our time. That put us twelve hours behind Rhiannon. "If the rest of our journey is a two-day, nonstop flight, can the dragons handle it?"

"With the energy they just received? I should think so."

"What about Ludek? We'll need him to meet us." *Ludek?*

No response.

Ludek!

Still nothing. The communication spell mustn't travel that great a distance. Unless their ship hadn't made it to the Divide yet.

Alajos arrived with the next flight. Before he blinked away, I leaped to my feet. "Alajos!" I jogged the distance between us. "Can you get a message to Ludek?"

"He's too far away to reach by spell, but the communication spell-casters back at the castle might get him a message. What do you want to say?"

"Tell him to land on Castle Bay's north shore, any crew member can tell you where it is, but make sure he reaches out to us before he lands."

"I'll do my best." He bowed and disappeared.

In less than an hour, we were ready to go. I clipped myself so I laid on Sakki, Hiisi strapped to my back. Sakki unfurled his colossal wings. With a burst of energy, he lifted off, and the ground disappeared in the darkness. Host to one hundred dragons, the sky transformed into a living tapestry of scales and wings. The wind, rushing past at exhilarating speeds as we ascended, carried the scent of adventure and freedom. Crisp and invigorating air enveloped me, and every effervescent breath refreshed my lungs. The air vibrated with the dragons' rhythmic beats, and that symphony resonated through my core.

Communication between the dragons echoed—a combination of roars, clicks, and rumbles, a language beyond words, a communion of unity and purpose. The flight ventured the skies as one, soaring in harmony, its sheer scale stirring the soul.

The dragons quieted and settled into a rhythm. Whooshing surrounded us as they flapped powerful wings, followed by a melody of whistles when they coasted. The moonlight and luminescent dragons brightened the night sky, and I imagined myself straddling a star traveling in a celestial cluster through the atmosphere.

I laid my head on Sakki's back and relaxed. His heartbeats lulled me to sleep, and I dozed off and on. Light brightened my eyelids, and wintry winds iced my hands. The discomfort hastened my departure from a forgotten dream. I unclipped my wrist to wipe my eyes and help them open. The morning sun presented itself over the horizon, putting the rolling hills glistening with frost on display. I shivered despite being sandwiched between Sakki and Hiisi as I loosened the other wrist strap to sit and stretch as best I could with Hiisi on my back. As I sat upright, he grumbled. Driving headwinds Sakki had protected me from now blasted me, deafening me in its steady howl. Hiisi pulled me in every direction as he stretched, yawned in my ear, then smacked his lips.

The hills rolled out their unending greenery for us and seemed to pass slowly. The dragons beat their wings harder, undulating like a dolphin pod swimming through mud. They had lost some of their glow. Or was it more difficult to notice in daylight?

Are we in the highlands?

Yes. Sakki flew through Rotko's southern barrier over an hour ago.

So I'd been sleeping better than I'd thought. I hadn't even noticed the Divide's waving wall of lights. *Are you getting tired?*

Sakki has plenty of energy.

Will you have enough to fly straight through with this headwind?

Yes, but if that changes, Sakki will tell Colleen.

That was good enough. We couldn't afford any more delay, but we couldn't go into battle with tired dragons either.

I occupied my mind by watching the dragons in flight. In an amazing display, they staggered themselves to fly close together despite their massive wingspan, without clipping each other. Some elves slept.

I dozed in and out throughout the day. Aches settled in, and I tried to change my position. But I had little freedom of movement. And I needed to relieve myself. If I needed to, others must too.

Sakki banked and turned, treating me to panoramic views. The hills leveled off, and rivers and forests became miniature wonders in the world's vast canvas. We must be leaving the highlands. It would be better to land now, before we entered the forests.

Niilo, we should land.

I agree.

At least the communication spell was still working. Maybe we were still in the veil too.

Within seconds, the dragons dipped down, preparing to land. But some of them caught wind instead, and it lifted them, so they deepened their dive.

Sakki's touched down on the frosty ground, his landing softer than usual. The wind wanted to toss him back into the air. He tucked his wings, and the wind exacted its vengeance on us with a harsher bite. Ninety-nine other dragons touched down, shaking the earth and crunching the snow.

"What's your plan?" Niilo called out to my right. He unwound his hands from the reins, cupped them, and blew warm air inside.

"We all need to take a quick break." I didn't want to spell it out for him. But if he didn't know, oh well. Sakki shielded me from view as I heeded nature's call.

Niilo must've figured it out. He took a moment of privacy under Ulla's wing.

"How's Ulla?" I asked when he emerged.

"She's doing well, despite the headwind. Now that we're descending out of the highlands, the flight should be easier."

"I hope so. We'll need them to be ready for whatever comes when we reach the castle."

"Don't forget. God is with us."

After Hiisi's turn, we swigged from the canteen and nibbled on our provisions. Just enough to quench our thirst, but not so much that we'd need to make too many stops.

The sky turned gray in the setting sun, stunting the sun's rays. Icy flecks pelted me and dribbled wet trails down my face. Sharp pings rang out as sleet collided with armor.

"We should get going again. As we fly south and at a lower altitude, we should escape this weather."

So, as quick as we could, we resumed our flight.

FORTY-THREE

W e spent the night flying over the forest with no more stops and landed in a clearing the following morning. The easterly wind died down, giving way to a westerly wind, and the skies cleared to allow for better travel. After one more stop, we arrived at the desert beyond the fishing village north of Castle Bay as dusk painted the horizon with sweeping orange and red brushstrokes. The dragons tucked their wings and dove toward the earth. The vast expanse of sandy terrain trembled under the weight of a hundred weary dragons, overreacting as if it were being attacked and retaliating with grainy sprays. I covered my eyes and mouth and waited for the sand to settle.

The scaly beasts had lost their ethereal glow. With measured grace, the dragons stretched their massive limbs, wings extending to their fullest span, and talons digging into the soft sand. The dragons indulged in the soothing embrace of the earth, a reprieve from countless hours spent aloft.

As riders dismounted, the dragons lowered their massive heads, the gritty earth cradling their snouts. Their eyes, once sharp and vigilant, now dulled with fatigue and closed. The atmosphere hummed sharp puffs of air as their breath etched twin rivulets in the sand.

Sakki was already asleep when I slid from his back. Niilo helped remove Hiisi from his carrier.

"How long should we allow them to rest?" I rolled my shoulders and twisted from side to side, but no movement touched the deep aches. "We need to move out under cover of darkness. Perhaps midnight?"

"That gives us about six hours. We'll set up a perimeter of elves to keep watch in hour shifts."

What kind of leader allowed their people to lose sleep while they slept? "I'll take a shift too."

"Me watch with you." Hiisi wagged a hand over his mouth, failing to conceal a giant yawn or catch a dribble of drool.

Niilo lifted a finger, about to make a point. "But, Your Highness—"

"I will take first watch." I cut him off with a sharper tone. If I fell asleep now, I wouldn't want to wake. Better to keep the momentum going and crash later.

After I'd trudged through the sand to the top of a dune overlooking the dragons, something thumped behind me. I spun.

"Sakki!" I pressed my fragile heart, incapable of handling the smallest of surprises, to keep it from pumping outside my chest. *What are you doing? I thought you were asleep. You* should *be sleeping.*

He dropped his big dragony rear and stretched out, laying his head beside me, almost in my lap. I snuggled into his soft scales while Hiisi curled into me on the other side. Both fought heavy eyelids as the sea of slumbering dragons, covering their elves and the dragonless, pulsed with steady breaths. They looked like sandy mounds, reminding me of where they'd come from just over a week ago.

I still struggle to believe we're here. The dragons and elves are alive. It seems like a dream.

Sakki gave a little grumble.

I wish I could talk to you again. I mean—I can. But it's different. It didn't run as deep. I didn't sense his emotions as I had. But this unseelie spell was better than nothing. If only I knew how long it would last.

Mmm.

But I'm glad we're together again and you don't have to be responsible for the Divide. There are others to care for it now. I rubbed his velvety ears.

He heaved a heavy sigh, sending streams of sand billowing away from his nose.

My eyes began to droop, but I startled awake to find him staring into the sky. I tracked his gaze to the black cloud sweeping toward us.

Is a storm coming?

No, the next wave of dragons.

As they drew closer and some light was visible between those on the outskirts, their flapping outlines took shape. The next hundred dragons were coming in.

"Ooh." Wonder replaced sleepiness in Hiisi's obsidian eyes.

They flew overhead, sending a gust of wind swirling my hair, disturbing the sand, and landed to the east. Though they were a ways off, as soon as they touched ground, they caused the earth to quake, and a sandy cloud descended upon us. Sakki covered us until the grit spilling over his wing subsided.

I pondered all I'd witnessed, then shifted my attention to the stars above. Mere pinpoints of light from my limited view, they were so much larger than me, the dragons, the realms—or anything happening on this puny planet. But most overwhelming was that, while God cared about all the little things happening here, they were nothing to Him, the Creator of it all. He was so much bigger. Larger than I could comprehend.

God, You are incredible. How could I ever doubt You?

Though I still fought heavy eyelids, my amazement sustained me while I awaited the next flight and the end of my watch, which came sooner than expected.

Niilo weaved through the mounds of sleeping dragons, disturbing some as he went, but they settled back once he passed. The sand squeaked beneath his feet. "First watch is over. Get some rest."

I wouldn't argue now. In a daze, I staggered down the dune with Sakki and Hiisi and collapsed. Sakki spread his wing over us. I cuddled close to his warm belly. He responded by vibrating with a comforting purr while Hiisi draped an arm over my shoulder.

As I drifted in and out of sleep, I was aware whenever another hundred dragons swooped overhead and landed nearby, ticking off another half hour. Between landings, concerns plagued each waking moment: Who was I to lead an army? What awaited us at the castle? Did the people even want me there?

They wanted to overthrow the monarchy. Many wanted me dead. Would they try to kill me too? I'd fled for Queen Rhiannon's help. If she was my only hope and reason to take the throne, was Ludek right? Should I have stayed away? Would Queen Rhiannon force me to become queen against their will? How long would my rule last before my assassination?

Despite these fears, blissful sleep came over me once again until I woke in extreme discomfort. My body buzzed, my heart thrummed, and my legs itched. I tossed and turned, trying not to disturb Sakki, but couldn't find a comfortable position. Though exhaustion weighed upon me, no way would I sleep more. Lying down felt torturous. I lifted Sakki's pinion to give myself more room. He turned, raising his wing. Soon soft rumbles came from his belly, and I got on my knees.

God, I'm not ready to lead these people.

Where you are weak, I am strong.

I jolted, bumping Sakki. He grumbled and offered me more headroom.

That voice wasn't me. Not the way I was feeling. Not with the thoughts plaguing me.

That was God.

I'd heard Him before, and His voice was becoming easier to recognize. Muscles I didn't know I had woke with renewed energy, ready to march. Kneeling, I straightened and faced skyward, though the underside of Sakki's wing blocked it.

"What do You want me to do?" I whispered.

Follow Me. Lead them.

"Follow You *where*? Lead them *where*?"

Put on the ring.

With my heart thump, thump, thumping, I fumbled with the chains on my neck, separating the ring from the bottle of sand collected at the Valley

225

of Bones. I dropped the ring. My heart thudding. The last time I'd delayed putting on the ring—

I scooped it up, blew away the grit, and slipped the ring on my grainy finger, praying my delay wouldn't be a problem.

Now rise.

I stood, breaking through Hiisi's arm and Sakki's wing without disturbing them.

Rise.

Without moving a muscle, I rose several cubits above the ground and hovered like a low-hanging star. The sky brightened as if the sun had raced ahead of schedule, chasing away the night like a bad dream as thousands of shining angels surrounded me.

Tell them to open their eyes.

I repeated God's words, and the mounds shifted as dragons retracted their wings, exposing the sleepy elves. They jerked from their slumber and snapped to attention. Ludek and his fae approached from the south, then sank to their knees. Once every eye aimed upward, God gave me more words to tell them.

"God has restored you and will return you to your lands. Darkness is descending on Talamh Sí, which threatens all the lands. Go to Talamh Sí. God is with us, and He is faithful."

The elves and fae basked in the angels' glow, mouths agape, faces lit. The light returned to the dragons' eyes and shimmering ripples crossed over their scales. Then the heavenly host surrounding me blinked out of existence like glowing embers in a night sky, and I lowered back to earth. After God's final command, I removed the ring and slipped it into my pocket. Everyone remained frozen, stunned. Then the hills erupted in activity. Elves donned their armor and weapons and saddled their dragons.

"That was quite the show," Ludek said. "You do this nightly?"

Were we on teasing terms? "I see you received Alajos's message." Except the part about reaching out to me before traveling here. "I hope you got plenty of sleep on the ship. It's time to face the queen."

His blue eyes alight, hands clasped, and shoulders erect, he could've come from a full night's sleep, not a long journey. "I gathered that."

Niilo came up behind Ludek and clapped him on the back. "Glad to see you made it. When did you come in?"

"Just now. We were ahead of schedule and decided to take advantage of the cover of night. I've got a few men with me." He waved toward a group of fae talking animatedly and motioning to the sky. "The rest are on the ship. When it's time to attack, I'll send a runner to alert the crew to sail to the castle."

"Very good." Niilo gave a sharp nod. "Once we've secured the castle grounds, we'll send them in."

"But you'll come with us?" God spoke through me, assuring us He was with us. While that was more than enough to embolden me, having Ludek and Niilo by my side would bring considerable comfort.

"I wouldn't dream of missing the opportunity."

"Good." I patted his arm. "Do we need more of your mixture of fae spells to stay hidden and communicate as before?"

White hair no longer contained in a topknot slipped over his shoulders as he inclined his head. "It's enacted until you inhale the antidote."

"What about the temple guard? He saw us."

Ludek inclined his head as if he hadn't heard quite right, his forehead crinkling. "In the Divide?"

"Might it have something to do with the temple itself?" Niilo raised his thin eyebrows. "It is God's holy connection to the dragons."

"That may be. Regardless, unless Rhiannon has wards we're unable to combat, no one will see you."

"Then we'll enact our plan as we did before and send in teams to test for wards. My father's castle has a similar place for waste to the south. With the continual crashing waves, iron gates, and no land access, my father always thought it secure. But the dragons can land on the southern cliffs and—"

"Did you say 'iron' gates?" Ludek sucked air through his teeth. "I'd forgotten how enamored King Auberon was with iron, despite his fae wife."

Right. Iron burned fae—permanently. There had to be a way to work around it. "Can't a dragon melt it with fire?"

Niilo nodded, sending his queue swaying over his armor. "It takes a formidable dragon with powerful lungs and stamina to create the heat necessary and a consistent stream to do the job quickly, but yes. It can be done."

"Good." I gave a sharp nod. "Make sure such a dragon accompanies the infiltration team."

"I will ensure there are two so they can work on taking the gate down. How thick are the bars?"

"I've never seen it. I just know it's there. My father sent defenders to check it. The south side cliffs are surrounded by sea."

"Then I don't need to worry about anyone seeing the flames?"

"Nay."

He rubbed his angular chin. "If it's not too thick, two dragons could break through in fifteen, thirty minutes, if that."

"Then send two with the perimeter team now and instruct the infiltration team to give them fifteen minutes before flying out."

Niilo spun and disappeared through the throng.

"Ludek, send your people to catch a ride with the dragons and alert your ship." I tightened the last saddle strap across Sakki's midsection. "You can join me."

Half of me was excited to be part of whatever God was planning. I still didn't know what that was. The other half didn't want to go where I knew we must. The castle. My temporary home. The place I betrayed my father. The place I last saw him alive. I fretted about the prospect as I prepared.

Niilo reappeared as a small flight of dragons swooped over us toward the sea. "The first team is airborne. The second team is counting down the minutes until their departure. What are your orders?"

Though half of my mind rebelled, the words escaped me. "We do as God said. We fly to Talamh Sí. I'm trusting God will show me what to do once we arrive."

"Very well." He spun on his heel, creating a divot that filled with sand as he departed, and returned to his readied dragon.

I poised Hiisi's carrier for him to step inside. "Are you sure you want to come?"

He gripped my shoulder for balance, then jabbed a thumb at himself. "Me go where you go."

"Okay, then." I crouched for him to climb onto my back.

He flung the straps over my shoulders and latched on while I found the other straps to attach him. We'd gotten pretty good at doing this without help. I climbed into my seat, and Ludek followed. Once we were all seated on our dragons, I thrust an arm in the air. "To Talamh Sí!"

The night sky erupted into a fury of rippling sinews and thunderous flaps as the army of dragons took flight.

FORTY-FOUR

A fingernail clipping of a moon hung in the eastern sky as we flew south over the sleepy fishing village. Moonlight reflecting on the water revealed dark huts lining the coast. Gentle waves lapped the shore beneath the primitive homes. It was difficult to spot individual people from this height—or sounds. Hopefully, we'd be difficult to make out too. Should a shadow-loving insomniac or a bleary-eyed villager wake and take notice of us, I hoped we'd appear as a passing cloud if the fae spells proved faulty.

But what did it matter? If someone saw us, they'd have no time to warn Rhiannon even if they wanted to.

With the village behind us and nothing but a rippling sea below, Sakki veered toward the moon, breaking away from the others as if an unseen force guided him. Something about it seemed right, and I trusted God guided us.

Niilo, follow us. We're entering the castle to the east.

Yes, Your Highness.

Hiisi and Ludek blocked my view to see if he followed, but after a few minutes, I glimpsed Ulla's snout. A silhouette of my father's castle stood against the darkened expanse of the sea. Moonlight, a silver cascade, spilled across the water's surface, weaving a luminous pathway from the distant horizon to the castle walls.

What awaited me there?

The shoreline whispers, once comforting, now carried an anxious undertone, as if the sea itself sensed the coming battle. Waves crashed against the castle's rocky coastline, trying and failing to beat it down.

Though I didn't know the state of the castle—who controlled it or how many guards they had—I hoped the infiltration team had worked their way inside and would take care of much of my opposition before I arrived.

Niilo, we will enter from my bedroom balcony.

Not to question Her Majesty, but is that the wisest course of action? Wouldn't the queen expect you to come to your quarters should you return?

She's not expecting me. She knows nothing of the dragons, and I wouldn't make it here on time any other way.

Doesn't the queen know of your dragon?

She knows we weren't together. Rhiannon's betrayal stung me afresh. Was everything a lie? Had she planned on fixing our bond? Had she cared about me? Or was everything she said calculated—a means to her desired end?

That may be, but Queen Rhiannon is crafty. Regardless of what she expects, I'm sure she's posted sentries.

He was right about that. I'd better learn, as he had, not to underestimate her. But it was the right course of action. Somehow, I knew it. *We are hidden. We can incapacitate them if necessary.*

If you insist.

I do.

Pinpricks of light from the castle pierced the darkness. Their wavering likeness shimmered on the ocean's surface. From out here, all looked calm, other than the waves battering the rocks. But what was happening inside? Had the humans decided on a ruler in my absence? Had they ransacked the place? Had Saors taken over, or had the Vapaus won out?

I didn't want to find out.

Whatever the case may be, my father wasn't there. Or Rhys. What about Iida?

Hope blinked within me. Iida. She'd always been on our side. Was she still there, working for us? Would they have her jailed for helping me? Or worse?

And where was Liam? My father didn't have cells in his castle. Would Rhiannon have locked him up in the Atonement Center? Should I look there first?

Nay. God had directed me here. I couldn't deviate from His plans.

Once the castle lay to our west, Sakki banked toward it. The rustling of their flapping wings sounded louder than it probably was, but it was necessary to land as softly as possible for such massive creatures. Still, I held my breath after Sakki thump-landed. Had anyone heard? Ulla dropped beside him, exhibiting more grace and making less noise. She tucked her wings slower, their rustle nearly silent. Sakki should take lessons from her on stealth. I slid into Ludek and squeezed into the sliver of space between the dragons, their tails dangling over the crowded balcony. Sakki morphed into a dog, and I stumbled and caught myself before falling.

Creeping crabs, Sakki! The double doors hung open, but nothing moved within. *Warn us before you do that.* I squatted for Hiisi to get his footing, then eased the clips free. Hiisi climbed from the carrier. *See? The rest of us can be quiet.*

Sakki lifted his snout and blasted me with smoke.

What are you doing, you daft lizard? I wafted it from the wide entry-way. *Someone might smell that!*

I peered into the dark chamber. *Please, God, don't let there be anyone inside. And if there is, I pray they didn't hear us, and the fae spell hasn't malfunctioned.*

Ulla shifted into a weasel. Niilo expected the change and caught the saddle. But then, Ulla must've had the decency to warn him, unlike my inconsiderate lump of scales.

I fought the temptation to tell Sakki we needed to work on our communication skills... and stealth. This wasn't the time, particularly while our bond remained broken. Guilt pestered me, and I stooped to kiss his furry forehead before tiptoeing into my old room. Mixed emotions blended in my belly, exciting me, yet slowing my feet. The spacious chamber unfolded in the night, the solitary tree imprisoned behind bars at its heart, bathed in the moonlight's enigmatic glow, while the deep recesses languished in mysterious shadows.

Memories and the echoes of emotions they evoked flitted across my mind and stabbed my heart. The uncertainty upon my arrival. The homesickness. The trepidation from knowing I'd have to betray the father I had come to love. He manipulated my memories and filled my head with false ideas and my heart with an unnatural contentment. But, despite all that, a genuine affection for him made the betrayal hurt all the more. But no matter who he was or what his intentions were, he had to be stopped.

Stifling a sigh, I shoved my emotions down and focused on my mission. I sneaked to the door past my old bed. What I wouldn't give to curl up in its comforting embrace now. But something wasn't right. I stiffened, and Niilo almost walked into me. The dim light revealed a lump under the covers. Was someone in my bed?

I closed in on the bumpy blankets. Sakki nipped at my heels. I swatted at him. I couldn't go any further without knowing my usurper's identity. Bright lights vanquished the shadows and hurt my eyes.

"Who's there?"

Iida?

My old maid crouched beside the light switch, her frizzy red hair as wild as her searching eyes. She stepped toward the bed. I shuffled backward on silent feet, but I tripped over Sakki, caught myself on a tea table, and toppled a cup to the floor. Her head snapped toward us.

"Is that you, Iida?" a familiar voice asked. "Why is the light on?"

With a grim recognition, not wanting my eyes to confirm what my ears already knew, I pivoted. The situation sank in as an unexpected face peered out amid the unfolding chaos. There, untangling herself from *my* blankets, sitting up in *my* bed...

"Ruuta?"

FORTY-FIVE

"Colleen?" Ruuta snapped awake, her neck elongated as she searched the room, then peeled back the covers. "Is that you?"

Creeping crabs! My heart pounded an aggressive staccato beat as we shuffled backward toward the balcony. I should've kept my mouth shut.

Hiisi hid behind my legs, trembling.

"This must be confusing. Please let me explain." Ruuta slipped from the bed and joined Iida. Both their faces twisted in confusion. Ruuta's normally pristine hair fell in matted tendrils from a pile atop her head. No glamors altered her, and yet, though her face appeared more real than I'd ever seen with pores and discoloring, she still seemed to wear a mask.

Where were their auras? I was back in Talamh Sí. Shouldn't I see them? Had something happened to them? To this place? Or to me? Had the witch broken my ability along with my bond?

Stop it, Colleen! Such errant ideas wouldn't sidetrack me. I had far more nefarious and pressing issues. What should I do? Flee? Demand answers? They were unarmed... other than the stone around Ruuta's neck. But she couldn't compel us all at once, and she needed to look her victim in the eye.

"I know you're there, Colleen. We're your friends. Please show yourself."

Ludek grasped my wrist. *I should secure the hallway. Can you handle this?*

I nodded to him, then followed so she'd think I opened the door. He eased the door open.

"Don't leave!" Her voice took on the tone of a child who didn't want their parent to leave them home alone.

Ludek peered into the hallway, then slipped through, closing the door behind him. I needed to conceal the others. She'd suspect I was with Sakki though. How else would I get up here? But then, by keeping him hidden along with the others, if she sensed another presence she'd assume it was his.

"Please, talk to me. Show yourself."

Think, Colleen. Think. Think. Think! I had to do something. Say something. My father's many clocks ticked the time away. I planted my feet and asked the most pressing question, steeling myself for the answer. "Why are you here?"

"Prove you're Colleen, and I'll tell you."

How could I show myself? I was under a fae spell I didn't understand. "You know my voice."

"Fae spells can mimic a person's voice."

I had a gift for veils. Maybe I could manipulate the air to reveal myself. But even if I could, would she sense the veil still hiding someone? Would she think it was more than Sakki? *God, please help me show myself and only me without removing the entire spell from any of us. I don't know what I'm doing.* I took a deep breath, grasped the surrounding air, peeled it away like a curtain, and closed it behind me.

Ruuta stopped advancing, her eyes wide. "It *is* you. I thought—I thought you were dead."

It worked. Somehow, I still saw the others. Did she see them too? I tried not to look at them straight on. "Clearly, I'm not, but that doesn't explain what you're doing in my bed."

"When we lost you, we returned to the castle for help." She stepped forward, hand outstretched.

Lies. Ludek's sources said Alpertti had apprehended them. I retreated further. "Where's Liam?"

She stopped and dropped her hand. "He's safe."

"Where?" Something about her wasn't right.

She cocked her head. "Are you afraid of me? Colleen, we're friends."

I hadn't realized my voice was shaking. Everything vibrated, building tension. I held back a scream to avoid attracting attention. My voice came out in a horrified squeak. "Where's Liam? What are you doing in my room?"

"I'm to be queen. My inauguration is tomorrow."

The rising tension plummeted to my feet, heaving my heart along with it. "That's not possible. You're not part of the royal family."

"Apparently, I am." A slimy smile slithered across her smug face.

"What?" I clasped my hands to keep them still. "No, you're not."

She sat at the end of her—*my*—bed and sighed. "Aunt Rhiannon confessed it all."

"*Aunt* Rhiannon?" Every ounce of my being cringed at those words coming from her mouth.

"You were right about Noita, the witch. She was Maija—my mother."

"Your mother?" The room swayed, and my legs gave out. I caught my fall on the tree's cage and lowered myself onto the soft cream carpet.

Ruuta crossed the floor and reached out to help.

"Don't touch me!" I smacked her creepy hand away. "Don't come near me!"

Ruuta yanked her hand back like a child wanting to pet a dog only to have her fingers snapped at. Anger flashed in her eyes, then calmed with a cleansing breath. "Yes, my mother. She fell in love with a human. Queen Rhiannon banished him to the Divide. My mother followed. Queen Rhiannon regrets not allowing the match."

I scrambled backward, dragging myself along the cage, away from her. An unsettling knot tightened in the pit of my stomach, a silent warning of something ominous. "What happened to him?"

Ruuta shrugged and quirked her lips. "He might be dead. Or he may have come here. The Divide didn't stop humans from escaping, only fae."

"What are you saying? You can take the throne and free Zorac?" Feeling sicker and sicker, I steeled my heart to keep from puking my emotions all over her vomit-inducing face.

Ruuta's eyes widened, aglow with greed and—What was happening to them? Were they pulsing? The ticking clocks grew louder.

Ticktock. Ticktock. Ticktock.

"Why didn't she tell you all this before? Why wait until now? Why not make you queen in the first place?"

"You're the rightful heir." She overenunciated each word as one trying to explain an obvious question to a feeble mind. "The daughter of King Auberon and Queen Delyth."

Something about her gaze was giving me a headache. I fought to clear my mind. "So, you can fulfill the prophecy and free Zorac, but you have no claim to the throne. Why will they accept you when they wouldn't accept me?"

Ruuta's gaze darted to Iida who'd been suspiciously quiet. And still.

Tick. Tock. Tick. Tock.

"Iida?" A frosty shiver crawled down my spine.

"You don't consider this a better alternative?" Ruuta inched closer along the bed, her pulsating eyes boring into mine. "You don't have to burden yourself with the crown. You can go home."

Tick. Tock. Tick. Tock.

I used the iron bars to hoist myself to stand and clung to them to steady me, moving from one rung to the next in my sluggish escape. While part of me wanted to block her out, another wanted to hear what she had to say. This was the first time anyone ever told me I was free to go home. I hadn't realized the depths of my desire to leave until the offer was laid before me. I wanted to go. More than anything.

"You don't need to take on the responsibility of an entire kingdom." She seemed to sense my desperation. Her voice became hypnotic, lower in pitch, heightening key words to calm and convince me. "You can return to Ariboslia. Don't you miss your family?"

How I missed them! They must be off their heads with worry. How long had it been? A year? Two? After my father manipulated my memories and the witch twisted my mind, I couldn't even guess.

Tick. Tock. Tick. Tock.

She took another tentative step toward me. Did she sense me weakening? Her eyes. Were they spinning? "Liam is here. He can go with you, and you can have a proper wedding with your family."

The room dimmed. My mind descended into a haze. A blurry vision of me dressed for a wedding, passing all my loved ones to stand beside Liam, beckoned. We stood, hand in hand, to pledge ourselves to one another. I wanted nothing more. It felt so... *real*. But nay, something was wrong. I squeezed my eyes shut and mashed a palm to my temple. Other images invaded, flashing between scenes of my wedding—Fergus, Carr and Fiske, the O'Donals—all the people I'd made promises to. Their faces broke through the obscurity, and I tried to focus on Ruuta. "What about the people?"

"I will take care of them." Her voice took on a velvety, melodic tone. Her swirling eyes gleamed.

The people's images disappeared, replaced by celebrating my new bond with my husband, my family beaming at me. I pressed my head against the bars, fighting to keep my mind here, now, not in a hypothetical future. "But—they're human. Elves." I swam through the haze, my mind clearing. "You're fae. Only part human. Even if you're a descendant of..." What was his name? "You're not from Talamh Si's royal line."

"Curses, Colleen. Don't worry about them!" Her face twisted, then smoothed as she regained composure at a psychotic speed. "They will accept me as their queen as Iida has."

Iida nodded, smiling. But it wasn't right.

Think, Colleen. Think. Clear your head.

"I can restore your dragon bond." Ruuta continued her slow pursuit.

Still clinging to the bars, I backed away.

"You'll talk to Sakki like you used to. Feel him." She reached for me. Her pulsing eyes, swirling, swirling, swirling.

Tick. Tock. Tick. Tock.

"I can teleport you, Liam, your dragon, and anyone else you'd like to accompany you back home. Would you like that?"

Images of Sakki standing beside me as I promised myself to Liam, surrounded by my family. She could give me these things. I'd be free. Unburdened. I stared into the depths of her spiraling ethereal-blue eyes. "Aye."

FORTY-SIX

Sakki morphed into his dragon form and blasted Ruuta with a warning flame over her head, singing the uppermost errant sprigs.

Ruuta howled, dropped her stone to her breastbone, and flailed in Sakki's general direction.

The stone. When had she grabbed it? Had she...? Had she...?

Think, Colleen. Think!

I rammed my fingers to my temples and blinked. With each blink, my mind cleared more. The pungent stink of burnt hair stung my nose. I gripped the bars tight and dragged myself away, rung by rung. What had I almost agreed to? How could I leave now... without taking care of all that I'd destroyed? All my father had destroyed? Ruuta would make a terrible queen. What might she have to do to get the people to accept her—a usurper to my father's throne? I couldn't do that to his people.

"Colleen?" Her eyes narrowed. Something ugly slithered behind them.

Tick. Tock. Tick. Tock.

"How can you be queen?" I cupped my palms against my ears to block the incessant ticking. "Why would they accept you?"

Iida threw Ruuta a nervous glance and tensed, ready to act the second her new master gave the word. But Iida was *my* friend, not Ruuta's. Something was wrong here. Very, very wrong. If I could clear my head—

Ruuta opened her mouth.

"Nay! Not another word. Iida, what's going on?"

"I'm certain I've no idea what you mean, miss?"

"Miss? Miss?" My legs gained their strength, and I stood upright, straightening my spine. "Since when do you call me miss?"

Iida faltered, glancing at Ruuta again. "Begging your pardon. I don't mean to anger Her Highness's guest."

What was this? Was she acting? There had to be a way to get her to reveal the truth. "Why are you talking to me like that, Iida? We're friends."

Iida stepped behind Ruuta.

"Please stop pestering my servant."

"Your servant?" A raging tornado swirled within me, gaining strength, pushing through the haze taking over my mind. "*Your* servant? What did you do to her? Where's Liam?"

Ruuta reached for the stone. My body reacted, pouncing, ripping the stone from her neck.

"Ow!" She howled with an unearthly roar and lunged.

Hiisi dove at her feet, tripping her. She caught herself on her palms. As she rose, Niilo unsheathed his sword and brought it to her neck in one swift motion. She stilled, her eyes wide at the invisible iron thrust against her. Her allergic reaction was setting in already, the site inflamed.

"That's an iron sword at your neck. I suggest you keep still unless you want a deeper wound that will never heal. Or worse." My stomach churned at the thrill of gaining the advantage and harming someone who'd been my friend, but what choice did I have? "I'm not alone."

Iida looked horrified. I'd gotten the advantage of her captor. She should look relieved. Was she under a—?

Curse.

How did I not see it before? Ruuta cursed her to be subservient. That's what Rhiannon was planning—to curse the people to follow Ruuta, behaving as my father had.

At the mere thought, a heart-stopping icicle of fear froze my veins. I opened the cage door. "Lock her in here."

Keeping the sword poised, Niilo positioned himself behind her and guided her toward the imprisoned tree.

Now that Iida guessed where Niilo stood in relation to Ruuta, she smacked at him. Sakki and Ulla fired warning flames, pushing her back. Her savage eyes, bright with fear, flicked in Sakki's and Ulla's general directions as invisible beings pushed her master into a cell.

The cure. I had a vial in my pocket. Might it work?

I pocketed the stolen stone, retrieved the vial, and sprayed her face. She faltered, sputtering and coughing. Graying red hair slipped from her bonnet as she scratched at her throat.

Ruuta spun and shoved Niilo through the air. He crashed into the armoire, and she made a run for the exit. Sakki slammed himself against the door before she could escape and shot her with another warning fire. She darted toward the balcony where Ulla blew out another blaze. Ruuta roared, frantic, her gaze darting every which way.

Sakki closed in, firing another short blast. The two dragons herded her to the cage.

Niilo limped toward her and jammed his blade against her neck. "Get inside if you prefer your head attached to your body."

With pure hatred flaring the sides of her eyes, Ruuta complied.

What happened to my friend?

Shuddering, I closed the cage, eager to lock her away. Creeping crabs! There was no lock. But it was iron, and she wasn't wearing her gloves. Still, she might throw something at it or kick it. "How are we going to lock it?"

Sakki and Ulla took turns sending warning streams of fire into the cell from random spots to keep Ruuta inside and unable to pinpoint their location.

"I have an idea." Bracing his lower back, Niilo hobbled to a plant on the wall.

"You're hurt." I wanted to help him, but I had to keep the door closed.

"I'll be fine." He removed the plant, set it on a table, and ripped the hanger from the wall. "She must've taken a potion to give her unnatural strength." His stride strengthened as he returned to the makeshift cell and placed the hanger where my hands held the cage closed. "Step back." He pushed me away, then waved to Ruuta. "You might want to stand back too." He turned to his dragon. "Care to assist?"

Careful to avoid Niilo's hand, Ulla blew a stream of fire that warmed me enough to retreat further. Ruuta hopped away from the split stream. Soon, the iron reddened, and Niilo hammered it with the butt of his dagger while Ulla worked on heating hanger's the other end.

Bang, bang, bang!

It was so loud. Would the thick walls cover it? Ludek had gone to secure the hallway. It must be clear. Even so, Sakki's gaze tracked mine, and he went to guard the door. While Niilo and Ulla worked, I dropped beside Iida, still crumpled on the floor, and leaned close to feel for breath and check for a pulse. Both were weak, but still there.

"She's not cursed. She's having an adverse reaction to your cure." Ruuta sneered. "When she dies, remember... you did this to her."

"Shut your gob." I blamed my foul language on my family's bad influence and the fury Ruuta had unearthed. Though my uncles would be proud. I focused on Iida. My innards raced to my throat, stopping my breath. *Please, God, don't let her die.*

"You should take more care, you fool. You know nothing about potions."

"She's not dead." *God, please, please, please don't let her be dead.*

"Yet."

I clenched my hands, fighting the urge to storm over to her and knock her teeth from her horrid mouth. What had gone wrong? For all her faults, she'd never been this terrible.

But what if what she said was true? I was sure Iida was cursed. If not my father's curse, something similar. Something where the same antidote might be helpful. But she was right. I shouldn't tamper with spells I didn't understand.

"That should hold her." Niilo prodded the iron fusing the door shut and jerked on the door. It didn't budge. He rushed to my side. "We should go."

"Please, a few more minutes. I need to know Iida's all right."

"He's right. You should leave. My guards are doing their rounds. They will check on me soon."

A nervous chill whipped through me, but I stayed.

Tick. Tock. Tick. Tock.

Iida coughed and rolled to the side.

My heart hammered like a woodpecker locked in on its prey. "Iida?" I wiped stray hairs from her face. "Are you okay?"

"I'm—oh." She groaned and gripped her head.

Thank You, God! She *seemed* to be coming out from a curse.

"Colleen!" She reached up for my face, then folded her fingers, packing them away in her palm. "I thought you were dead."

"Sounds like that's the common theme," I joked.

"The castle—!" She bolted upright, nearly colliding with my head. "It's–it's—" She wobbled.

"What about the castle?"

"We were attacked. They threw something inside, and pink smoke billowed in." She pointed to Ruuta. "Her. Queen Rhiannon. The fae. They cursed us."

FORTY-SEVEN

"Did you curse the entire city, or is it contained to those in the castle?" I gripped the bars and glared at the silent animal who used to be my friend. "Are you using the same curse my father used? That's how you planned to become queen, though you have no claim to Talamh Sí's throne?"

She didn't reply. Instead, she looked bored and smoothed a hair by her brow, not seeming to realize her entire head was a disaster.

I worked it all out aloud, speaking to no one in particular. "The reaction to the cure was a little different. Rhiannon must've tweaked it some. Who's it geared toward? Allegiance to you or Rhiannon?"

"Or both," Niilo said.

"Ruuta." Iida winced, rubbing her temple. "We were cursed to follow her and make her our new queen."

"If you had the coronation yesterday, you might've had a chance." I scoffed.

"You think you've won? Have another think, *princess*." Ruuta sneered.

I gaped at the flesh that used to house my friend. "What happened to you?"

She collapsed into a heap and thrashed on the pebbly ground. Foam bubbled from her lips, and her eyes rolled back in her head.

"Ruuta!" I rushed to the door, but it wouldn't budge. "Ruuta!" I slammed my palms against the iron as she writhed.

She stilled.

Ulla morphed into a weasel and slipped through the bars to check on her. Sakki changed into his cat form and followed.

She's still breathing. Ulla's voice spoke into our minds, and I relaxed some.

Whispers of a diabolical presence rode the air currents, leaving an ominous trail. The atmospheric pressure shifted, and an unearthly chill iced my veins. "Get out of there!"

I retreated, putting distance between the cage and me. Something was there. I couldn't see it, but it suffocated me, making it hard to breathe. It wanted to destroy me. All of us. A wave of nausea crashed through me. "God, help us."

The presence vacated, and the air normalized. The dragons made their way out, toward me. Ruuta woke, holding her head and groaning. Had she been under a curse too? She was reacting as someone being freed.

"Colleen?" She tried to stand, but she fell onto her knees and retched. When she finished heaving, she shrank away from the stench and crawled toward me. "I thought you were dead."

"Didn't we already have this conversation?" I'd never been so thoroughly confused. Not even when my father was manipulating my memories. Okay, maybe I had been more confused.

She pulled herself to the bench to sit. "Zorac. He—" She buried her face in her hands and wept.

If only I had the strength, I'd peel the iron bars away. "What did he do?"

"H–he—" She looked up at me with tearful eyes, then tore at her chest, and screamed.

I'd never seen her like this. Part of me wanted to break through the door to comfort her while another part wanted to keep a safe distance. Was this another trick? Nay. The sickening realization seeped in. "Did he... *possess* you?"

She hung her head, her gaze downcast again, and nodded with a muffled yes.

I sucked in a breath. How long had he been there? Just now or—

My mouth soured, and I swallowed a thick, slimy helping of disgust. My body absorbed the nasty mass and tried to reject it with a deep shudder. However long he'd been there, I'd been talking to a demon. I again fought the urge to puke. I smacked my lips, trying to eliminate the nasty taste and formulate words. "W–where'd he go?"

She slumped. "To Rhiannon, probably. I'm no longer of use to him trapped in here." She choked on a sob. "Thank you for freeing me."

"But why not possess Rhiannon in the first place? Why you?"

"To force me to take the throne and free him." Her voice cracked as her teary eyes pleaded. "I wouldn't have done it, Colleen. You must believe me. I wouldn't rule over cursed people. Not willingly."

"But I thought he couldn't cross the Divide?"

"With a host, he can. But he can't last long without one." She shuddered and scraped at her arms as if part of him was still in there and she would tear herself apart to get him out.

"And if the Divide falls...?"

"He won't need a host." Her watery eyes appeared bigger and bluer. An ocean of sorrow swelled within. "I'm sorry I doubted you. You were right. He–he's evil." She folded over with a fresh batch of tears.

Even she, without understanding God's goodness, at least, not *fully*, finally understood what evil was.

"I need to free you." I yanked on the immovable door.

"No!" She held her palms up. "I'm safer in here. If I'm trapped, he can't force me to claim the throne."

"All the more reason to get you out—to hide you."

"There's no time. He's probably already on his way with reinforcements. You should go. Now."

A sickening thought renewed my nausea. "Where's Liam?"

Ruuta pressed her lips together and closed her eyes as she shook her head, shaking out more unruly strands from her hamster-nest hairdo.

Creeping crabs! We'd wasted too much time. "Is there anything else I should know?"

She blinked, and a light came into her eyes. "Queen Rhiannon believes you're dead. She knows of the rebellion against her and assumes they killed you to stop her plans."

I nodded, absorbing all that meant. She wasn't expecting me or my army. That was something. But if Zorac went to her, she knew now. *God, where should we go from here?*

An idea came, and I hid myself in the veil once more.

"Colleen?" She stood and, with an outstretched hand, stepped toward the door. Then, remembering the bars were iron, she withdrew her hand and touched the cut on her neck. "Are you still here?"

"Sorry, Ruuta. I can't let you know our plans. He might return to you." I didn't *have* a plan, but she needn't know that. But where was he? His presence had gone.

"Hiisi, can you fit through those bars?"

"Hiisi's here?" Ruuta asked.

"Aye. He tripped you. Or... Zorac. That was a good move, my friend."

He smiled at me and sucked in his stomach to squeeze, but his oblong head and the iron beams wouldn't give. He slumped. "Me no get in."

"I'd hoped you could stay safe inside with her."

"Me stay and watch her."

I wasn't sure about leaving him, but I didn't want him to come with me either.

"Me stay and hide."

Good enough. "Okay. Be careful. Call out to us if anything happens." I turned to Ruuta. "How long can Zorac last in spirit form?"

"I don't know." She sat on the bench as if she were a fragile old lady.

Creeping crabs. That was no help. *God, how do I fight a demon?*

Forty-Eight

I tiptoed to the massive door and pressed my ear against it. Despite my excellent hearing, the thick wood stifled all sounds. Ludek must've cleared the hall.

Ludek, where are you?

No response. My stomach soured. Had he gotten captured? Why hadn't he come back? Why didn't he answer me? *Ludek?*

We'll find him. Niilo nodded to the door.

I grasped the handle and twisted until it had turned as far as it would go. Then, holding it in that position, I eased it open and peered outside. My trapped breath escaped. It was empty. Nothing but rows of hanging clocks and more ticking. I led the others to the right to my father's quarters. Rhiannon probably slept there now, unless Zorac had gotten to her.

Though my feet stumbled, trying to disobey my commands, I inched along. Sneaking outside his door like this reminded me of eavesdropping on his conversation with Alpertti on the teleview.

Where was Alpertti?

I gripped the door as I had before and edged it open. The dragons squeezed through in their cat and weasel forms. Niilo pushed past me with his sword raised. We neared the bed, ready to attack, but the sheet lay flat.

I flicked the light switch and stared at a bed that hadn't been slept in. "Where is she?"

We searched my father's quarters and balcony, but she was nowhere to be found.

Creeping crabs! Did she know we were here? Was she setting up a counterattack even now? Was Zorac with her? Had he chosen a less obvious host? He might be in anyone. Anywhere. How long could he survive outside a host? Better yet... what would happen to him if he strayed too long without one?

If this came down to a fight between him and me, I was done for. I'd better take out as many of his underlings as possible. Whatever else happened, we needed to gain control of this castle. If I died, I died. As long as no one freed Zorac.

I waved Niilo and the dragons to follow me back into the hallway. I poked my head inside my room to ensure Ruuta was still there and found her hunched over, weeping into her hands in the cage. As much as I wanted to rescue her, she was right. She was better off there until Zorac no longer threatened her.

We passed Rhys's old room. Grief panged in my chest. I peeked inside the empty space. Then, at the end of the hall, I opened the door to find two defenders stationed there.

"Wha—" one of them said as I blasted him with the cure.

Niilo knocked the other one out. I leaned over his slumped form and sprayed his face too. Though he had passed out, he coughed on the cure. Hopefully, it would work.

But if Rhiannon stationed guards there, where was Ludek? Had he gone up into the towers? Or gotten captured?

I couldn't worry about that now. I had a demon to hunt.

We wound our way through the castle. Thankfully, they seemed to have kept the posts as Auberon had them stationed. Some were already unconscious from the elves who'd been here before me. I sprayed everyone I came in contact with. Then I sneaked through the servants' quarters where the daytime shift of defenders slept. I moved from cot to cot, spraying their faces until one woke and noticed something suspicious.

"Who's there?" a female voice asked.

The defender on my next cot began to wake. "What are you—"

I sprayed him. He coughed and fell back. Even with only the scant moonlight shining through, she must've seen something.

"Ehren? Are you all right?" Terror grew with her pitch. "Who's there?"

Rather than continue in order around the cots, I ran to hers and sprayed her face. "Who?" Cough. Cough. Hack. Wheeze. "Are—" Then she crumpled back onto the bed, nearly falling off. I caught her and shoved her onto the mattress.

Quickly, they're waking! Niilo spoke into my mind.

One leaped from his bed and attacked the air where Niilo had been. "Show yourself!"

I hurried to spray each alarmed face, no longer concerned about where they fell. Sakki guarded the door, and Ulla covered the window so none would escape. When anyone got too near, they breathed a warning spray of fire until everyone ingested the cure.

They began waking and questioning.

"It's me, Princess Eerika, Auberon's daughter. I helped free you once from my father's curse, and now I'm freeing you from Queen Rhiannon's. Alert the others as they wake. Tell them the elves and dragons are on your side and to fight with us."

Good thing I'd freed them in the past and there were undeniable sensations of coming out from under a curse when one's mind returned to them, so none doubted or questioned me. None could think *I* was cursing them now. I slipped out and ran straight into an armored chest. My heart nearly broke through my rib cage while I tried to stifle a scream, but it was just an elf.

"Forgive me, Your Highness." He stepped aside. "We've secured the perimeter and captured the guards and servants. They're being kept in the ballroom under guard."

"Is Rhiannon there?"

"We haven't located her yet."

"What about Liam?"

He shook his head. "I'm afraid we haven't found him either."

Defenders began streaming out of their sleeping quarters and breaking off in two different directions.

I splayed a hand on the elf's chest to stay him and let the defenders go. "Queen Rhiannon cursed the humans to follow Ruuta and make her queen. These defenders have received the cure. They're on our side."

"Yes. Niilo has been keeping us apprised of the situation through the fae communications."

It hadn't occurred to me that the elf hadn't moved to stop them. I dropped my hand. "Have you heard from Ludek?"

"We've tried to reach him, but no." The elf frowned. "He hasn't responded."

That was bad. Very bad. But it would have to wait. "We still have Zorac to deal with. His only goal is to get Ruuta—or me—on the throne. She's locked up in my room. We need to guard her... to make sure she stays there."

He placed a hand up. "I'll assign guards to watch her."

Niilo and I ran through the castle, peering out the windows to check the grounds. The sun's early rays bathed the sky in gray. The city would wake soon. Even now, early risers would be awake. Were they cursed too? Or was the new curse isolated to those within the castle?

I checked Father's study and the library, then remembered the secret library. I pulled out books until the right one opened the door. We couldn't see anyone inside. I entered to investigate the shadows and make sure Liam wasn't tied up in a corner. A layer of dust coated everything. No one had been here for some time.

Niilo ran his fingers along the holy texts my father banned. "Your father collected these?"

"Apparently." I shrugged. "He didn't want his subjects to read them. Particularly youths yet to be atoned."

"But why keep them? Why not burn them?"

"Maybe he couldn't bring himself to do it. He must've believed. He was saved in the end."

"Was he now?" Niilo faced me, but his gaze didn't quite land.

"No one is beyond saving."

"How true. How true." He blinked, seeming to pull himself from a trance. "We must find Rhiannon."

Several footsteps headed toward us, fast. Niilo and I crouched in the shadows, weapons raised. A small body appeared in the entryway, their features obscured in darkness. A child?

"Who goes?" came a gruff voice. That was no child.

I stepped out from the veil with Niilo close behind. "It's Princess Eerika. Are you—"

He thumped his chest in the traditional pech greeting and bowed. "Loring, at your service."

My heart leaped like a frog surrounded by flies. "Is Hadwin here?"

He turned to allow me to pass, the light falling on his red beard and bulbous nose. He looked like Pepin, but younger. "I believe he's in the ballroom helping your invisible army round up prisoners, Your Highness."

"What of Queen Rhiannon?"

He grunted. "No sign of her yet."

Why hadn't anyone found her?

FORTY-NINE

Niilo and our dragons followed me through the magnificent halls full of images of the royal family and members of the court, including my father and me. The clocks he had obsessed over tick tick ticked away my time and revealed my irregular heartbeat. On my way to the ballroom, something made me pause. The pressure changed in the atmosphere, chilling me.

Zorac.

I halted. "Loring." I threw him the cure. "Get this to the others. Spray anyone cursed to follow Ruuta—in the face."

His dark eyes twitched, and his mouth opened. But rather than question me, he sped off.

I turned to Niilo. "You should go too. Zorac is here."

He stood in an unnatural stance, like he had frozen midstep. "I can't move."

Sakki and Ulla appeared to share Niilo's predicament.

We're trapped, Sakki said.

But I wasn't. Though my body wanted to spit up my soul to spare it the ugliness to come in the presence of such evil, I continued like a prisoner prodded at gunpoint toward the executioner. My hands felt tied, immobile. My heavy feet pressed onward.

Help us! Niilo yelled in our minds. *The throne room. Send everyone you can spare to the throne room!*

As soon as I entered, all the doors slammed shut, echoing in the chamber. The sensation of being trapped in a sealed tomb encased me. But help was on the way. Rhiannon and Zorac didn't know about the elves. Or did they?

As I continued my slow walk past the bronze beams encircled with leafy lines and dots—symbols of my mother and father's lineage, my hand lifted to my upper arm. My socrú. This throne room and I possessed the same mark. This was where I belonged. To take the throne was my destiny. My heritage. My right.

I entered the circle with the gleaming triskelion embedded in the obsidian floor symbolizing allegiance to my father. This. This was how I could repay my betrayal—by accepting the crown my father so desperately desired for me.

But only if it wouldn't free Zorac. And if God willed it.

"May the sun shine upon you, niece." Queen Rhiannon stood beside the throne. She didn't sound like herself. It was her voice, but something in the way she spoke—the tone, the inflection—something was off. It sounded more like Ruuta had in my room.

Zorac had possessed her.

Zorac, in Queen Rhiannon's body, clapped a slow, condescending clap. "You've thwarted my alternate plans by undoing my curse and trapping my host. But"—they shrugged—"that's of little consequence now, isn't it? You're the rightful heir, returned from the dead."

My throat seized. I searched for an escape as I gulped for air. *Sakki!*

"No one can help you here. We've sealed this room. No one can get in or out." They laughed, then cut it unnaturally short.

Could they hear me calling Sakki?

"Your tricks don't work here either. I see you. And you can't call out to your dragon or anyone else. Nor can you teleport, though I doubt you'd be able to do that on your own anyway, even covered by a continual spell."

"What do you want with me?" The air hung heavy. Like breathing sludge.

Their shoulders sagged. "You're not that daft, are you?"

"I won't take the throne. Not as long as it serves you."

"Oh, I beg to differ. What did you expect after thwarting my plans for your understudy? But no matter. She was an undesirable second choice should my original plans fail. And the original players are back on stage." They beamed a beautifully horrific smile, making my stomach reject itself, and thrust their arms out as if welcoming a loved one into their repulsive embrace. "You, the rightful heir of the crown, a hero to those who rejected you the first time. Now that you've saved them a second time, how can they reject you again? Now I've no need of any curses. Your subjects will follow you without magical aids. I couldn't have planned it better. Thank you, niece. You've outdone us all."

"What makes you think I'll do as you ask?"

"Oh." They tsked. "You and I both know you will, and why." They waved a hand, and a veil I hadn't sensed dissipated. There stood Liam, fighting invisible binds, struggling to speak against an unseen gag.

"Liam!" My desperate voice rang out.

"It's a shame inhabiting him wasn't an option. With Rhiannon on my side, this is a waste of resources, but you've gone and ruined him for me. Such a pity."

My heart plummeted, smashing on the floor. I ran to him, but something stopped me midrun. I fought to move, but an unseen force bound me. "Release me!"

"We need a little chat first, dear niece." They coughed a laugh. "Or should I call you great-granddaughter? Forgive my inability to calculate how many greats should be in the title. Let's have one suffice, shall we?"

I glared and continued to fight to move from my unnatural midrun stance.

They stepped down from the dais, sauntering toward me. "If I'm to dirty myself entering these foul bodies, how wonderful to be in one as powerful as Rhiannon's. That Ruuta. Ugh." He spat. "Thank you for sparing me putting her on the throne. Now"—they walked in slow circles around me—"let us chat about *you* taking the throne. You've had your reservations, but consider this, great-granddaughter. Consider taking your father's rightful place with Liam by your side. You will be free to rule as you like."

Now that he was making yet another offer that included Liam, I recognized what he'd tried to do to me before. I wouldn't give in to the temptation.

"You have compassion for these dirt sacks? Very well. Make their miserable little existences comfortable. Do what you can to aid them before they return to the dirt from whence they came. I don't care what you do. I won't stop you. You'll have complete freedom." They motioned to Liam. "And he is all yours."

How tempting that sounded! "And what do you get?"

"Bah!" They waved it off. "I'll receive the same as everyone else—freedom. Doesn't everyone deserve freedom?"

"And what will you do with your freedom?"

"What does anyone do with freedom? I'll come and go as I please."

"Possessing souls?"

"What need will I have of carrying around heavy dirt sacks when my body is so much more comfortable? And pretty. Wait until you see it. I'm sure you'll agree."

"To manipulate them."

"Do you understand how easy it is to influence these bags of dirt?" They huffed a staccato laugh through their nose. "I don't need to possess anyone to manipulate them. They destroy their lives well enough on their own."

"Because of you! You destroyed the elves' bloodline, tainting their souls with sin."

"Exactly!" They threw their arms up. "What more can I do?"

My brain chugged to keep up with their meandering trails of logic. If he'd already tainted the elves by turning them into fae and didn't plan to take any more hosts, what more harm could he do? Meanwhile, I might do a lot of good as queen. And with Liam?

Wait.

He was doing it again.

My insides wanted to explode and implode, anything to stop my topsy-turvy thoughts. What *was* I thinking? Was I considering giving in to the demon? He lied. There was no truth in him. He wouldn't happily skip about the realms with complete freedom without causing chaos. He'd twist their thoughts even as he now twisted mine. I couldn't give in. Ever. I had to remember it came at a price. A great price. "Nay! I'll never serve you!"

"I didn't ask you to serve me. Take the throne. Allow me to place the crown on your head, and you will rule with this dirt sack by your side."

"Never."

They frowned at Liam. "Well then, I fear for whatever befalls your little friend."

I choked on my heart. "No!"

"No?" They completed another circle around me and paused, pressing their face mere fingers from mine. Zorac's demonic soul raged in Rhiannon's icy eyes. "Dear great-granddaughter, I'm afraid you don't quite understand. Either you take the crown or I kill your friend. You can't have it both ways." They pulled away and resumed their slow pace around my frozen form.

Liam fought against his restraints, but it was futile. His neck strained and his face reddened, but he only made slight movements and minor grunts.

God, what should I do? I can't allow him to kill Liam.

Put on the ring.

Queen Rhiannon's demon-possessed body recoiled. "Are you speaking to God?"

How? I'm stuck!

Tell him you'll comply.

You want me to lie?

You are *complying... to Me.*

"Stop!" They moved an arm toward Liam, sweeping him into the air. "Stop talking to God, or I will crush him!"

"No! Please, no! Let him go!" My thrumming heart stopped beating so fast. The soul within my frozen body slumped. "I'll comply."

They narrowed their icy eyes at me, not moving.

"Please, don't hurt him."

Liam's fighting increased. If he were free, he'd be yelling at me not to do this. He wouldn't understand that I was obeying God. But he'd find out eventually. If I had the chance to tell him. Just because God willed it, didn't mean I'd survive it. But either way, Liam would be free, and I would be too —whether that was on this earth or in heaven. Either way, I had to obey.

"I'll comply."

Zorac must've sensed something. He moved from his contemplative stance and twisted his hand like spinning an invisible dial. I fell forward from my midrun, but it allowed me to sneak the ring from my pocket as I righted myself. Then I slipped it on my finger.

"What?" Queen Rhiannon's voice sounded confused as Zorac's rage penetrated the spiritual realm. "How dare you defy me!"

I sensed his intent to harm Liam and did the only thing that came to mind. I flung myself at Zorac to do something—anything—to stop him.

FIFTY

N ow in the spiritual realm, I thrust my hand into Rhiannon's chest and tore a hole into the physical realm to seize her heart. *Remove the ring.*

I complied. Still gripping her heart with all but my ring finger, I slid it off and yanked my hand away in that brief moment between realms. The slimy lump pulsed in my hold. I dropped it on the tile with a squishy thud.

A guttural gasp escaped Rhiannon. Her eyes widened. Limbs trembling, her body convulsed as if trying to resist an unseen force. A strangled cry clawed its way out of her throat. With a final, rasping breath, her body slackened. The spark of consciousness behind her eyes extinguished, and her body slumped to the obsidian floor in an unnatural, unqueenly posture.

Wear the ring.

Though I couldn't comprehend the reason for the command, I knew better than to disobey. I worked to put the ring back on my grubby hand in time to watch the inky blackness ooze from Rhiannon's eyes and mouth. Like with Noita, the ground absorbed her soul into hell.

Is that it, God? Is he finished? Did he die with Rhiannon?

Not yet.

Oh, come on! What more do I have to do? Whatever it was, I'd better free Liam before Zorac used him against me again. I ran to his side and ripped a hole in the atmosphere to grip Liam and pull him into the spiritual realm with me.

"I'm free?" He studied his hands. "How did you free me?"

"We're in the spiritual realm. I'm hoping this works." I hauled him away from where he'd stood, though that probably made no difference. Then, at God's command, removed the ring.

"Can you move?" I studied him.

He threw himself at me, nearly toppling me before holding me upright in his tight embrace. "I was so worried about you. They told me you were dead."

"That seems to be the consensus." I wrapped my arms around him, breathing him in. His familiar woodsy scent calmed me. "Yet, here I am."

"Yes, you are." He held my face, his thumbs brushing my cheeks. His ocean eyes swelled with a turbulence as he stared into mine.

I gripped his hands. My heart skipped, mirroring the emotions in his gaze.

"I can't believe you're here." He kissed my forehead, then moved in to kiss me, but the evil spirit swept past, sending an icy chill down my spine.

Right. We weren't alone—or done.

"Did you feel that?"

The color drained from Liam's face. His hands slipped to my shoulders, squeezing. "Zorac."

I searched the emptiness as if I might find the demonic presence. "Do you think Rhiannon's spells will keep him trapped in here? Since he can't inhabit either of us and can't last long without a host, maybe he'll die in here."

"We can only hope." He released me and raked a hand through his hair. "If only we knew how long 'not long' is."

"You safe!"

"Hiisi?" I scooted from the little gargoyle between us. "What are you doing here? How'd you get here?"

261

He tackled my legs in a tight embrace and peered up at me. "You ask? Me appear in käärme and unseelie lair and you ask?" He saw my hands and backed away. "You hands?"

I forced myself not to puke at the already-drying blood. "I—"

"You killed the queen? She's dead?" Ruuta's voice came from behind me.

"Ruuta." A chilling current slithered through my soul. "What are you doing here? It's not safe."

"Me bring her." Hiisi jabbed himself with his thumb. "Queen dead. She safe."

"No, Hiisi." Dread oozed over me, the foul gunk seeping into my soul. "She's not."

Ruuta folded forward like something hit her in the chest. Her breath whooshed out. She lifted her head, her smile sly. "You're right. It's not safe. How did they get through Rhiannon's impenetrable wards?" He waved a hand. "No matter. Rhiannon is a sad loss, but I've got all I need in this room. *You* will rule in Talamh Sí. *She*"—he pointed to his host—"will rule in Seelie Clós. And *I* will be free."

Roaring, Liam pounced on them, but they pushed back, sending him flying and skidding along the throne room floor like a skipping stone on a smooth lake.

Use the sand.

What sand? My hands flew to the bottle of sand from the Valley of Bones strung on my neck. *This sand?* I yanked the vial free and uncorked it.

Liam regrouped and lunged at them, and I shook out some sand and flung it in their face. They coughed and sputtered as Liam wrapped his hands around their throat. She gasped a soundless gasp, fighting for air. Still, Liam choked the life from her.

I couldn't do this again. I couldn't watch another person die. Not Ruuta. Not after showing hope for salvation.

Put on the ring.

What in Ariboslia? What good would that do now? But I complied.

Enter her.

What?

Jump.

If I'd learned anything, it was to follow without question. I jumped at Ruuta and disappeared inside.

FIFTY-ONE

Where was I? The blackness surrounding me was so complete I might be thousands of cubits below ground where nothing survived. No sound existed. No air moved. But I had to be somewhere in the spiritual realm. My body moved without limbs. I wasn't aware of breathing or a heartbeat. But as I traveled in every direction, no matter how far, I found no walls. Nothing. Just the pervasive darkness.

"Colleen?" Ruuta materialized in the blackness, though no light illuminated her. "How are you here?"

"It doesn't matter." I was aware of a heartbeat slowing. Hers. No breath came. "You're dying."

"Yes." She nodded. "I'm sorry I couldn't help you. But it's better this way."

"Better?"

"I'd rather die than coexist with him." She pointed into the darkness.

The nauseating sensation came over me again. A beautiful being appeared in a robe cinched with a gold sash. If I didn't know any better, I'd have thought he was an angel. But the aura of evil emanating from him made it clear. "Zorac."

"Look at me. Didn't I say I was pretty? Admit it, great-granddaughter.

You could stand looking at me in the real world. And you, my other great-granddaughter. I wouldn't remain in you forever. Only until I escape Rhiannon's trap and inhabit another body. Then one of you will take the throne and remain unburdened by me forever. Sound good?" His light tone darkened and deepened until it sounded like a thousand voices talking at once. "Call off your friend before she dies! He'll do nothing but kill her. He won't stop me. I'll find another host."

"Don't," Ruuta said. "He can't get to another host in Rhiannon's trap. Just let me die."

Nay! I couldn't let anyone else sacrifice themself. "God! Why did You call me in here? What can I do?"

Another figure appeared, this one barely visible beyond the bright light surrounding Him, but I knew who He was. Peace washed over me despite Zorac's presence. "Ruuta, do you know who I am?"

"Are You... Are You the God Colleen speaks of?" Her voice thickened.

"I am."

"Why are You here?"

"For you." He reached out for her.

"Go away." She collapsed to her knees and sobbed. "I served a demon. I'm not worthy."

"No one is worthy, dear child. And yet, you are loved." He laid a hand on her shoulder, and a soul-purging wail escaped her.

Ruuta sounded like she was trying to say something, but it came out as blubbering.

He knelt before her and clasped her chin, forcing her to look in His eyes. "You can have what Colleen has. What Liam has. I can save you too. And when you die, you don't have to be separated from Me. You can be with Me forever. Would you like that?"

Her tears dripped onto His sleeve as she gazed upon Him through watery eyes. "How?"

"Do you believe that you deserve death? That you need a Savior?"

Her face crumpled, and she lowered it to stare at his knees. "Yes."

"All you need to do is believe that I am that Savior." He lifted her head again and wiped away her tears. "I died for you. I can wipe your sins clean if you only believe."

"Is it that simple?" Her voice cracked.

"It is that simple for some. Most difficult for others." His sympathetic smile tugged at my heart. I fought the urge to run to Him. This was Ruuta's moment, and I was honored to take part.

"I believe." She choked and straightened. "I believe with all that I am."

"Then it is done." He grasped her hand and stood, bringing her to her feet, and kissed her forehead. "Your sins are forgiven. You are saved."

He approached me and stroked my cheek. His electric touch energized me. "Your job is done, Colleen."

I reappeared in the throne room beside Ruuta's fallen body, with Liam slumped over her.

"Well done, my good and faithful servant. Your faithfulness has restored you and your bond with Sakki. You are free. I've dissolved the fae magic over this room and the people. Now rule the kingdom as your father should have and remove the ring." He gave me one last embrace, kissed my forehead, and blinked away.

Though I wanted to bask in the space still warm from His presence, I didn't delay. I tried to capture the moment in my heart, to hold it there forever, even in the physical realm, and removed the ring from my clean hand.

Liam groaned and peered up at me. Recognition sank in. "You're back! I thought that demon had done something to you." He scrambled like he was about to jump up and hug me, but then such sorrow dulled his eyes. He ducked his head and touched Ruuta's shoulder. "I killed her."

I collapsed beside him and hugged him. Footsteps echoed in the hall, and we parted.

"Ludek?" Liam limped from the shadows. "Where were you?"

"Here. Queen Rhiannon captured me. She trapped me in a veil." Ludek's gaze lowered to Ruuta's fallen form. "What's that?"

Thick blackness oozed from her facial orifices.

"No!" I clamped a hand over my mouth as the floor swallowed up the goop. "It can't be. He saved her. I was there. A witness. He saved her." This couldn't be happening.

"I told you," Liam said in a flat tone. "She's dead."

"Nay, she's not. I was inside her... soul? I don't know, but I saw her. She was saved." Then it occurred to me. "I'm not wearing the ring. How can I see her soul?"

With a sharp gasp, Ruuta sat upright. Liam and I jumped backward, and I screamed.

After a couple of heartbeats, when the worst of the shock wore off, I scrambled to her. "You're alive?"

"Oh, thank God!" Liam dragged a hand down his face.

"But how can that be? I saw a spirit come from you and descend into hell."

"That wasn't me. You saw—Jesus saved me." She smiled. "It was Zorac. Being in my renewed body with the Holy Spirit killed him. The two couldn't occupy the same space."

"What's happened?" Alpertti's advancing footsteps slowed as he took in the scene. Rhiannon's fallen body. Her heart lying next to her. "What did you do to the queen? This is treason. Traitor!"

Ruuta stood and squared her shoulders. "Your queen is dead. The demon you serve is dead. You are the traitor."

His green eyes darkening, he backed away. When he spun and fled, Liam overtook the stiff man with ease.

Colleen?

Sakki?

I sensed him nearby. The doors burst in, and Sakki morphed into a dog, charged, and leaped, then shifted into a cat midair. *Our bond. It's restored.* I nuzzled his head with my cheek, his purr loud in my ears.

EPILOGUE

A *month later...*

My hands trembled as I paraded through the mixed crowd of humans, elves, fae, and pech adorned with golden flags waving. Sakki wanted to be something more regal for the occasion, so he paced at my side as a white tiger. The adornment on my head tickled my forehead, and I fought the urge to scratch. The crowd turned to stare, clapping, as attendants carried the long train of my robe. Äiti waved. Kohl clapped. I smiled at them, then Alajos and Egon. Even my would-be kidnapers made it out to celebrate today.

On the other side, Fergus shook a fist in the air. He came down from tending his sheep in the highlands for this?

My faithful driver, Vilppu, and my maid, Iida, stood together, smiling and waving.

A sharp whistle snagged my attention, but I didn't recognize the man's face or the adorable little girl beside him.

I scanned the faces as I continued forward.

"Colleen!" a familiar voice called.

I searched the crowd. There, toward the front, I found her. Fallon. I stopped, halting the procession though the symphony carried on.

It couldn't be.

My family? My chest tightened, then swelled, and a sob almost burst out. They were all there—my mother and father, my uncles, and all my siblings. How in Ariboslia were they here? I nearly ran to embrace them. But I had to continue marching toward the stage. Then, as I passed them, Pepin peeked down the aisle.

Pepin! The pech must've found him. That explained how my family was here. Was that—Aunt Stacy? They all hooted and hollered for me. There was no holding the emotion back now. Tears coursed down my cheeks.

Creeping crabs! I was supposed to be noble. Royals didn't cry.

On the opposite aisle, Hiisi stood on his chair, hopping up and down.

I climbed the steps, catching the supportive gaze of every person on the stage to the throne, stopped, and faced my audience. My hands shook more than ever when Liam approached, holding a scepter.

I trembled so badly, the vibrations should've sent me skittering across the floor. My heart increased its incessant pattering.

He knelt at my feet, propping himself up with the scepter. "My queen, as the leader of the army, I'm honored to present you with the golden scepter—a symbol of justice and a reminder of your pledge to rule in a just and fair manner." He held the scepter out to me.

I reached out a shaky gloved hand and gripped the metal. I fought to steady my voice and say the practiced words. "I accept the golden scepter and promise to rule in a just and fair manner."

He bowed, then stood, and returned to his place on the stage, making way for Hadwin.

His posture stiff, his wild hair slicked back, and his graying beard trimmed and oiled for the occasion, Hadwin sank to his knees as Liam had. He laid a pillow at my feet. The velvet cushion cradled a sphere with a cross engraved on it. "My queen, as the leader of the church, I'm honored to present you with the golden orb—a symbol of your dominion over the earthly realm and a reminder of your connection to God and your pledge to rule under God's divine authority." With both hands, he lifted the pillow to me.

I fought to contain tears and steady my voice. "I accept the golden orb and promise to rule under God's divine authority."

After Hadwin bowed and returned to his position, Reko advanced with the crown on another pillow. "My queen, as the leader of the government, I'm honored to present you with the golden crown—a symbol of our highest position of power and your pledge to act as sovereign for the good of your subjects."

The crown. The same one I'd seen on my father's head. His absence stung. And Reko was a reminder of Pirkko, Taneli, Valtteri, and others I'd lost on my way here. But I could almost see them among the smiling crowd, cheering me on. "I accept the golden crown and promise to act as sovereign for the good of my subjects."

Reko stood and placed the crown on my head. Its weight was more than the precious metal and jewels adorning it, but the heavy responsibility that came with it.

Once the crown sat firmly atop my head, he raised his hands to the audience. "All rise and pledge loyalty to your queen."

The hushed audience broke out in rustling as they stood. Then they began chanting, "All hail the queen! All hail the queen! All hail the queen!"

Reko lowered his arms, and the witnesses sat.

Niilo drew near with Ulla draped over his shoulder like a live weasel scarf. He knelt, then touched the bulb on the scepter I extended, and stood to offer a string of gems. "Your Highness, as leader of the elfin army and ruler of Rotko, I pledge my elves and dragons to your service, so long as you reign under God's divine authority. I bestow you with this bracelet. Let it serve as a reminder of our unity and peaceful alliance between Talamh Sí and Rotko."

I bowed. "I accept and confirm the peaceful alliance between Rotko and Talamh Sí, so long as you rule under God's divine authority."

He strung the bracelet around my wrist, then gripped my arm. "Our people are united under God."

Ludek did the same thing. "Your Highness, as leader of the fae army and with Queen Ruuta's blessing, I pledge my fae to your service, so long as you reign under God's divine authority. I bestow you with this bracelet. Let it serve as a reminder of our unity and peaceful alliance between Talamh Sí and Seelie Clós."

Again, I bowed. "I accept and confirm the peaceful alliance between Seelie Clós and Talamh Sí, so long as Queen Ruuta rules under God's divine authority."

After Ludek clamped the bracelet in place, he clasped my arm. "Our people are united under God."

Reko motioned for me to sit. "All who wish to address Queen Eerika of Talamh Sí, uniter of the realms of Betören, may do so now."

Though Reko moved into the audience and motioned my family up first, they jumped up to be the first in line. Ryan scrambled to be in front.

Reko draped a hand on Ryan's head. "Please wait for the queen to lower her scepter before you approach."

First thing I'd need to do was loosen some of these rules. I wouldn't survive in such a stuffy environment. Even so, I lowered the rod, and Ryan threw himself into my lap and hugged me.

My crown nearly tumbled from my head, and I laughed. "It's good to see you too, buddy."

My mother hugged me next.

Her familiar scent comforted me and teared me up. I breathed it in. "I was so worried about you."

"You were worried about us?" She cupped my ear and rubbed my temple with her thumb like she did when I was little. "Sweet girl, I knew where you were the whole time."

"You did?" My already aligned spine from the layers of formal wear straightened more. "How?"

"Sully."

"Huh?"

Pepin pushed through the rest of my family and squeezed my hand. "Sully told me long before he died what would become of you."

"But I was just a child!"

"And yet." Fallon lowered her hand, grazing my cheek as she stood back. "He knew about me before I was even born."

That man was a true prophet. My heart went soggy thinking about him. If only I could see him now. But I would, one day, along with other loved ones I'd lost. "So, you knew I would go through the megalith?"

Pepin's beard lifted in the corners with his grin. "That I did."

"So, I was stupid to hide it from you?"

He barked a gruff laugh. "All happened according to God's plans."

"Yeah." My father stepped forward and kissed my cheek. "We worried. How could we not? But knowing you were doing God's will as we have comforted us."

One by one, they came up to kiss my cheek, even my brother Corwin, who I would've expected to break out in hives if his lips contacted my skin. They were all dressed and groomed for the occasion. Clearly, they hadn't just arrived. "How long have you been here?"

"Last night." Fallon quirked her lips in a partial grimace as if expecting a rebuke. "Pepin wanted it to be a surprise."

"So it is! How long will you stay?"

"As long as we can. And we'll be back for your wedding too."

I gave up being a stoic queen and let the tears trail down my cheeks. The one thing I wanted most at my wedding, besides my husband, was my family. Still seated on the throne, I spun to my adopted dad. "You'll be able to give me away?"

He kissed my hand. "I wouldn't miss it."

"Have you met my fiancé?" I looked over at Liam, still standing in his spot with the other leaders. He winked at me, making me all gushy inside.

"Yup!" Ryan nodded, his black hair flopping. "But Pepin made everyone keep it a secret under pain of death." He made a grotesque face and slid a finger along his neck.

"Oh, he did, did he?" I tousled the morbid little boy's hair.

He reached a tentative hand out to Sakki. "You have a tiger?"

"This is my dragon, Sakki."

"I heard you had a dragon. He can change shapes? Sake!" He put his hands by his head and made an explosion sound.

"I'll show you later. Maybe we can go for a ride."

He sputtered nonsense, and Fallon pulled him back, draping her arms over his shoulders and clasping her hands, trapping him.

"I can't believe you're a queen." Nialla touched my crown.

"You're royalty too, Princess Nialla, and you're always welcome here."

Her eyes went wide, and her mouth fell open.

Hiisi decided not to wait for his turn. He pushed through my family and climbed into my lap. I introduced him, and he became Ryan's new best friend.

Reko came to my side. "My apologies, Your Highness. But many other attendees want to greet you, and we have a dinner to attend. Your family will be at your table. You can talk more then."

"We shall visit more soon. You are loved, sweet girl." My mother blew me a kiss and gathered my family.

They moved along with Hiisi's hand in Ryan's, and I began the tiring work of greeting all my subjects and guests from the other realms. Most of them gave a quick greeting or blessing. But those I knew lingered longer. I promised to make more time for them later to hurry the procession.

Äiti approached with Kohl cowering behind her. After showing the proper respect, she snagged my hand and held it for dear life.

"Äiti, I'm surprised you waited in this line to see me." We'd spoken many times after rescuing her and her church friends who tried to save Liam and Ruuta, thanking each other profusely.

"Oh, I'm not here to thank you for rescuing us again. This time, I want to thank you for restoring my home. I never dared believe the seelie court would submit to God's rule. "

"Have you had time to return to see it?" I thought I saw her the other day.

"No, no. Not yet. I was waiting to return until after your coronation. No, I heard rumors from those who've arrived about how much Ruuta has changed it already, and I had to thank you. I'm so eager to see it. I plan to return tomorrow." She raised her eyebrows appreciatively. "Though I might have to return for a wedding, I hear."

I laughed. "You are always welcome here."

"I also wanted to thank you for making my friend the leader of your church. He'll do a fine job."

"Hadwin? You know Hadwin?"

Her eyes sparkled. "Remember the slave boy I told you about? The one who told my äiti and me about God?"

"That was Hadwin?" If my mind could have exploded, it would.

Äiti gave my hand one last squeeze, and with a smile full of gratitude, she sauntered off, yanking Kohl with her.

I flexed my gloved fingers to get the blood flowing again.

More humans thanked me for curing them from the curse, restoring their family, or reestablishing order. Within those thank yous, many expressed one concern or another to which I promised to hear them out at a later date. Then the man who had whistled neared with the little girl.

"Do you remember me?" The girl squealed, revealing neat rows of baby teeth. Her soulful eyes looked familiar. Then I imagined her with a pig nose. "Silja! Is that you?"

"Yes." A smile took over her small face as she curtsied. "Thank you for freeing us! I got to go home to my mother."

"Your mother is alive?"

A large fae blocked the line behind her. Other than his size, he didn't remotely resemble the ogre he'd been.

A pretty woman I hadn't noticed standing with them bowed at my feet. "Thank you for returning my family."

"You're Silja's mother?" Dumbfounded, I couldn't think of anything better to say. "What happened?"

"I thought she died entering the Divide at our banishment." Silja's father had the same gruff ogre voice. "But they were forcing so many of us through at once, and we got separated." His already gruff voice thickened with emotion. "So many were burning up upon entry...."

"And I thought they'd died." She wiped a tear from her eye. "The witch's curse confused us."

"So you were all there, all along, in Rotko?" How horrible to be raised without a mother when she was there all along. "I'm so sorry."

"You've nothing to be sorry for." Silja's mother patted my hand. "Jumala, or God, as you say, saw fit to reunite us through you."

"Thank you, Queen Colleen," Silja said in a singsong voice, waving as her parents ushered her away.

After a few more friendly blessings, another familiar face emerged.

"Fergus! You made it all the way down from the highlands?"

He removed his hat with a sweeping bow. "Ol' Fergus at yer highness's service."

"Who's tending your sheep?"

"After the Divide fell, a young lad stumbled upon me cottage. He's there now." He scrunched his eyes at me. "I've had an easier time of it, without defenders coming to claim all me hard work. But I'm in need of supplies. What's to happen now?"

"I don't know. But I will make sure you have all you need. We'll talk more before you return home, okay?"

He gave a sharp nod. "That'll do."

TWO MONTHS LATER...

I stood on the western balcony overlooking the courtyard below and my kingdom beyond. *Does this feel like a dream to you, Sakki?*

He lifted his doggy head from his paws and snuffed. *It feels like a lot of time lying around on hard surfaces.*

Listen to you, sounding so depressed, like you haven't been flying with the dragons Niilo left for our army. I stooped to pet him. *And don't think I haven't noticed that girl dragon you've been frolicking around with.*

He showed his teeth, making him look like he was grinning.

Footsteps advanced, and I rose.

"Permission to approach the queen?" Liam's ocean eyes sparkled.

"Always."

He reached out for me. "Permission to embrace the queen?"

"Of course."

He wrapped me in his arms, his face closed in on mine, and he whispered, "Permission to kiss the queen?"

I closed the gap and kissed him. When we parted, we stayed close.

"I take that as a yes." He smiled a body-melting smile.

"Nay. It's an aye." I kissed him again. "A most emphatic aye for the rest of our lives."

"Well then." He kissed me more deeply. "How is life as a queen so far?"

"Exhausting." I sighed. "I'm in over my head."

"How can you say such a thing? You have support from everyone in every kingdom in Betören. And without curses or manipulation of any kind. No royal has ever achieved what you have."

"But there's still the keino issue—"

"The people have created an alternative energy source using food scraps."

"But they haven't created enough to serve everyone. I hate having to institute blackouts."

"That will get resolved in time. This is a new process. The people understand."

"And I have a long list of subjects who want to speak with me. Remember the O'Donals? The man who tried to shoot you? He wants to talk about his farm. And remember Fiske from Sáile? The one who tried to turn us over to the defenders? He wants to discuss the terms of their fishing. The list goes on and on."

"Stop overthinking." He pressed his palms to the sides of my head. "Just deal with one thing at a time. You have me and many others to help, and God is with you."

"I know."

"For now, be with me, your husband." He pulled me into his chest, and I snuggled in, his heartbeat calming me. "You are loved."

THE END.

Shameless Request for Reviews

Authors need reviews! They help books get noticed, and I love to know what my readers think of my stories. So, if you enjoyed this book, please consider leaving a review on Amazon, Goodreads, BookBub... anywhere you think a review might be helpful. I'm forever grateful!

You are loved,
J F Rogers

Acknowledgements

God, thank You for inspiring me, giving me purpose, and, well, everything. It all comes from You. Please use my stories to further Your kingdom.

Rick, thank you for putting up with me, being a sounding board, reading my work before it's done, and dealing with much confusion amid many changes. Thank you for your suggestions—I take them sometimes! I couldn't ask for a better husband. I love you!

Em, you're halfway around the world and yet still here in my heart. Your adventurous spirit and love for other cultures and languages inspire me! I love you, and I'm so proud of all you're accomplishing.

Special thanks to:

- Dierdre Lockhart with Brilliant Cut Editing. My one and only faithful editor. God knew what I needed when He brought me to you. Thank you for making my stories shine.
- 100 Covers and the infinitely patient Phyllis Ngo. You're always on the ball. Thank you for your stunning covers, graphics, bookmarks... all the things!
- My faithful local writer friends, Sharon Gamble, Amanda Ovington, and Marlene McKenna. You're more than writers. You're prayer warriors, sisters in Christ, accountability partners, and friends. Thank you for praying for me and keeping God at the forefront of all I do.

- Julie Bernier and Sarah Daniels—You both have encouraged me in incredible ways. You're traveling companions to conferences, in my writing journey, and in life. Thank you for always showing up and supporting me. And congrats! You're now published authors! Woo Hoo!

- Claire Gagne—God did me such a huge favor when He brought you into my life. I'm supposed to be mentoring you, but I think I'm getting the better end of the deal. Just seeing your face month after month is more encouraging than I can express. You are a gift. I can't wait to see what God does in and through your life.

- Azalea Dabill - We were baby writers together in my first ever critique group! It good to work with you again in your writer's collaboration group. I'm grateful to all the writers involved and to you for arranging it. Thank you!

- Ron Descoteaux - In a short time, you went from neighbor to fellow author and friend. You are always encouraging me and I can't express how much I appreciate you. Thank you, Cap'n!

- My beta readers - Angel Cross, Gina Detwiler, Claire Gagne, Carla Greathouse, Vickie Grider, Debbie Harris, Maureen Henn, Birgit Lehmann, and Deb Shaw. You have faithfully read through each book in the Cursed Lands series, offered valuable feedback, and encouraged me. Thank you!

- My street team - Nicole Burns, Dani Coquat, Angel Cross, Sarah Daniels, Claire Gagne, Steph Gagne, Angela Grimes, Debbie Harris, Barbara Harrison, Maureen Henn, Bill Long, Pamela Anne Reinert, Mariel Renaud, Sharon Selig, Deb Shaw, Monique Summers, Jackie Tansky, and Lena Karynn Tesla. Book after book, you show up to read my stories and share them with the world. There are so many hurting people out there who need to know that they are loved. You help bring that to them. Thank you!

- My ARC readers, clan members, church, family, and friends - Thank you all for reading, showing up, or giving me a timely word of encouragement or advice. I'm so grateful for you.
- Realm Makers - Thank you for offering great conferences and retreats and connecting me to so many incredible writers.
- And to my readers. I pray my stories encourage you, strengthen your faith, and remind you that you're not alone. There is a God who loves you. He sent His Son to die for you. And I pray you all believe it with all your heart and know—you ARE loved.

So many people showed up to encourage me along the way in God's perfect timing. I am beyond blessed. Thank you! I love you all!

You are loved,
J F Rogers

ABOUT THE AUTHOR

J. F. Rogers lives in Southern Maine with her husband, daughter, pets... and an imaginary friend or two. She has a degree in Behavioral Science and teaches a 5th and 6th grade Sunday School class. When she's not entertaining Tuki the Mega Mutt, her constant companion and greatest distraction, she's likely tap, tap, tapping away at her keyboard, praying the words will miraculously align just so. Above all, she's a believer in the One True God and can say with certainty—you are loved.

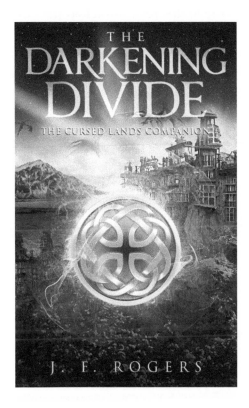

A jaded elf. A feisty dragon. And a deadly curse that threatens them all.

Samu would do anything to be bonded to a dragon, even serve a king he doesn't trust. But when a strange mist falls over his city and the humans massacre the elves, the last thing he wants is to come to the king's rescue.

Then the dragon eggs are threatened, and the Divide grows dark.

This was no ordinary curse.

Someone... or something... is staging an extinction-level attack against the elves and their dragons.

But Samu won't let that happen. He can't. He'll rescue the dragons or die trying.

The Darkening Divide **is the action-packed prequel to** *The Cursed Lands* **Christian fantasy adventure. If you enjoy mixing up genres with elves and dragons in a steampunk world infested with humans, download** *The Darkening Divide* **today! You'll love this intro to J F Rogers's exciting new series.**

http://jfrogers.com/free-book/

MORE FROM J F ROGERS

THE ARIBOSLIA TRILOGY

Astray

A mysterious amulet leads Fallon to everything she's ever wanted...and possibly her death.

Adrift

Fallon returns to Ariboslia to save lives...but the creatures she wants to save want her dead.

Aloft

Fallon and Morrigan face off for the ultimate battle ... in their minds.

Alight

Three friends. Evil seeks to corrupt them. If they survive... what will it cost?

Pepin's Tale

Can one small peach make an eternal difference?

STANDALONE NOVELETTE

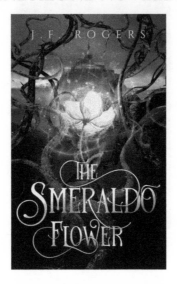

The Smeraldo Flower

Beauty and the Beast meets the Phantom of the Opera in the Secret Garden in this standalone novelette. A retelling of the Italian folktale, La Citta di Smeraldo, inspired by BTS's song *The Truth Untold*.

STILL LOOKING FOR MORE?

Be among the first to know when new books are released.

Join her clan at jfrogers.com/join/

Milton Keynes UK
Ingram Content Group UK Ltd.
UKHW010948220224
438207UK00013B/79/J